Praise for L[illegible]
K[illegible]

D1012212

"With a few highly origi[illegible] [illegible]nda Lael Miller follows *Pirates* with another ingenious time-travel romance. . . . Using her many talents and her special storytelling abilities, she spins a magical romance designed to capture the imagination and the heart with wonder."

—*Romantic Times*

"As her readers will expect, Linda Lael Miller whips her fiery characters into yet another clock-bendingly happy ending."

—*Publishers Weekly*

"Charming! *Knights* entertains and enthralls from beginning to end with a clever plot and memorable characters!"

—*The Literary Times*

"Ms. Miller's talent knows no bounds as each story she creates is a superb example of exemplary writing. By the end of one of her masterpieces, the reader will know that not only have they enjoyed the story, but lived intimately with the characters through all their journeys—be it love, joy or pain. Keep it up, Ms. Miller, your stories are just one of the many reasons we love romance."

—*Rendezvous*

"*Knights* is a fun-to-read weaving of elements from a time-travel romance into a magnificent medieval romance. Dane and Gloriana are superb characters deserving the empathy of the audience. Linda Lael Miller's ability to paint a bygone era so vividly that it appears to be more a video than a novel makes this work a one-of-a-kind reading experience."

—*Affaire de Coeur*

Acclaim for Linda Lael Miller's First Time-Travel Novel, *Pirates*

"*Pirates* is Linda Lael Miller at her scintillating best. This first-class piece of entertainment is earthy, humorous, and lively. Ms. Miller creates warm and moving characters who are realistic in either century. This novel is a one-sitting tale that has bestseller written all over it."

—*Affaire de Coeur*

"Read this one for fun, stay for the gentle observations. I hope [Linda Lael Miller's] brand of humor shows up in her next two time-travel stories, *Knights* and *My Outlaw.*"

—*Heartland Critiques*

"*Pirates* is a heartwarming time-travel tale with that special Linda Lael Miller touch. Love, hope, redemption and belief in magic transcend the pages of this glorious little novel to whisk the readers away on a cloud of joy."

—*Romantic Times*

"Linda Lael Miller's magical pen has woven its wonder again. . . . I was so enthralled by this exciting, intriguing story that I couldn't put the book down. . . . A glorious, sensuous love story with tender, sensitive emotions on every page."

—*Rendezvous*

Rave Reviews for Linda Lael Miller!
Linda Lael Miller "Enchants Readers"
—*Romantic Times*

"Funny, exciting, and heartwarming. . . . Another romance that's as wonderful and hot as you'd expect from Linda Lael Miller!"

—*Romantic Times*, on *Caroline and the Raider*

"Ms. Miller's unique way of tempering sensuality with tenderness in her characters makes them come alive and walk right off the pages and into your heart. . . ."

—*Rendezvous*, on *Emma and the Outlaw*

"Every novel Linda Lael Miller writes seems even better than the previous ones. She stirs your soul and makes you yearn along with her characters . . . encompassing every emotion and leaving you breathless."

—*Affaire de Coeur*, on *Daniel's Bride*

"The love . . . shimmers from the pages just as the sexual tension sizzles. Ms. Miller writes a wonderful story."

—*Rendezvous*, on *The Legacy*

"Linda Lael Miller continues to prove that she is one of the hottest romance authors writing today. This is a novel filled with passion, mystery, drama, humor, and powerful emotions. Her love scenes sizzle and smolder with sensuality."

—*Romantic Times*, on *Angelfire*

Books by Linda Lael Miller

Banner O'Brien
Corbin's Fancy
Memory's Embrace
My Darling Melissa
Angelfire
Desire and Destiny
Fletcher's Woman
Lauralee
Moonfire
Wanton Angel
Willow
Princess Annie
The Legacy
Taming Charlotte
Yankee Wife
Daniel's Bride
Lily and the Major
Emma and the Outlaw
Caroline and the Raider
Pirates
Knights
My Outlaw
The Vow
Two Brothers
Springwater
Springwater Seasons series:
  Rachel
  Savannah
  Miranda
  Jessica
A Springwater Christmas
One Wish
The Women of Primrose Creek series:
  Bridget
  Christy
  Skye
  Megan

For orders other than by individual consumers, Pocket Books grants a discount on the purchase of **10 or more** copies of single titles for special markets or premium use. For further details, please write to the Vice President of Special Markets, Pocket Books, 1230 Avenue of the Americas, 9th Floor, New York, NY 10020-1586.

For information on how individual consumers can place orders, please write to Mail Order Department, Simon & Schuster Inc., 100 Front Street, Riverside, NJ 08075.

Linda Lael Miller

The Vow

POCKET STAR BOOKS
New York London Toronto Sydney Tokyo Singapore

The sale of this book without its cover is unauthorized. If you purchased this book without a cover, you should be aware that it was reported to the publisher as "unsold and destroyed." Neither the author nor the publisher has received payment for the sale of this "stripped book."

This book is a work of fiction. Names, characters, places and incidents are products of the author's imagination or are used fictitiously. Any resemblance to actual events or locales or persons, living or dead, is entirely coincidental.

An *Original* Publication of POCKET BOOKS

A Pocket Star Book published by
POCKET BOOKS, a division of Simon & Schuster Inc.
1230 Avenue of the Americas, New York, NY 10020

Copyright © 1998 by Linda Lael Miller

All rights reserved, including the right to reproduce this book or portions thereof in any form whatsoever. For information address Pocket Books, 1230 Avenue of the Americas, New York, NY 10020

ISBN: 0-671-00399-2

First Pocket Books printing April 1998

10 9 8 7 6 5 4

POCKET STAR BOOKS and colophon are registered trademarks of Simon & Schuster Inc.

Cover art by Lina Levy

Printed in the U.S.A.

For Debbie Korrell and Tamra Clark,

for whom the impossible
only takes a little longer

One

Annabel Latham McKeige's return to Parable, Nevada, some twelve years after her scandalous departure, might have equaled the Second Coming for spectacle, if an angel or two had taken the trouble to show up.

In the misleading chill of that Independence Day morning, 1878, Annabel's sky blue surrey, with its liveried driver and dancing fringe of gold, came trundling over the rise a quarter of a mile east of town, emblazoned like a living icon in the glorious aura of dawn. In attendance was a retinue that seemed to represent fully half the United States Cavalry—a noisy multitude of blue-coated soldiers with brass buttons gleaming and the hooves of their horses raising billows of sun-gilded dust. Two huge black hounds trotted along on either side of Miss Annabel's rig, their fancy collars catching light.

Einar Grubb, who mucked out the Samhill Saloon on a daily basis and served as night guard at the town jail, on the rare occasions when there was a prisoner, claimed ever after that he'd been the first to take note of the Approach. There were others who disputed this contention—Miss Bethesda Deed, for one. An early riser by habit, she'd been standing at an upstairs window at the time, admiring the sunrise. She said the whole thing put her in mind of Hannibal crossing the Alps.

Marshal Jacob Swingler, returning from a tryst with a certain pretty widow, considered himself to be the first witness, but he was less vociferous in the matter, for reasons of chivalry as well as prudence.

In any event, it was Grubb who raised the alarm, sending the swinging doors of the saloon crashing inward and charging halfway up the staircase on the far side of the room before thinking better of the idea and stumbling to a halt on the first landing.

"Gabe!" he bellowed, sounding plaintive, like a cow up to its belly in a mudhole. "Gabe McKeige! Godamighty, get down here quick—*she's come back!*"

A general racket erupted then, not only there in the gloom of the Samhill but all over that small cattle town, as if the fuse on some giant firecracker had finally burned down to the powder.

Whores with tumbledown hair and fading ruffled nightdresses lined the railing overhead like tawdry flowers of unlikely hue, fussing because they'd been awakened at such an unholy hour. A few of the regular patrons hopped and hobbled along the hallway behind them, like blind rabbits spilled out of a feed bag, wrenching on boots and fastening trousers as they bolted toward the back stairway, making damn near as much racket as the throng of soldiers outside.

Then Gabe McKeige himself appeared, fully dressed and in no apparent hurry to save his skin. He was a big man, lean but powerfully built in the arms and shoulders, and he shoved both hands through his straw-colored hair as he glowered down at Grubb.

"What the hell . . . ?"

In that moment Einar was sore glad he had just cause for rousting McKeige out of his mistress's bed, because the look in Gabe's blue eyes was fierce enough to back down the devil's gatekeeper.

"It's Miss Annabel—Mrs. McKeige, I mean," Grubb sputtered, pointing in an easterly direction. "She's come back to Parable, and she's brought the army with her."

Gabe swore under his breath and descended the stairs, pushing past Grubb and striding across the sawdust floor. When he reached the doors, he was momentarily dazzled by a storm of brass and new-minted sunshine.

He narrowed his eyes against the glare, and sure enough, right there in the center of the exhibition was Annabel, sitting primly on the cushioned-leather seat of that surrey and looking down at him with all the disdain of a queen come to conquer and redeem a backward people.

Something tucked far back in Gabe's heart tightened briefly at the sight of her, but he put that down to annoyance. The clenching sensation in the pit of his belly defied explanation.

Annabel must have ridden a long while in that rig, and left in the dark of night to do it, since the nearest settlement, Fort Duffield, was nearly eight miles away. Still, she looked as fresh as a new bride. Her abundant red-brown hair gleamed in a tidy arrangement, beneath a prim little hat, and her sherry-colored eyes were bright with intelligence and disdain as she assessed him.

"I might have known I'd find you here, Gabriel

McKeige," she said, with a little sniff and an indignant motion of her chin, indicating the Samhill Saloon looming behind him.

Gabe wanted to grin, but did not indulge the urge. Dealing with Annabel required serious concentration, a difficult feat after a night spent drinking, arguing politics, and losing at cards. "Your judgment is as flawless as ever, Mrs. McKeige," he allowed.

She flushed slightly—prettily—and one of the fancy hounds came whimpering to Gabe to nudge his thigh with a long muzzle. Idly, without looking down, Gabe acknowledged the dog's greeting by wrestling its ears around a little.

"Champion!" Annabel scolded, giving her fringed parasol an irritated little spin against her shoulder. "Heel—at once!"

With a whine, the beast skulked back to its station beside Annabel's ridiculous rig. The dust was still settling.

Gabe folded his arms and watched his wife in silence, wearing the faint smirk he knew would nettle her.

The soldiers, evidently come to town on business of their own, dismounted at the command of a cavalry captain, who, like the two dogs, kept what appeared to be an assigned place near Annabel.

"I have come to discuss a matter of grave importance," Annabel said. Though she was perfectly controlled, as she almost always was, Gabe could tell that she wanted to close that fussy little umbrella and clout him over the head with it.

He counted the fact as a minor victory.

Smiling, he spread his hands in a gesture of cordial forbearance. "I'm listening," he said.

Annabel's color heightened again, but her gaze was unflinching. "You cannot think I would speak of personal matters in front of the entire town," she replied coolly.

Gabe shifted his gaze to the army officer, a man he did not recognize, then back to Annabel. "I guess we could talk at the ranch," he reasoned. "You do remember where that is, don't you?"

Annabel glared. "Please do not speak to me as though I were stupid, Mr. McKeige. Of *course* I know."

Gabe made a show of dragging out his pocket watch, flipping open the case, frowning at the time. "I'll meet you there," he said, ignoring her remark entirely, or at least pretending to ignore it. In truth, every word she said lodged itself in him somewhere, there to sting like a nettle. "In, say, an hour?"

Annabel cast a telling glance toward the uppermost story of the Samhill Saloon—where Miss Julia Sermon kept private rooms. "I would not like to inconvenience you," she replied pointedly.

Gabe grinned widely. "Oh, you won't," he answered, with exaggerated charm. Then he turned his back on her, walked back into the saloon, and climbed the stairs, humming under his breath.

Julia's girls watched open-mouthed as he passed, but the saloon was filling up with youthful soldiers bent on making good use of their free time. No one employed by the Samhill Saloon would be idle for long.

As Gabe entered Julia's sitting room, he heard the first tiny chords of a spritely tune rise through the floorboards. Someone had resurrected the piano player.

The long couch where Gabe had passed the night was still a tangle of blankets, and Julia stood in the doorway of her bedroom, clad in a floaty silk dressing gown, her dark hair brushed and hanging free to her waist.

"Annabel has come home," she said.

Gabe picked up his hat, tossed onto a chair the night before, then set it aside on a table. "No," he said gruffly, avoiding Julia's gaze while he tried in vain to work out what he felt and how he wanted it perceived. "No, she wants something, that's all. Most likely this is about Nicholas. She probably has some silly idea about making a gentleman out of him."

"Sit down," Julia said quietly. "Get your wits about you. She's got you rattled, Gabe, and if you don't take the time to think, you might do or say something you'll regret."

He sat, stretching out his long legs and crossing his feet. He was silent for a long while, staring pensively at the scuffed toes of his boots, and then he gave a great ragged sigh. "Damn," he said, without looking at Julia. "I didn't expect this. Her coming back all of the sudden, without a word of warning, I mean."

"I imagine that's why she did it, at least partly," Julia answered. She was as placid as a sheltered pond, as usual, taking a chair opposite his, all delicate and mannerly. She was probably the best friend he'd ever had, and not for the first time, he wished he could have loved her in another way. "Annabel is obviously a woman who puts great stock in the element of surprise"—she paused, struggled with a muted smile, and gave in graciously to defeat—"not to mention stagecraft."

"It's got to be about Nicholas," he mused aloud. Their son, his and Annabel's, was nineteen and full of the devil. Gabe wondered how the boy, off by himself in the foothills for the past ten days, would feel when he learned of his mama's return. Annabel and Nicholas weren't close, as far as Gabe knew, but they'd stayed in contact over the years, exchanging letters.

Nicholas never said much about Annabel or what passed between them; when a vellum envelope bearing her monogram came to the ranch, the boy would tuck it unopened into his shirt pocket and go off somewhere by himself to read it. Although Nicholas, as hardheaded at seven as he was now, had hated Boston from the first and promptly demanded to be sent home to Nevada, he had surely missed his mother. Gabriel knew better than most how hard it was to grow up without one, since his own had vanished into another world before he could lace up his shoes.

"Maybe she's here about Nicholas," Julia said, more out of politeness, Gabe thought, than true agreement. "Still, it seems to me she would have gone looking for *him*, if that were the case. Whatever Annabel's business is, she's nervous about it. Otherwise she wouldn't have needed the U.S. Cavalry for moral support."

Gabe sighed again and shoved a hand through his hair. He hadn't thought much about Annabel's military escort, except to figure that she'd merely happened by Fort Duffield when there was a detail headed in the same direction. It wasn't uncommon for the army to offer its protection to lone travelers, especially ladies of consequence, like Annabel.

"The last I heard," Gabe said, still thinking aloud, "Annabel was in England, living high on the hog. I confess, I'm mighty curious to know what brought her all this way."

"You've got to tell her the truth, Gabe," Julia said. "About us, I mean."

He glanced at her, the woman everyone in and around Parable believed to be his mistress. Her mother had been his father's housekeeper and cook after his mother was carried away, living with her young daughter in the attic of the ranch house. Gabriel and Julia, two lonely children, misfits even in a land populated by mavericks and outcasts, had formed a bond truer and deeper than most. "Even if I thought the truth was any of her business—which I don't—I wouldn't waste my breath. Annabel wouldn't believe a word I said. Hell, nobody would."

Julia looked down at her elegant white hands. In its present state, the relationship served a different purpose for each of them, but she had never been comfortable with the situation, at least where Annabel was concerned.

"Mrs. McKeige is still very much your wife."

"*Mrs. McKeige* abandoned me and our son a long time ago."

Julia spoke firmly, though in her usual ladylike tones. In many ways she was like Annabel, though of course it would have infuriated his wife to know he held that opinion.

"I remember it somewhat differently," she said.

Gabe closed his eyes against an onslaught of recollections, which only gave them greater power, color, and impact. When their second child, a little girl named Susannah, had died suddenly of a fever, Annabel had gone into a deep and bitter melancholy. He'd been sad, too, of course—brokenhearted, in fact. God knew, if no one else did, how many times he'd gone off to some private place and given himself up to grief.

Still, there came a time when a person had to fetch up and go on.

Annabel had not been able to do that; sorrow had swamped and saturated her. In time, things had disintegrated to such a point that one day while he was away on a cattle drive, she'd packed her trunks and left. She'd taken Nicholas, then seven years old, and gone back east by train, leaving nothing personal behind except a terse note and the harp that Gabe had given her as a wedding gift.

Even after a dozen years the recollection of coming home after weeks on the trail and finding his family gone sent the old pain echoing through his gut.

He squeezed the bridge of his nose between a thumb and forefinger.

"Gabe," Julia said. "Look at me."

He wouldn't. Or couldn't.

"You love her," she told him gently. There was compassion in her voice, in her bearing. "You always have and you always will."

"No," he said. The word scraped his throat as it passed, like some small clawed creature torn, unwilling, from its lair.

She sighed. "Go home, Gabriel McKeige," Julia ordered quietly, and this time she sounded weary. "Whatever the good people of Parable may believe, I will not entertain a married man in my private chambers if there is the least chance of a reconciliation between him and his wife."

Gabe stood, half hoisting, half thrusting himself out of the chair. It was the sturdiest one in the place and still too spindly for comfort. "Once again, Julia," he growled, "Annabel is not here to mend matrimonial fences."

"Whatever you say," Julia chimed sweetly, examining her fingernails. "Don't forget your hat, Mr. McKeige."

Directly following the interview with Gabriel, Annabel dismissed her driver, Mr. Hilditch, for the day, with strict orders that he take care not to spoil his uniform. Then, after politely refusing Captain Sommervale's offer of a further escort, she took up the reins of the surrey and set out for the ranch house. The hounds, Hercules and Champion, trotted obediently along beside the rig, pink tongues lolling.

The trip was two miles long and took a little over half an hour, to the best of Annabel's recollection. Moments before the substantial three-story house came into view, she pulled a lace-trimmed handkerchief from the sleeve of her dress and dabbed furiously at her face. No one else needed to know that Gabriel McKeige—once again—had made her cry.

When Annabel was quite certain that any vestiges of her weeping could easily be ascribed to a sensitivity to dust and pollens or to the violent brightness of a July morning, she raised her chin, squared her shoulders, and with a flick of her wrists, urged the horses to a more resolute pace. With luck she would have a few minutes of privacy in which to prepare, both physically and mentally, for the coming confrontation.

The sight of the rambling log house brought a great lump to her throat. She and Gabriel had been so happy there, once. . . .

Annabel brought the surrey to a halt in the dusty driveway, secured the reins and brake lever, and climbed down with the dignity and grace she had cultivated from earliest memory.

The very private hope that Nicholas would appear

in the doorway, smiling, to greet her, was quickly dashed. She had not written her son to forewarn him of her visit and her purpose. Had not had the courage.

Nicholas was nineteen; she had been a year younger than that when he was born. What a handsome, sturdy babe he'd been, substantial and stubborn from the very moment of his birth, as if he'd known his life's purpose even then, and meant to pursue it straightaway. He had never seemed to need her very much, so independent was he. Not at all like sweet, fragile Susannah, his sister.

Nicholas had been so like his father then—and he was now, too, if his irregular letters were to be credited. Right down to his propensity for breaking her heart.

"Mrs. McKeige?"

The familiar voice startled Annabel out of a reflection dangerously akin to self-pity, and she looked up to see Charlie Gray Cloud standing a few feet away, on the porch. He was exactly as Annabel remembered him—squat and sturdy, with a cobbler's apron around his middle and a cooking pot in his hands. There was only a trace of gray in his cropped black hair, and although she could not see his eyes and seek a welcome there, she had heard kindness in the timbre of his voice.

Her smile was genuine. "Hello, Charlie," she said, approaching him. "It is so good to see you again."

Charlie was clearly delighted; he moved quickly to open the front door for her. "We—I have missed you."

Annabel stepped over the threshold and into the cool dimness of the house with an aplomb that was assumed rather than spontaneous. "Nicholas isn't here?" she asked, holding her breath for the answer even as she scolded herself for expecting too much. They'd made headway over the years, she and Nicholas, but there was still a long way to go.

Charlie shook his head. "Darn fool boy—prowling around in the foothills all the time. Thinks he's an Indian."

Annabel subdued a rush of disappointment and reminded herself yet again that she had not told Nicholas she was coming and thus could not expect him to be there, waiting for her. "I wonder if I might have a basin of water," she said, tugging off her kid gloves and stuffing them into her drawstring bag.

Charlie nodded toward the stairway. "I'll bring a pitcher to your room, Mrs. McKeige," he said, and was gone before Annabel could protest that she would prefer to perform her ablutions in the little washroom off the kitchen.

Out front, the hounds barked as a rider thundered into the yard.

Annabel scurried up the steps and along the wide corridor to the master bedroom. She paused at the door, assailed by memories that would have been easier to bear if they'd been bitter instead of sweet, then turned the knob and went in.

The great four-poster bed stood in the same place as before, between two windows. Her own armoire towered at one end of the room, and Gabriel's bureau was at the other, just as she recalled. Beside the fieldstone fireplace was her harp, the beautiful instrument Gabriel had given her the day they were married.

An angel, he'd said, ought to have a harp to play. . . .

The bellow from downstairs startled Annabel so thoroughly that she cried out softly and pressed a hand to her throat.

"Charlie!" Gabriel shouted.

Annabel spun round and was startled again, for Charlie stood in the doorway, extending the promised pitcher of water, not releasing his grasp until her own hold on it was steady. The Indian's innate quietness of spirit calmed Annabel; she nodded her gratitude.

Charlie went out, closing the door behind him.

Moments later she was splashing her face with blessedly cool water, silently rehearsing, for perhaps the thousandth time, the persuasive speech she would make to Gabriel.

His voice rose from belowstairs, countered by Charlie's measured, even responses.

She'd probably been flattering herself, Annabel thought, by ever believing that persuasion would be necessary. Only one thing could be worse than Gabriel's flat refusal of her request, and that was his ready acquiescence.

"Annabel Latham McKeige," she muttered before Gabriel's shaving mirror, as she dried her face, "you are indeed a fine fool."

Gabriel was standing at the foot of the stairs, one leather-gloved hand dwarfing the newel post, when she came out of the bedroom, hair smoothed, face scrubbed clean of road dust and the traces of imprudent tears.

Annabel called upon every resource she possessed simply to descend in a graceful and unhurried way; actually, her heart was pounding and she could barely breathe. Gabriel was forty, and more attractive for the passing of time, damn him. The years had lent his patrician features a rugged cast, hardened his muscles, given him the lean, stealthy prowess of a mountain cat.

"Charlie was kind enough to offer me a place to

refresh myself," she said, eager to establish a mundane reason for being in the room she and Gabriel had shared so long ago.

"Charlie," Gabriel drawled, peering at her with narrowed eyes, "is the *soul* of kindness."

The barb reminded Annabel that Gabriel was an adversary, and a worthy one. Inwardly she braced herself for combat—and for devastating success.

"I see no reason to delay matters any further," Annabel announced, meeting and holding Gabriel's gaze. "Perhaps we might speak in your study?"

Gabriel executed a deep bow, meant to mock her love of all things gracious and civilized. "As you wish, my lady," he answered.

Annabel was sustained by an upswell of righteous fury; she swept past Gabriel with her head high and her shoulders back. The hem of her heavy skirt made a whispering sound against the smooth pinewood floor.

Inside the study, she stood near Gabriel's vast cluttered desk and watched as he closed the double doors and turned to look at her.

He folded his arms. "All right, Annabel. Speak your piece. I have work to do."

She battled a dizzying need to hurl something heavy at his head and commanded herself to speak calmly. A few words, nothing more rigorous than that, and it would be over, done with, the task she had rehearsed and dreaded these many months.

"As you may know, I have been living in England in recent years."

Gabriel said nothing, but only waited, revealing nothing of his feelings, if he had any in the first place.

"I should like to receive gentlemen callers," Annabel rushed on. "As a married woman, I have not thought that proper, but I am thirty-seven years old, after all, and, well, time is passing."

Gabriel arched one golden eyebrow. "And?"

Annabel's cheeks stung smartly, as if he'd slapped her. She drew herself up and held her chin high. "And I have come to ask you for a divorce."

He was silent and as still as stone, and Annabel suffered an agony of suspense, awaiting his answer. It was, for her, as though all the air had somehow been drawn from the room in one great inhalation.

"Absolutely not," he said, precisely when Annabel thought she might swoon for lack of breath.

She was stunned and, at the same time, relieved, though there would be no confessing this latter emotion, of course. Gabriel was refusing the divorce out of sheer cussedness, not some tender sentiment.

Overcome, Annabel spread a hand over her bosom and eased to one side of the desk, there to fall into a leather-upholstered chair.

"What?" she whispered. "Gabriel—*why?* Why would you refuse now, after all this time?"

He crossed the room to bend over her, his hands resting on the arms of her chair, his face so near her own that she could feel his breath on her skin. "Why? Because we made a promise, you and I. We took a vow."

Annabel's heart fluttered painfully. She looked away from Gabriel's hard, unreadable face, then back again, angry and wounded. "A promise you have plainly held in *high* regard these many years!" she gibed, too frustrated to maintain her composure, precious though it was.

"I have indeed," Gabriel said quietly. "Have you?"

Annabel flushed. The world was different for women than for men; she could not take lovers with the same impunity as her husband, had not even wanted to do so. She had been faithful to Gabriel. "Yes," she spat, still imprisoned in her chair, between his two arms. "Yes, Gabriel, I have honored our wedding pledges, believe it or not. But I am tired of living half a life. I want a husband, babies."

"Babies?" He looked surprised, as though he couldn't imagine such an ancient and dried-up creature bearing children. He straightened and retreated a step. "Babies?"

Annabel glared at him defiantly. "Yes!" she cried. "Is that so difficult to believe? I am not a crone, Gabriel. Women my age have children all the time."

He thrust himself away, moved to the liquor cabinet on the other side of the room, drew the lid from a crystal decanter, and splashed brandy into a snifter, heedless of the fact that breakfast had yet to be served.

"You have a husband, Annabel," Gabriel said, taking a sip and then raising the glass in a toast. "And like it or not, for better or for worse, you're stuck with me."

Annabel closed her eyes in a desperate bid for self-control. "Will you force me to return to England and live in scandal?" she asked in exasperation.

Gabriel regarded her thoughtfully. "I don't see how taking lovers would be any worse than presenting yourself to society as a divorced woman—that pretty much means ruin out here. But then, maybe that's accepted in your more sophisticated circles."

The words stung, as they were no doubt meant to do. Although divorce was common enough in certain sets, Annabel was at heart a traditional person. For her, ending the marriage before taking callers and proceeding with her life was a matter of honor.

"Damn you, Gabriel—why must you make this difficult?"

Gabriel set the brandy aside, barely touched. "Difficult? I think I've been pretty patient with you, Annabel. You left me while I was on the trail, and you took my son with you. A lot of men would have followed you back east and dragged you home by the hair."

She looked away for a moment, backward through time, remembering how she had waited for him during those first awful months away, how she had prayed he would come back east to collect her and Nicholas. But no, he hadn't cared about anything but his damnable ranch, his cattle, his mines and timber.

And Julia Sermon, of course. Oh, yes, he'd cared about her.

"Please, Gabriel, do not play the wronged husband. You were probably glad to be rid of me."

Gabriel went to the door, laid a hand on the brass knob. "There will be no divorce," he said. And then he was gone, leaving her sitting alone in that rustic study and very much at a loss. She had simply never troubled herself to plan beyond an initial refusal, convinced as she had been that Gabriel wished to be free.

It seemed she'd been mistaken. More than freedom, he wanted revenge.

Gabriel went outside to stand on the porch with one upraised arm braced against a support beam. In the distance he heard the first Independence Day firecrackers shattering the early morning peace. Annabel's silly-looking hounds lay nearby, in the fragrant, dark purple shade of an overgrown lilac bush, curled up close together, their muzzles resting on their paws. They looked up at Gabe with baleful eyes.

The surrey was gone. He had personally ordered it moved before he entered the house to confront Annabel; the team had already been unhitched, watered, fed, and curried. At present, though, he wished he'd reserved the task for himself, for he was in profound need of distraction.

Annabel wanted a husband, a home, babies.

Their son had survived, if not their daughter. He'd given her a fine house, a bank account, all the clothes and trinkets and gewgaws a woman could ask for or expect. He'd loved her with all his being, damn it, and if she'd troubled herself to stay, there would surely have been more children after Nicholas and Susannah.

If Annabel had wanted a family, why had she left in the first place? It made no damned sense.

"I sent Ben and Jimmy to bring Nicholas back."

Gabriel stiffened at the sound of Charlie's voice, embarrassed, as if his thoughts and regrets and private injuries were outside his skin, for anybody to look at. "Damned Indian," he muttered. "When are you going to stop sneaking up on me that way?"

"No time soon," Charlie answered easily. "Got to admit, though, there's not much challenge in it anymore. You're getting old."

"Annabel wants a divorce," Gabe said, without planning to speak at all.

"So she claims," Charlie replied, showing scant interest. "You'd better wash up, boss. Breakfast's on the table, and my guess is you'll be needing your strength."

Two

NICHOLAS MCKEIGE WAS BARELY A MILE FROM HOME, his mind on one of Charlie's home-cooked meals and the forthcoming Independence Day celebrations in Parable, when he came upon Ben Evans and Jimmy Conroy. They were riding hard, but when they saw him, they both drew up fast, which indicated to Nicholas that he'd been the object of their hurry.

He greeted the ranch hands with a grin but did not rein in his own gelding, a bay named Homebrew. Ben and Jimmy were both younger than Nicholas, yet they'd been working for his father for several years—people grew up fast out west, or else they didn't grow up at all. They fell in on either side of him.

"It's a lucky thing we found you," Jimmy blurted. He was a good hand, but he would never change the world.

Nicholas pushed his hat to the back of his head and waited. Despite the smile he sustained, as impudent as he could make it, as usual, he was worried. For two of Gabe McKeige's men to come looking for him in such an almighty rush was not a good sign—something had to be wrong at the ranch. His father took life seriously, and he wanted all of the men on the place doing their part, all the time. It was one of the reasons they fell out so often, the two of them.

"It's your ma," Ben put in eagerly, his little eyes wide in his pockmarked face, and right then Nicholas's whole gut tightened up like a fist.

The grin fell off his face like a rock skittering down a cliffside. "What about her?" he demanded, drawing the trotting bay to a stop and thus forcing Ben and Jimmy to hold up, forming a two-man, two-horse half-circle in front of him.

The young ranch hands looked at each other in silent consultation.

"She's back," Jimmy said, after due deliberation.

Nicholas stared, at once relieved and stunned. "What?"

Ben gave a high, delighted giggle, like an old maid imparting scandal with tea and cookies. "She's here, yes, sir, right here on this ranch. You ought to see the rig she showed up in—fancy as a circus wagon. And she's got two dogs with her, near big as ponies." He reached out to poke his smaller companion in the ribs. "Jimmy here could ride one of 'em."

Nicholas spurred Homebrew forward, breaking through the crescent of horses and men like Moses parting the Red Sea, but he held the reins taut, let the gelding walk. Leaning forward to brace one forearm against the pommel of his saddle, he pondered the state of affairs awaiting him at the ranch house.

"Was my father around when she arrived?"

The boys tossed another happy grin back and forth between them.

"Yup," said Jimmy. "Word spread clear out to the ranch in no time. She found him at the Samhill Saloon, bunkin' in with Miss Julia Sermon."

"Jesus," Nicholas breathed. Just imagining the scene made the back of his neck prickle with sweat. "Was there bloodshed?" Nobody laughed, which was just as well. He hadn't meant the inquiry as a joke.

A few minutes later he was home. He handed Homebrew over to his companions to be taken care of, a responsibility he had been strictly trained never to shirk, and, after one rueful glance down at his dirty clothes, entered the house by the kitchen door.

Charlie was washing dishes at the big metal sink. He gave Nicholas a look of quiet assessment, taking in his wind-tangled shoulder-length hair and otherwise generally sorry appearance. "You'll never make an Indian, boy, if you don't learn to spruce up once in a while."

Nicholas chuckled, but in the next instant he was sober again. "Is it true? That Miss Annabel's come back?" He couldn't think of her as "Mother," even in the privacy of his own mind. Where she was concerned, he had a lot of contrary feelings, and though he'd often tried, he'd never been able to sort them out. Not with so much ground and water getting in the way.

Charlie nodded, never pausing in the scouring of a pan. "It's true, but the peace in this place is mighty delicate right now. Your pa ate his breakfast here in the kitchen, while Mrs. McKeige took her meal at the dining room table, as a lady could be expected to do."

Nicholas got a mug down from a shelf and poured himself a dose of coffee from the pot on the stove. "Where are they?" he asked warily, after a bracing sip. Charlie's brew tasted like corral mud, but it could be depended upon to give a man a sudden sort of stamina, if he didn't mind the vertigo.

"Mrs. McKeige is upstairs, resting. I imagine your pa is outside someplace, gnawing down a tree with his teeth."

Nicholas grinned. Nearly twenty, he was a man grown, with his own interests, his own money, his own women, but it still pleased him to have both his parents under one roof, figuratively at least. The situation put him in mind of two barn cats sealed up in the same five-gallon lard can.

Yes, sir, things were bound to be interesting around the homeplace, at least for a while.

"What do you want first?" Charlie asked, drying his hands on that ever-present apron of his and turning to face Nicholas straight on. "Breakfast or water for a bath?"

"Breakfast," Nicholas said, after another gulp of the poisonous coffee. "I'll go down to the spring to wash up."

"Well, get yourself outside and scrub off the top layer of dirt anyhow," Charlie demanded. "You aren't clean enough to eat at my table."

Obediently—and because he was hungry and damn tired of his own cooking—Nicholas set aside the mug, pumped a bucketful of water at the sink, and carried it outside to the wash bench. Charlie had a clean shirt and a towel ready by the time he was through lathering the upper half of his body and splashing off the suds.

He was seated at the table, tucking into a plate of eggs and venison hash, when his father appeared, making a noisy entrance through the back door.

"There you are," he said to Nicholas, as he poured coffee for himself.

Charlie quietly vanished. He was probably the smartest person on the ranch.

"Here I am," Nicholas replied, with the faintest hint of insolence in his tone. He supposed he loved Gabe as much as any man had ever loved his father, but that didn't mean they got along well. They were too much alike, too bullheaded and fractious, bent on having things their own way, an insight Nicholas had come to at a fairly tender age.

Gabe brought his coffee to the table and sat down on the bench across from Nicholas. "You might want to move out to the bunkhouse for a while," he said.

Nicholas widened his eyes for a moment. "Why?" He couldn't remember ever seeing his father look so bewildered; in a man like Gabe McKeige, one of the most powerful ranchers in Nevada, the quality was entertaining indeed. "Is there going to be a reconciliation?"

Gabe gave him a warning look that took some of the grease off his wheels. "No," he replied. "There's going to be a war."

"I wouldn't want to miss that."

Gabe glowered. "Too bad. It's private."

Nicholas finished off the last of his hash and downed what remained of his coffee. He wouldn't have to worry about falling asleep before the Independence Day celebration got under way in town that night; thanks to Charlie's paint remover, he'd probably be wide awake for a week.

Not, he thought to himself, that he'd miss the fireworks by staying home.

Nicholas made the charitable decision to let up on

Gabe, since the man looked as if he'd been dragged over rough ground behind a horse weaned on Charlie's coffee. "How is Miss Annabel? She's well, isn't she?"

Gabe looked rueful. "Annabel appears to be in fine health."

"What brings her all the way out here? Last letter I had, she was in England, riding to the hounds and all that."

Gabe's face tightened into hard lines and sharp angles. "You'll have to ask her about that." He stared into his coffee for a few pensive moments, then met Nicholas's gaze squarely. "Annabel's real eager to see you, and she's come a long way. You be kind to her, or you'll give an accounting. Do I make myself understood?"

Charitably, Nicholas sloughed off a rush of resentment that Gabe thought he had to be told how to treat his mother; after all, it was barely ten in the morning, and the old man had already been through a full day's misery. "Miss Annabel and I worked out our differences long ago," he said, though in fact he often thought of how she'd dragged him away from everyone and everything he loved, all those years ago. And the memory still burned like the touch of a branding iron.

Gabe rose somewhat awkwardly from the bench—despite his size, he was an agile man, still limber even at his advanced age. "We've had a lot of strays lately," he said, keeping his broad back to Nicholas while he set his cup in the sink. "Too many for coincidence. I'd like you to ride fence with some of the boys tomorrow and see if you can find the leak."

Nicholas nodded, even though Gabe wasn't looking

at him. "You taking Miss Annabel to the picnic and the Independence Day dance?"

Gabe stiffened visibly but didn't turn around. Nicholas recalled what Ben and Jimmy had told him—there'd been a scene when Miss Annabel showed up that morning. A public one, likely to live on in local legend. "I have work to do," he said.

Nicholas shrugged. "I don't reckon she'll lack for dancing partners," he remarked lightly. "I remember her as a mighty handsome woman."

Gabe crossed the room in a few strides and went outside, slamming the door behind him with such force that Charlie's tin dishes rattled on the shelves.

Nicholas smiled to himself as he carried his plate and silverware to the sink. It looked like the fourth of July would last a lot longer than one day that year. At least in terms of loud explosions.

Annabel awakened, refreshed, after a brief catnap. She was not a woman to sleep when the sun was up, even at the end of a long journey. The familiar sounds of a working ranch made a strange, rustic music, and she hummed as she dressed, donning a cheerful blue gown over her camisole and petticoats.

Before the full-length beveled mirror, which had belonged to Gabriel's beautiful mother before the tragedy of her abduction, Annabel brushed her hair vigorously, plaited it into one long braid, and wound that loosely at the nape of her neck. Bending close to the glass to pin the soft coronet in place, she looked for gray hairs and found nary a one.

That morning's conversation with Gabriel came back to her—indeed, it had never truly gone, having haunted her like a specter even while she dozed—and her recollections brought a rush of color to her cheeks. Why had it surprised him so, the news that she longed for love, for more children, for a real home?

Annabel turned sideways, inspecting her reflection in the looking glass. Never one to indulge in false humility, she knew she was a beautiful woman, with far more to offer than any mere girl. She'd been barely seventeen when she and Gabriel were married, and though she'd loved her husband wildly, she had been woefully ignorant in many ways.

They had learned lovemaking together, she and Gabriel, and they had taught each other well. They had built the ranch from a homestead Gabriel inherited from his father, one of the earliest settlers in the area, and, most importantly, they had created Nicholas.

Annabel turned and looked sadly at the big bed that dominated the room. Their son had been conceived there, born there, and so had their daughter. When Nicholas was very small, only two, and stricken with scarlet fever, she and Gabriel had tucked him in between them every night, as if to shelter him from death itself.

He'd rallied, and a few years later Susannah had fallen ill, and they'd done the same. The loss pierced Annabel's heart afresh, old as it was.

Why, she wondered, had that tragedy driven her away from Gabriel, when it should have propelled her into his arms? He'd tried to console her, there was no denying that, but her grief had been consuming, all-encompassing, trapping her in an airless place, like a firefly in a jar.

She went to the window, pulled aside the gauzy curtain, gazed out over the land. Off by itself, on a small hillside, she could see Susannah's monument, a stone angel, standing guard over the tiny grave.

Julia Sermon had been part of the problem, of course—Annabel had always been jealous of her odd closeness with Gabriel—but it wasn't as simple as that. Sure, he'd spent a lot more time with Miss Sermon after Susannah's death, but now, after more than a dozen years, Annabel was ready to take at least part of the blame upon herself.

In her sorrow she had not been a real wife to him. She had not been unwilling to respond to his attempts to reach her; indeed she had never drawn a breath without loving him since the first day they met—she fifteen, he sixteen—in the churchyard in Parable. No, she had been unable to respond.

The illegitimate child of a handsome disinherited Englishman with a penchant for gambling, drinking, and wandering, Annabel had no recollection of her American mother, though she'd known her maiden aunt, Beatrice, well enough to flee to her, in later years, with a young son in tow.

Ellery Latham, Annabel's father, had been a remittance man, the ne'er-do-well second son of a prominent family, with a past so infamous that even as an adult, having spent much time in England, Annabel did not know the full extent of his youthful sins. Nor did she wish to be enlightened.

In the end, what mattered was that Ellery had been paid, by his grandfather, to stay out of England forever, and denied all access to the family home, a spectacular place called Evanwood, within hailing distance of Warwick Castle.

All the while she was growing up, being dragged from one city to another, and finally, when her father had made too many enemies, from one town to another, Annabel had heard stories of the family home. And she had ached to go there, to be received as a member of the dwindling Latham clan, before it was too late to be accepted.

To her, faraway Evanwood had seemed almost magical. There, the child Annabel had dreamed, she would not be the child of a penniless, if charming, vagabond. There she would be a member of some respectable group, a person who belonged.

That fantasy of mending the breach and fitting in had never come true, despite Annabel's efforts, though it had consumed her youth and practically obsessed her. She had often been a guest at Evanwood, now the property of her sickly, suspicious and snobbish cousin Peers, but she was still a stranger.

These days she kept a manor house nearby, thanks to a generous allowance from Gabriel, complete with liveried footmen and inside servants, and she had a circle of amusing friends. Evanwood and the life that should have been hers were as elusive as ever; indeed, she had long since stopped wanting them.

Annabel set her jaw. She wasn't ready to give up on the things she did want, however. She was constitutionally incapable of that.

After another quick glance in the mirror, Annabel left the room, with its great, empty bed and its multitude of sweet and bitter memories, and progressed along the corridor and down the stairs with studied grace.

Charlie was in the entryway, presenting an incongruous picture as he swiped at a massive coat tree with a feather duster. His smile was gracious, genuine. Would that Gabriel might have met her with even that much civility. Would that he had been anywhere but at the Samhill Saloon, having just passed the night in the arms of Miss Julia Sermon, his devoted comforter.

"Feeling better, Mrs. McKeige?" Charlie asked.

Annabel smoothed her hair, even though she knew it was perfect, had taken care that it should be. "Much better, thank you," she replied.

Charlie went right on dusting, having progressed to the long, slim marble-topped table where Gabriel always tossed his hat when he came in. "Might be somebody you want to see out at the corral," he suggested, twinkling a little.

She felt a rush of sweet tension. Gabriel? Perhaps he had relented, realized how unreasonable he was being about the divorce. The thought left her oddly deflated.

"Nicholas is home from the hills," Charlie prompted gently. Annabel had forgotten his unnerving knack for guessing what people were thinking.

"Nicholas!" Annabel's joy was sudden and ferocious. She had not expected to see her son for days, since he had not been present upon her arrival, and now, suddenly, blessedly, the reunion she had so long anticipated, and rehearsed over and over in her thoughts, was at hand.

"Take that little umbrella of yours along," Charlie suggested, ever practical. "Sun's hot."

Annabel was too anxious to see Nicholas to bother with retrieving her parasol. She nodded at Charlie in insincere compliance and dashed out of the house and across the porch. Her dogs, waiting faithfully in the shade of the lilac bush, got to their feet and trotted after her.

Holding her skirts at ankle height, Annabel hurried across the sweet grass in the side yard, past a line of men's clothing drying in the breathlessly warm air.

Rounding the corner of the house, Annabel spotted the corral in the distance, and the fine figure of a youthful man leaning against the high fence, looking on with interest as one of the ranch hands broke a horse to ride.

Annabel stopped, filled with a wild and instant fear. When she'd last seen Nicholas, he'd been a small, recalcitrant boy, Gabriel in miniature, solemnly informing her that if she didn't send him back to Nevada, he'd run off and find some way to get there on his own. She'd never questioned the fact that he'd been entirely serious about the threat. Nicholas had never really been a child at all, except physically.

Now he was grown up, almost as tall as Gabriel. His hair was fair, like his father's, but longer, and tied back with some kind of narrow cord. He wore black trousers, boots, and a loose-fitting shirt, but no hat.

Annabel's heart pounded with anticipation and a terrible anxiety. Despite the letters and one or two photographic likenesses that she and Nicholas had exchanged over the years, she was not well acquainted with the man he had become. She couldn't guess how he would receive her, for though his letters had been cordial enough, he had said little or nothing about his feelings and had pointedly ignored her every reference to the past. Not one of her hundreds, possibly thousands, of explanations and apologies had ever drawn a response from him. He'd written about a succession of horses and dogs, hunting trips and cattle drives, and passed on a lot of innocuous information about his father and his beloved aunt Jessie. In recent years he had mentioned numerous young women, though always with a forbearance that had made her smile.

Now, as if he sensed her presence, Nicholas turned to look in her direction.

Annabel stopped, frozen in midstride, wanting desperately to approach him, take him into her arms, tell him how dearly she loved him, but afraid. Dear God, if he rejected her, she did not know how she would bear it.

He started slowly toward her, and that enabled Annabel to take one tentative step, follow it up with another, and another.

They met exactly halfway between the corral and the house.

"Miss Annabel," Nicholas said, with a polite nod. His blue eyes, so like Gabriel's, betrayed no expression other than simple civility.

"Nicholas," Annabel marveled, and the name came out as a hoarse whisper. "Oh, *Nicholas.*" Where she could not move before, now she could not hold herself back. She stepped forward and put her arms around her son. Her child.

Although Nicholas did not embrace Annabel, neither did he resist. He simply stood there, within the tight grasp of her arms, betraying nothing—no tension, no anger, no love.

She stepped back, her eyes clouded with happy tears, and cupped his clean-shaven face in her hands. Although beards and sideburns and mustaches were very much in fashion, neither Nicholas nor Gabriel wore them, and Annabel was glad.

"You look wonderful," she said.

"So do you," Nicholas replied, with a slight smile, indicative of nothing.

"I have missed you more than you could ever

imagine." And it was true; Annabel had grieved every day and every night for the lost years, for the man Nicholas, and for the determined, unbiddable little boy she had begged to remain with her in Boston so long ago.

Nicholas made no reply. He closed his hands over hers, brought them away from his face and yet continued to hold them.

"You are the image of your father."

Nicholas grinned, did not release Annabel's hands. There was hope in that, at least. "So they say. I've cherished the hope that I'm not as cussed, but I'm probably fooling myself."

Annabel laughed through her tears. "You are," she answered and, impulsively, recklessly, stood on tiptoe to kiss his cheek. He smelled of soap and youth and clean Nevada air. "Fooling yourself, I mean."

At last Nicholas opened his grasp, but he offered his arm to Annabel in almost the same motion. "Come inside, Miss Annabel, and tell me what you're doing here. Pa wouldn't."

It wounded Annabel that she was Miss Annabel and Gabriel was Pa, but she supposed it was natural enough. Gabriel had raised Nicholas while she'd been far away, first in Boston, then in England, chasing phantoms. Or had she been running from ghosts instead? Not for the first time it occurred to her that she had paid far too high a price for her pride and for those precious, persistent dreams.

Annabel took Nicholas's arm and found it strong, as she had expected. The American West, despite its many and varied perils, was a good place to grow up, breeding strong young men and women who knew their own minds and feared little or nothing.

As they walked toward the house, Annabel found

herself dreading the task ahead, even though it would surely come as no surprise to Nicholas that she wanted to divorce his father. Any sensible person would have wondered why they hadn't ended the farce long ago.

Gabriel was crossing the entryway as they entered, obviously ready to go out. He wore the Colt .45 Annabel had always hated, strapped low on his hip in that way peculiar to men practiced in the use of lethal weapons. Comfortable with them.

"I see the two of you have met," Gabriel said dryly, "so I won't trouble myself to make a formal introduction."

Annabel was stung by the verbal thwack, but she was careful to hide the fact. Before she could respond, Nicholas spoke, and while there was no rancor in his tone, his azure eyes flashed.

"Miss Annabel and I are about to have a private conversation. After that, we'll be heading for town. Don't look for us to come back until after the dancing is over. Fact is, we might even impose on Aunt Jessie for a place to spend the night."

Gabriel looked, for a moment, as if he'd have liked to throttle his son, but the exchange was largely lost on Annabel. Jessie was Gabriel's sister, older than he by nearly twenty years, a banker's widow and a beauty, as their mother had been, and she had probably been something of a substitute mother to Nicholas over the years.

Still, Jessie had never forgiven Annabel for leaving the way she had—she'd written a series of blistering letters early on that left no room for doubt—and there would be no passing the night at her house.

"You do whatever you want," Gabriel said coldly, and though he addressed those spare words to his son,

Annabel knew they were meant for her as well. At the door, he tugged his hat onto his tawny head and added, "Be sure you're back first thing in the morning, that's all, ready to ride the fence lines. I want to know where those missing cattle are."

Nicholas executed a faintly insolent salute, barely civil enough, Annabel suspected, to prevent Gabriel from backhanding him. She had always assumed that her husband and son were close, perhaps even united against her in their blasted alikeness, but now she saw that there were hidden, even dangerous, dynamics at work in their relationship.

"Say hello to Jessie," Gabriel said, in parting, and then he was gone.

Annabel was struck by a confusing and downright disgraceful sense of loss fit to make her grasp the newel-post at the foot of the stairs.

Nicholas gazed at the door for several seconds, as if he could see through it, but—as was typical of him, Annabel was rapidly discovering—his expression was unreadable.

She touched Nicholas's hand tentatively, to bring him back to her, then led the way into the parlor without speaking. Best to get the inevitably difficult conversation over with and see what, if anything, could be salvaged.

It was plain upon entering that the large, once happy room was seldom used now, and the realization deepened Annabel's growing sorrow. The furniture was covered, the fireplace had been swept clean, the piano looked forlorn, though Charlie had obviously made a point of dusting it.

The wooden floor shone, but the rugs, selected with great care from the catalog of an eastern mail-order house, had been rolled up and pushed up against the walls. The painting of Gabriel's mother, the legendary Louisa, who had been stolen by a band of Sioux warriors when Gabriel was a small boy and never seen or heard of again, hung in a shadowy corner. Forgotten, Annabel thought, as a woman who has suffered such a travesty should not be forgotten. The painting and the piano were the only monument to Gabriel's mother on the ranch; Louisa's journals and few pieces of jewelry were in Jessie's keeping.

"Has there been no word of her in all this time?" Annabel asked, distracted for the moment by the fate that had befallen Louisa McKeige. No one had ever seen her after the day the Sioux rode in and snatched her up while she weeded her vegetable garden. Jessie had been long married, with a home of her own, and Gabriel was inside the cabin, recovering from the measles, when it happened. Nick, the children's father and Louisa's devoted husband, had been away, hunting in the foothills.

The first Nicholas McKeige had been destroyed by his wife's disappearance, had searched for her frantically, and then slowly descended into drunkenness, finding some solace there. Eventually the combination of whiskey and despair had killed him.

Nicholas came to stand beside Annabel, gazing at the painting, as she did. "Rumors, once in a while. Nothing more."

Annabel turned to study her son's inscrutable face. "What kind of rumors?"

Nicholas shrugged. "That she was eventually married to one of the braves who kidnapped her. A trapper claimed to have seen her once, while he was trading with the Sioux." He sighed. "Probably just a yarn."

Annabel clasped her hands together in resolve and

turned her thoughts away from poor lost Louisa McKeige. The horrors she might have suffered after her abduction did not bear considering. "Nicholas . . ."

He took her arm, as though she were ancient, led her to a chair, and pulled the sheet away. "Sit down, Miss Annabel. You look as though your knees are about to buckle."

Annabel sat, gratefully, and looked up at her tall son with blurred vision. "Can't you call me Mother?" she asked, in a voice barely more forceful than a whisper.

Nicholas looked away. "No," he said quietly. "No, I can't. I'm sorry."

She pressed her lips together, breathed deeply through her nose, and made no reply. Nicholas, meanwhile, uncovered another chair and drew it close, facing hers.

"All right," he said. "What brings you to this place you hate above all others?"

Annabel swallowed a protest that she did *not* hate the ranch or the house. Too many cherished memories were secreted here; her own lost child was buried only a short distance from where they sat.

"I came to ask your father for a divorce."

Nicholas, who had been leaning forward in his chair, sat back with a sigh and crossed his arms. "What did he say?"

Annabel recalled the confrontation in Gabriel's study with irritation. "He refused. I cannot think why, except that he wanted to thwart my wishes in any possible way. After all, this would leave him free to marry Julia Sermon at long last."

Nicholas frowned. "Marry Julia? She'd never have him—not for a husband, anyway."

"They've been lovers for years, since before we—I—left Nevada," Annabel sputtered, truly taken aback. Gabriel was handsome, virile, strong, and intelligent. He was wealthy, with silver mines that seemed to spew money and more cattle than there were angels in heaven. Why would any woman—*especially* one like Julia—refuse such a man?

Nicholas smiled thoughtfully. "Maybe," he said. "But I think there's more—and at the same time far less—to that alliance than most folks would imagine."

Annabel's mouth might have dropped open if she hadn't trained herself so well. She straightened her skirts with a fidgety motion of both hands and drew a deep breath. "You are quite wrong, Nicholas, but decency constrains me from pursuing the subject further, and I would not like to prejudice you against your father."

"Why did you travel all this way when you could have sent a wire or had your Boston lawyers contact Pa for you?"

Annabel wet her lips and looked away for a moment, then, staunchly, back again. "I wished to see you, Nicholas. And I knew you would not come to England."

He did not look entirely convinced. "You were right about that," he said. "I belong out here, same as Pa does. Do you ever wish you'd had another child after Susie—a son, maybe? Somebody who suited you better than I did?"

She smiled, despite a fathomless need to weep. "I would like daughters, and sons as well, Nicholas," she confessed, "and I intend to have them. But I could never wish for you to be any different than you are."

He seemed puzzled by the news that Annabel

wanted more children, though less insultingly so than his father had been. He pushed back his chair and rose, offering no comment to Annabel's statement.

"Is there somebody you want to marry?" he asked, after a few moments.

Annabel felt heat rise to her cheeks, and wondered why it was that this young man and his father could make her blush so easily, when no one else could. "No," she said. "But I should like to find someone, and I can't do that while I'm married."

"If you want babies," Nicholas said reasonably, "why not have them with Pa? Wouldn't that be easier?"

An unseemly rush of heat raced through Annabel's system at the thought, and settled in a place that caused her to squirm slightly.

"I would die first," she said.

Three

IT WAS A GOOD THING SHE WAS NEARLY INDEFATIGABLE, Annabel told herself, as she returned to town later that morning, traveling in one of Gabriel's lightweight wagons, after a private visit to Susannah's grave. Nicholas held the reins, and the basket of cold food Charlie had prepared was perched on her lap. Still another hurdle awaited her—meeting and greeting the curious and ofttimes self-righteous populace of Parable.

Except for the kidnapping of Louisa McKeige more than thirty years before, Annabel's up and leaving Gabriel, and taking Nicholas with her, was surely one of the most discussed and speculated-about events to take place since the arrival of the first settlers. The bolder members of the community would not hesitate to put their questions to her straight out, and the more cowardly ones were sure to whisper behind their hands.

As the child of Ellery Latham, probably the most winsome swindler ever created, Annabel, by the time she was twelve years old, had already met with all the social disapproval she ever wanted to encounter. She craved respectability with an intensity that made her ache.

Annabel made a point of straightening her backbone an extra measure and meeting the gaze of everyone she could as Nicholas drew the rig to a stop among a dozen others like it, in the shade of a massive oak tree. There was a legend that the tree had been planted by a white woman nearly a century before. The story went that she'd been taken by the Indians, like Louisa McKeige, only way back in Kansas or Missouri, traded from one tribe to another, and eventually carried west. All that wretched woman had had to remember her true home and family by, it was said, was a handful of acorns, snatched up in the initial struggle.

From the day she'd first heard it, that tale had given Annabel the shivers, but now she wondered if it had ever happened at all. The West was a place that spawned spectacular stories as well as strong children. The survivors, whether they were myths or the mortals who passed them on, were durable indeed.

Like a gentleman, Nicholas secured the brake lever and the reins, then came around to help Annabel down from the wagon. His resemblance to the young Gabriel filled Annabel with a certain sweet sorrow, and she found herself wishing, once again, for a second chance. She should have been stronger, should have fought her way out of the darkness, to Gabriel. Should, at least, have made Nicholas stay with her, instead of returning to Nevada, whether he liked it or not.

Dear heaven, she'd made so many mistakes in her life, and giving both Gabriel and Nicholas up without a fight had been among the greatest. Instead of running away, taking refuge in faraway Boston with an embittered old aunt, and waiting there for her husband to come and fetch her, why hadn't she held her ground, right there in Nevada? Why hadn't she waited for her grief to pass, or at least become manageable, before acting so rashly?

She closed her eyes, and the regret was so strong in that moment that she must have swayed slightly on her feet, for Nicholas took a quick, firm grip on her arm.

"Miss Annabel?" he asked quietly. "Are you all right?"

Oh, to hear the word "Mother" from him, spoken with tender regard. But she had surrendered that precious right, by her own choice. By giving in to a child's demands to go home.

She steadied herself, met her son's inquiring but otherwise impenetrable gaze, and managed a smile. *I'm so sorry, Nicholas,* she wanted to say. *Please forgive me.*

"I'm fine," she said instead.

Nicholas grinned at her in that mischievous and vaguely impertinent way that was his alone and, taking the picnic basket in one hand, offered his other arm. "Shall we?"

They had barely reached the edge of the churchyard, where all such community events were held, there being no other appropriate place, when Jessie approached.

Gabriel's sister had aged with grace, like her brother. Her beauty, as classic as that of a finely wrought Greek statue, had only grown more refined, more marked, over the passing years. Her fair hair, the same spun-gold shade as Gabriel's, was loosely bound atop her head, and her figure, always magnificent, remained trim. No doubt it was only the marked lack of eligible men in Parable that had kept the widow from remarrying.

"Annabel," she said coolly, by way of a greeting.

"Jessie," Annabel replied, with a nod and an offered hand, well aware of the censure snapping in those McKeige-blue eyes.

Jessie hesitated a moment and then, probably for Nicholas's sake, reached out to clasp Annabel's palm and fingers in a slight squeeze. "You look well," she said, then made a point of peering around Annabel. "Where is Gabriel?"

Nicholas interceded then, bless him. "He'll be along," he said smoothly, and leaned forward a little way, to kiss his aunt's cheek.

She beamed at him. Jessie had never had children of her own, and in the early days, when she and Annabel were still friends and Jessie's wealthy husband, Franklin, was still living, she'd confided her despair.

"Will you be staying in Parable long?" Jessie asked, linking her arm with Annabel's in a way that might have been amicable, were it not for the subtle stiffness in her countenance. "It's a pity, isn't it, that after all this time, our town is still without a hotel?"

Only fierce pride prevented Annabel from blushing at this oblique reference to her own temporary residence at the ranch. She supposed people were already cogitating on the possibility that she would be sharing Gabriel's bed, despite her long and, in their eyes, unwarranted absence from it.

Annabel offered her warmest smile. "Gabriel has

been kind enough to surrender his room," she said, "and I am quite comfortable."

"Will you be staying long?" Jessie asked sweetly, still holding Annabel's arm in a grip that more resembled being taken into custody than simple companionship. They had reached the edge of the festivities by then, and, as Annabel had expected, several of the folks in attendance were tossing not-so-inconspicuous glances in their direction.

"As long as it takes to complete my business," Annabel answered, with about the same degree of affection Jessie had shown. "I must locate my driver and have Gabriel assign him a place in the bunkhouse." She turned as her son stepped away from her side.

Nicholas seemed oblivious to the small drama, plainly distracted. He wore a solemn expression, and if Annabel had been asked her opinion, she would have said he was looking over the assortment of young ladies scattered among the other picnickers—maybe assessing them, maybe searching for one particular girl.

It pained Annabel that she did not even know if her son had a sweetheart, and the realization that he might well have confided in Jessie sent a rush of sorrow surging through her spirit. Nicholas had told Annabel very little in his letters, though he'd written regularly for a decade, beyond superficial things like describing the weather or relating the news of a train robbery or a trip to Virginia City, but he'd still managed to make it clear that he spent a fair amount of time with Jessie. In fact, he had a room in her house.

"Do come and sit with me," Jessie said, with quiet

insistence, half dragging Annabel toward the blanket Gabriel's sister had spread in the welcome shade of a carefully nurtured elm tree. "We have so much to talk about."

"Will you excuse me?" Nicholas asked, his attention still diverted, and he was gone before either his mother or his aunt could reply.

Jessie smiled indulgently, as though Nicholas were her son, not Annabel's. And maybe, in some ways, she did have a claim on him. She'd surely been the guiding feminine force in his life, imparting whatever grace and refinement he possessed. God knew, Gabriel couldn't have managed the task.

Jessie took a seat on her picnic blanket, and because she was still holding Annabel's arm firmly, Annabel had no choice but to follow suit. She landed with unnecessary force beside her sister-in-law and gained the time to recover her dignity by smoothing and arranging her skirts.

"Why have you come back, Annabel?" Jessie asked, in a moderate but wholly implacable tone of voice.

Annabel met Jessie's unflinching gaze. "I have asked Gabriel for a divorce," she said. "He has, not surprisingly I suppose, made up his mind to be as difficult about the matter as he can."

Jessie blinked; perhaps she had not expected such a direct reply. "Oh, dear," she murmured.

Why, Annabel wondered, did everyone seem taken aback by her wish to be set free from an empty marriage? Simple reason indicated that either she or Gabriel should have taken steps long ago to put the union out of its misery, like an injured horse or a mad dog.

Before she could give voice to her opinion, however, Jessie looked past her and exclaimed again. "Good heavens!" she said.

Annabel turned and saw Gabriel striding through the gathering, tall and wrenchingly handsome in dark trousers, polished boots, a white shirt, and a vest. She almost smiled, despite the sudden and inexplicable swelling in her throat, to notice that he'd forsworn both coat and collar, in typical Gabriel fashion. His expression, far from celebratory, was instead ominous and glowering, as though he were silently daring anyone to comment on his fancy clothes.

It seemed to Annabel, as she watched him walk toward her and Jessie, that time had slowed down to the pace of a stereoscopic machine, showing each passing instant as a separate, if similar, scene. With his patrician features and graceful movements, he looked, if anything, like an archangel, sent to earth disguised as a rancher, but Annabel doubted that he had ever even considered his appearance, beyond the simple demands of everyday grooming, let alone realized how magnificent, how classically *beautiful,* he truly was.

No, Gabriel's self-confidence stemmed from nothing so shallow as his looks; his belief in himself was rooted in the very substance of his being. He was, Annabel realized, a man who had been tested in more than one crucible, a man who had learned to place implicit trust in his own mind, body, and soul.

A path naturally opened for him as he made his way through the gathering, grumbling what was probably a greeting of sorts to this one and that one. Whatever Gabriel's business was, it had nothing to do with socializing at the Independence Day picnic.

He came to a stop, after what seemed like an

inordinate length of time, at the edge of Jessie's blanket. Both women looked up, Jessie shading her eyes with one hand, Annabel forced to squint. The fierce July sun rimmed him in crimson-gold and rendered his features indistinct.

"Join us," Jessie said.

Reluctantly, Gabriel lowered himself to his haunches and, in that instant, became clearly visible again. His gaze, narrowed and more than a little ominous, was fixed on Annabel.

She couldn't resist taunting him just a little, though in truth the sight of him had stolen her breath and speeded up her heartbeat until she could feel it pulsing in every part of her. Maybe she was trying to get back at Gabriel for that, for the seemingly unconscious power he still held over her; she didn't know. "I could have sworn you said you didn't have time to celebrate the Fourth of July," she said.

He glared at her, without so much as a glance or a how-do-you-do for Jessie. "What are you doing here, Annabel?" he rasped.

"I told you," Annabel replied, nettled. "I came to ask for a divorce."

"That isn't what I meant," Gabriel pointed out, with acidic brevity. "You don't belong at this picnic, making a spectacle of yourself."

Annabel's right hand rose automatically to her breast, and she could feel her temples throbbing. Maybe Gabriel McKeige was handsome enough to warrant a place on Mount Olympus, but he was also the most maddeningly presumptuous man Annabel had ever known.

"Making a spectacle of myself?" she echoed, in a soft and measured voice. She wondered if Gabriel remembered how dangerous it was when she took that tone. "I am merely sitting here, on a blanket, having a quiet conversation with your sister. How does that constitute making a spectacle?"

"Gabriel," Jessie said, in a creditable attempt to intercede and defuse the situation.

"You know damn well," Gabriel answered, looking straight at Annabel and ignoring Jessie completely, "that these people"—he paused to gesture with one hand—"are wondering, *gossiping* . . . Thunderation, Annabel, if ever there was a private matter, this is it!"

"I have not so far climbed onto the bandstand," Annabel said carefully, with only the mildest tinge of sarcasm, "and announced to the town of Parable that you and I are getting a fancy eastern divorce."

"After the scene you made this morning," Gabriel whispered furiously, "you don't have to!"

Annabel straightened her skirts with small, swift plucking motions of her fingers. "I confess that was a bit theatrical," she said. "However, you might have been spared the embarrassment if you hadn't spent the night upstairs at the Samhill Saloon, in the embrace of your mistress."

Somewhere behind Gabriel, a firecracker went off. It seemed puny in comparison to the incendiary suspense building between the two of them, and neither Gabriel nor Annabel so much as flinched at the sound.

"If you want to discuss Julia," Gabriel said ominously, "we will. But not here. Damn it, Annabel, where you're concerned, I've put up with all the scandal I'm going to."

Annabel opened her mouth to make a scathing reply, but Jessie silenced her by reaching out and placing a cool hand on hers.

"That's quite enough from both of you," Jessie

said. "If you're wise, you'll be civil to each other, enjoy the picnic as best you can, and hold a shouting match later, when half the county isn't there to hear it. I'll ask Nicholas to spend the night in town."

Gabriel gave a sudden dazzling and slightly chilling grin at his sister's words, though his eyes never left Annabel's pinkened face. "That's a good idea," he said, and then, in a single motion, he clasped Annabel's hand and drew her to her feet as he stood. "Come along, Mrs. McKeige. The games are about to begin. Let's join all the other happy couples."

Before Annabel could even get her breath, she was being dragged across the picnic grounds by one hand. With horror, she saw that Gabriel expected her to participate in, of all things, a sack race.

She pulled up hard, but simply did not have the strength to counteract Gabriel's forward momentum.

"Here," he said, upon reaching the starting line, where other pairs were preparing to compete, and thrust a burlap sack into her hands. "I think we can win this if you can stay upright and hop fast. That rail fence up there is the finishing line."

Annabel looked up into her husband's face and saw that, while his mouth was set in a determined line, his eyes were dancing. She tried to shove the bag back at him—other women were already scrambling into sacks of their own, stuffing their skirts in around their hips and pulling upward on the hems of the bags—but Gabriel would not accept it.

"Gabriel McKeige," Annabel whispered desperately, "I *will not*—"

He arched an eyebrow. "Don't they have sack races in England, Lady Annabel?" he asked, his voice brimming with false benevolence.

"If you wish to avoid a scene, this is hardly the way to do it," Annabel pointed out tightly.

Gabriel appeared concerned. "Are you afraid?" he asked.

She opened her mouth to say that if Gabriel wanted to enter the sack race he could damn well be the one to wear the sack, but before she got the words out, she spotted Nicholas at the edge of the group. He was laughing, helping a pretty young girl into a bag, and something about the sight took all the heart out of Annabel.

She thrust the bag into Gabriel's hands, turned on her heel, and walked away, mortified. While she didn't give two hoots in hell what Gabriel thought of her, in this instance at least, or the town as a whole, Nicholas's opinion mattered. She wouldn't be made a fool of with him looking on.

Gabriel pursued her, backed her up to a tree trunk, with the race going on somewhere behind her. He tossed aside the bag, but the gesture seemed more one of resignation than fury.

"I'm sorry, Annabel," he said.

She took a few deep breaths, in order not to cry, and wished with all her heart that she were the kind of woman to participate in a sack race. "Who is that girl with Nicholas?" she asked, when she could safely speak, looking over her shoulder.

"That's the marshal's daughter," he answered. "I think her name is Ellen. Or maybe Sally."

The participants were lined up on the starting line, which was really just a length of twine stretched across the grass. "Is she his sweetheart?"

"Maybe this week she is," Gabriel said, with a benign lack of interest. "Nicholas is a fickle soul." He paused. "I can't imagine how he comes by such a sorry trait. Can you?"

Annabel spun round to look at him. "Yes," she responded. "He gets it from you."

Gabriel grinned. "I won't pursue that argument, Mrs. McKeige," he said sweetly. "Which is fortunate for you."

The pastor, appointed to signal the beginning of the race, stood at the far end of the starting line with one arm raised. "Now remember, ladies," he called out cheerfully. "To win the prize, you have to hop down to the fence and back, get out of the sack and give it to your partner. Then he's got to do the same thing. Falling down is all right, long as you get back up. Is everybody ready?"

Annabel smiled, watching.

"Go!" the pastor yelled.

Nicholas's friend Ellen-or-Sally had taken an immediate lead. Several of the other women were already on the ground, struggling to get up, their laughter rising through the still green leaves on the trees, ringing like music in the shimmering heat. Their husbands and sweethearts cheered them on from behind the finish line, and friends and family added their own boisterous encouragement from various other vantage points.

"Annabel?"

She turned back to Gabriel, unprepared for the quiet, searching look in his eyes. "Yes?"

He curved his fingers under her chin, made a soft smudging motion on her mouth with the pad of his thumb. And then he kissed her.

Annabel, caught off guard, knew a long-forgotten joy, so piercing and sweet that it brought tears to her eyes. During that kiss, innocent though it was, her whole being seemed to awaken from some ancient trance. A delicious ache flowed through her, settling heavily between her hips.

When at last Gabriel drew back, Annabel was so disoriented that, for the briefest fraction of a second her entire past eluded her. Except for the part that concerned Gabriel, of course.

Then he drew back, turned away. His obvious regret was harder to bear by far than her own outlandish reaction to the interlude.

Annabel hesitated a moment, unsure what to do or say, then threaded her way back through the trees and people, making for Jessie's picnic blanket. When Gabriel followed, only seconds later, he seemed so completely unmoved, unchanged by what had happened between them that she was injured. The power of the attraction had been unmistakable, and yet he would deny it, pretend to be unmoved.

Nicholas wandered over presently, without the girl he'd kept company with earlier, and his mood remained solemn. He didn't speak to either Gabriel or Annabel, and since they weren't speaking to each other, that made things even more awkward. When Jessie served her nephew a plate filled from her own picnic basket as well as the one he and Annabel had wheedled from Charlie, he looked at the food as though it were a foreign substance.

Annabel sat a little to one side of the others and, without thinking, raised her arms to secure the strategically placed pins and combs in her hair. Gabriel, stretched out in the grass a few feet away, watched her breasts rise, with a somber interest that should have annoyed her but didn't.

She blushed and quickly lowered her hands, but she still felt as though her bodice were transparent.

Gabriel's smile was demonic. When Jessie gave him a plate, he set it aside and took a plum from the basket instead, taking a bite of the fruit and then languidly running the tip of his tongue over his lips to catch the juice.

Annabel looked away, but it didn't help. All of a sudden she felt dizzy enough to swoon, and her eyes went straight back to Gabriel as though they were under his control instead of her own.

He finished the plum, tossed the pit aside, and licked his fingers, one by one.

Inwardly, Annabel groaned. She bit her lower lip and stared at Gabriel in helpless fascination, praying that none of the others knew what was happening, that he was wooing her, preparing her for his bed. She remembered that he'd been accomplished at such games when they were young—and in their time apart, he must have become an expert.

"Have something to eat," Jessie said gently, urging Annabel to take the plate she had apparently offered before. "You must be half starved after the day you've had, not to mention tuckered out."

Annabel had no appetite whatsoever, but she wanted Jessie's friendship, or at least the pretense of it, and she needed a distraction from Gabriel, so she accepted the meal and murmured her thanks. Nicholas, intent on something or someone else, wandered away without a word, carrying a drumstick and a slice of the cherry pie with him.

Gabriel was still lying on his side, one elbow on the ground, his head propped in his hand. Annabel knew, even though he surely presented an irreproachable picture to any other observer, that he was remembering things they'd done together. Furthermore, he was fully *aware* that she knew.

Jessie chatted with passersby and occasionally commented on someone's dress or potato salad or political opinions, but she seemed completely heedless of the silent exchange taking place between her brother and his estranged wife. She nibbled at a delicate slice of the cherry pie, then excused herself and went off in search of some friend.

Annabel, in an effort to keep her there, barely restrained herself from clutching at Jessie's skirts as she walked away. She and Gabriel were alone, for all intents and purposes, for although everyone in town must have been present, with few exceptions, the populace seemed to stream around them like water around a brook stone.

"Stop it!" Annabel hissed.

Gabriel looked bewildered—deliberately so. "What?"

"Stop trying to make me want you. It won't work!"

His expression was entirely unfitted to a churchyard. "Won't it?"

"No!"

He only wanted to torment her, of that she was certain. He'd discerned from her reaction to the kiss that she still desired him, and if she succumbed, he would no doubt make a mockery of her.

"I think you're mistaken in that, Mrs. McKeige. No doubt we'll find out, later on tonight, though, won't we?" He lowered his voice to one notch above a whisper, and the sound of it was plainly erotic, softened by promises and at the same time made rough by some very private memories that belonged to both of them. "Don't worry, Annabel. It's Independence Day. Nobody will notice a few extra skyrockets."

Four

BY MIDAFTERNOON THE YOUNGEST INDEPENDENCE Day picnickers had ceased running and shrieking through the crowd, their games won or lost, the attendant prizes cherished or mourned. They lay curled up on family blankets, eyes closed, breathing deeply and slowly, tendrils of moist hair clinging to their cheeks.

The older children were subdued as well, some wading in the creek that flowed behind the churchyard; some, homemade lines and poles in hand, complaining that the others were scaring off the fish. Their fathers played horseshoes on the far side of the cemetery, collars undone, coats shed. They swapped lies, laid wagers, and passed around flasks of whiskey and fat cigars. Gabriel was among them.

The women sat in little groups in the sweet grass, talking quietly, fanning themselves with special editions of the *Parable Testament*, a one-page newspaper passed out to everyone, free of charge, by the publication's eager new editor, Lucius Wickcomb. Nicholas had not yet decided how he felt about Lucius; the man was pleasant enough and pretty game, for an easterner, but he asked a lot of questions and he had a way of watching a person that was downright unsettling.

Fresh from a poker game, and a few dollars richer, Nicholas sat on a low branch of the fabled oak tree, which grew almost parallel to the ground, his back to the trunk, one leg dangling, one bent at the knee. There in the leaf-dappled shade, he drew on a slim cheroot in a leisurely way, his attention now focused on his mother.

Miss Annabel sat only a few feet away, on an outlying corner of Jessie's blanket, legs curled up beneath her voluminous skirts, hands folded in her lap. She must be exhausted, Nicholas thought, having traveled so far in recent weeks, including the eight miles between Fort Duffield and Parable before dawn, and yet she showed no visible sign of fatigue. Jessie was close by, eyes closed, newspaper fan in slow, steady motion, lips curled in a serene smile.

Nicholas ground out the cheroot and tossed it aside. He had things to do, should by rights have been on the road already. Miss Annabel's unexpected return was a bewildering thing; he hadn't decided whether it was bad or good or just plain indifferent.

Funny, he thought. As a little kid, he used to lie in bed at night and pray she'd come home straightaway. He'd wanted her to love him, to love his father, the way other mothers and wives did. But she'd lost interest in him after Susie died; he'd come up short by comparison to his little sister, he reckoned. Had never had her sweet, pliable nature.

Nicholas looked back cautiously on those times, so early in his life, when things had gone so very wrong. After Miss Annabel had sent him home from Boston, he'd made a lot of promises to God. If only his mother could be on the next stage, full of smiles and love for his father, for the ranch, for him . . . he'd do his lessons at school and memorize his Bible verses at church, stop dropping frogs in the water buckets out in the bunkhouse, give up spinning yarns about how his grandmother had married an Indian chief and become a princess. Back then, of course, he'd known a whole lot less about everything.

God hadn't kept up His end of the bargain, but then, neither had Nicholas. He'd gone right on with all the mischief that seemed to come so naturally to him, and God had kept Miss Annabel far away.

Until today.

Nicholas sighed, propped his crossed arms on his knee, and tilted his head back, closing his eyes. After all this time, all those prayers, Miss Annabel was home again. He just hoped she wouldn't stay long enough to see him hanged.

"Nicholas?" The voice was soft, tentative, and definitely female.

He opened his eyes to see the marshal's daughter, Callie, standing beside him. The tree branch was only about chest high, and thick as a horse's girth.

"Hello, Callie," he said, trying not to sound weary. She was a sweet girl, and so pretty it sometimes made him ache all over just to look at her, with her masses of bright brown hair and her wide-set green-gray eyes, but she was young and probably a virgin, though he'd heard speculation to the contrary—speculation he'd answered with a sucker punch.

Nicholas did not make conquests among the innocent, and yet he was a man, with a man's desires. Too much time spent with Callie meant bedding an older, more experienced woman, whether it was convenient or not.

She smiled at him in that angelic way that always roused contrasting wants in Nicholas. "You going to the dance?" she asked.

He took another cheroot from the pocket of his shirt, only too aware that Miss Annabel had taken notice of the exchange. To give his mother proper credit, she did look like she was trying not to listen, but that was nigh unto impossible at such a short distance.

"Maybe," Nicholas said.

Callie raised one small, dark eyebrow, as trim and silky as the wing of a tiny bird. "So you may not be there at all."

"Maybe not," Nicholas allowed, watching his mother out of the corner of his eye. Miss Annabel was still studiously *not* watching him, while Jessie appeared to be absorbed in one of those love novels she was always mailing away for.

"You won't mind, then," Callie said.

Nicholas sat up a little straighter, couldn't help himself. "Won't mind what?"

"That I'm going with Jack Horncastle."

Horncastle had been educated in Parable's one-room schoolhouse, like Nicholas, but he'd gone away to some college in Illinois afterward, planning to become a lawyer, then come back as nothing in particular. Nicholas, connected to the ranch by some mystical umbilical cord, had never wanted to do anything else but live and fight, love and die, on the land—McKeige land—but that didn't mean he hadn't hungered for learning. He'd devoured his father's eclectic collection of books, then gone on to consume every volume his aunt Jessie had proffered as well, except for the love stories.

"You have a good time," he told Callie evenly, with a little smile. Fact was, he wanted to find Jack, get him by the lapels, and slam him up against the nearest wall a few times. And not just because of the marshal's daughter.

Callie showed just the slightest flicker of disappointment, it seemed, but Nicholas figured he might have imagined that. When he finished watching her walk away—what a bittersweet exercise *that* was—he was startled to turn and find that his mother had crept up on his blind side.

"She's a pretty girl," Miss Annabel said.

"Yeah," Nicholas admitted, and there might have been a sour note to his voice; he couldn't have said for sure.

"What's her name?"

Nicholas narrowed his eyes at Miss Annabel, unconsciously mimicking his father, and thought he saw her wilt slightly, like a tender flower under a glaring sun. "Callie Swingler," he answered, unwilling to give away much more than that.

Miss Annabel sighed softly and leaned against the tree limb, gazing up into his face. "I'm not your enemy, Nicholas. I hope to prove that to you."

"That will be hard, Miss Annabel," he replied quietly, striking a match to the sole of one boot and touching the flame to the cheroot between his teeth. The smell of sulfur scented the air between them. "You being in England, and me being here."

Miss Annabel watched with an expression of gentle disapproval as Nicholas drew on the acrid smoke. "So you admit it. You *do* think of me as an enemy."

Nicholas regarded his mother in silence for a few

moments. "No, Miss Annabel," he said, at some length, and with neither bitterness nor regret. "The truth is, I don't often think of you at all—these days, anyway. I did a lot when I was little."

She flushed, and Nicholas was sorry if he'd hurt her, but at the same time he couldn't rightly have taken back what he'd said. As a boy he'd pondered the mystery of Miss Annabel and her disaffections until his mind was raw, but as a man he had other concerns. Serious ones, some of which, if misunderstood, could cost him everything.

"Did they tease you about me—the other children, I mean—when you were small?" Miss Annabel offered the question tentatively, and yet the look in her eyes plainly showed not only that she wanted the answer but that, in some strange way, she needed it.

"Never more than once," Nicholas replied truthfully. He'd bloodied a few noses and blackened a few eyes—Jack Horncastle's among them—and after a while the other kids had known enough to speak politely of Annabel McKeige, if they mentioned her at all.

She smoothed her hair back from her forehead, sighed again. "I may be in Parable awhile," she said presently. "At least until I can make your father see reason. During that time I hope to find my way back to you. Are you going to make that difficult?"

The honesty, the forthrightness, of Miss Annabel's assertion took Nicholas aback. While he wasn't ready to be vulnerable to her—he suspected his father wasn't, either—he didn't, couldn't, hate her. "No," he said, examining the crimson tip of his cheroot with idle interest, as if it offered some small revelation. "But I will offer you some advice, if you'll take it."

She smiled. "What's that?"

"Change those dogs' names. The poor creatures have enough against them, being so stupid-looking and useless. Being called Champion and Hercules is adding insult to injury."

Miss Annabel chuckled. "Very well. What would you call them?"

"Stupid-looking and useless," Nicholas reiterated, but he was grinning. A little. "Hell, I don't know. Out here, dogs have names like Shep and Blackie and just plain Dog."

She moved, smiling, to touch him, then changed her mind.

Nicholas felt both relief and regret. The old questions, unwelcome and unbidden, popped into his head: *Was it something I did, something I said, that made you stay away? If I'd been better or different, older or younger, smarter or dumber, or a girl, would you have stayed? Did you ever love me, or even love my father?*

Nicholas couldn't bring himself to ask aloud, but he wondered, all right, just as fervently as he had when he was small. Probably, on some level, he'd never stopped wondering.

"Will you be staying in town for the dance?" he asked instead.

Miss Annabel smiled again, though sadly, found the distant horseshoe players with her eyes, and nodded. "Oh, yes," she said softly and with the fathomless pride that Nicholas suspected was both her blessing and her curse. "I won't have one person in this town thinking I'm hiding anything."

Nicholas grinned. By that time he'd heard the full and glorious tale of his mother's spectacular arrival that morning. He especially liked the part where she showed up at the Samhill Saloon, where his pa had passed the night in Miss Julia Sermon's apartments, and confronted him right there on the sidewalk, in front of God and everybody. "I don't suppose anybody has that impression," he said.

Gabe, Nicholas noticed, was walking slowly toward them, wending his way between scattered maples and oaks planted by settlers nostalgic for easterly homes, sidestepping blankets where babies slept and work-worn women chatted, worked at their sewing, or simply daydreamed. He looked younger to Nicholas all of a sudden, with his collar open and his shirt grass-stained because his long frame didn't fit on a picnic blanket. Younger and vulnerable in a way Nicholas had never thought he could be.

Suddenly he feared for his father, and understood so much that he'd overlooked before.

He felt a flash of anger as he swung his gaze back to Miss Annabel, who was watching Gabe's approach and thinking thoughts of her own. Solemn ones, Nicholas guessed, by her expression.

"If you're going to hurt him again," he said quietly, "leave now. Leave Parable and don't ever come back."

Miss Annabel was startled, and, like anybody else, her first instinct was surely to defend herself, but after biting her lip, she got control. The faint flush that had risen to her cheeks at Nicholas's warning receded slowly. "I will be gone," she said, "as soon as I have your father's promise to set me free."

Nicholas swung deftly to the ground. Suddenly he wanted to join the horseshoe tournament, though more for the circulating whiskey flasks than for the game itself. With a curt nod he turned his back on his mother and walked away. As he passed his father, so close that their shoulders brushed, he nodded again.

Jessie kindly invited Annabel to her house to freshen up before the dance. Gabriel was nowhere about, a fact that Annabel tried not to be concerned about, but it was hard. She should have been glad, she supposed, considering that, thanks to his shameless flirtation that afternoon, not to mention that stolen kiss, she was painfully conscious of him, but she wasn't glad. She kept worrying that he'd gone to the Samhill Saloon to pass some time with Miss Sermon.

"That is a lovely dress," Jessie commented from the doorway of the guest room she had allotted to her sister-in-law. Annabel had sent her driver, Mr. Hilditch, to the ranch for the emerald-green gown, after advising him which trunk it could be found in.

"Thank you," Annabel said. The garment was one of her simplest, for while she wanted the men and women of Parable to know she'd come back with a purpose in mind and her head held high, she wasn't one to flaunt expensive belongings. She'd left her jewelry and better gowns in Boston after the crossing from Southampton, safely stowed in the grand, gloomy house she had recently inherited from her ancient aunt, the woman who had given her shelter so long ago, when she had fled home and husband.

She turned away from the mirror, satisfied with her appearance, and admired Jessie's soft green gown. "I declare," Annabel said, in all honesty, "you are *ageless.* No doubt Captain Sommervale and all his young soldiers will be swooning at your feet tonight."

Jessie smiled thinly; it was clear she had perceived Annabel's compliment as shallow, meaningless flattery, and she brushed it off without comment.

"They're here because someone has been stealing their cattle, between Gabe's ranch and the fort," she said. "They lost two hundred head not long ago."

Annabel had no doubt that Gabriel could handle the situation, and said so, somewhat briskly, as Jessie led the way down the corridor toward the main staircase.

Jessie turned at the top of the stairs, her face shadowed in the thin light of early evening. "I quite agree with you," she said. "If that were the worst of it, I'd rest easy of a night."

Annabel, who had been wondering which of the closed doors along the long hallway opened onto Nicholas's room, was suddenly alarmed. "What do you mean?" she asked.

To her credit, Jessie met her gaze and did not look aside. "There are those who say Nicholas is involved. In the rustling, I mean. And in other things, too. Worse things."

Annabel's stomach turned ice cold and then clenched so violently that she thought she might be sick. "That's impossible!"

Jessie turned, started down the steps. "Is it?" she asked, tossing the question over one shoulder without looking back. "Nicholas was a very troubled boy, Annabel. He's been in trouble more than he's been out. He drinks too much, fights too much, and holds the record for the most nights spent in the town jail. He's broken the heart of every girl in town over the age of fifteen, with the exception of Marshal Swingler's daughter, Callie, and it looks like he's working on her."

"Jessie McKeige," Annabel said at the foot of the stairs, her tone forcing Jessie to look at her, "why didn't you write to me?" Jessie had taken her maiden name back after her husband's death.

"I figured you would have been here if you'd wanted to be," Jessie answered reasonably. Coldly.

Annabel ached to raise her hand and slap the other woman hard across the face, but she restrained herself. She thought of her father and all his wastrel's ways, and the inevitable comparison between Nicholas and his worthless grandfather chilled her. "What of Gabriel? What kind of father stands back and watches his own son become a drunkard and an outlaw?"

"One who knows people have to make their share of mistakes, for better or for worse," Jessie said. "Gabriel believes in Nicholas, and so do I. He'll straighten out on his own one day, if he doesn't wind up on a scaffold or in the territorial prison first."

Again Annabel felt the urge to do violence. It was all she could manage not to grasp Jessie by her straight, slender shoulders and shake her. "Perhaps you and Gabriel are willing to stand by and watch my son destroy himself," she said, in a furious whisper, "but *I* am not! I intend to *do* something!"

"Like what?" Jessie asked evenly.

Tears of frustration and frantic worry burned behind Annabel's eyes. "I don't know," she said miserably, "but before God, I will think of *something.*"

There was a rap at the door, and then it opened and Gabriel was standing there in the foyer, looking handsome even in the same shirt and trousers he'd worn in the sack race, with his hair slightly mussed and the beginnings of a golden beard glimmering on his chin and jaws.

He nodded to Jessie, then raked Annabel with those blue, blue Viking's eyes.

"I want to talk to you!" Annabel announced, and stormed forward to take his arm and half-propel him outside, onto Jessie's dark porch. Jessie politely shut the door between herself and them.

The night air was not merely warm but hot, scented by midsummer roses, and the sky was spangled with stars, as if adorned for the holiday. The irregular pop of firecrackers echoed from near and far.

In the light of a bright moon, Annabel could see that Gabriel's brow was furrowed in consternation. "If this is about the divorce . . ."

"It's about Nicholas!" Annabel interrupted, barely able to contain her outrage. "How dare you, Gabriel? *How dare you?*"

"How dare I what?" Gabriel demanded, annoyed now as well as baffled. His nose was half an inch from Annabel's, and she felt his breath on her face. To her chagrin, it made her lips tingle and started a veritable avalanche of other visceral sensations within. If he'd kissed her then, even in the state she was in . . .

She shook off the images that threatened to flood her mind and divert her from this most important of purposes. "Why didn't you tell me that Nicholas has been in trouble? Why didn't you send for me?"

"Every kid gets into trouble, if he's got any imagination or gumption at all," Gabriel said. His eyes were flashing, bright as any Chinese rocket. "As for my sending for you—why would I? You made it pretty damn obvious from the first, Mrs. McKeige, that you didn't give a damn about him!" *Or me.* He didn't add that last, but he might as well have; the phrase pulsed between them, like the echo of a war drum.

Annabel went to the porch rail and grasped it with both hands, fighting tears. Her back was stiff, and she felt as if her knees would give out, not from weakness, not from fatigue, but from the sheer, ferocious intensity of her emotions.

"I had my reasons for leaving, and you well know it," she ground out. "Furthermore, Nicholas refused to remain in Boston with me. I had no choice but to send him back."

"You might have come with him."

She whirled, ablaze with indignation. "And you might have come back east to fetch us!" she cried.

"What for?" Gabriel asked, and he looked genuinely confused. "That would have been stupid. You'd already made it clear enough how you felt by leaving in the first place."

"Damn you," Annabel gasped, raising both fists in an ineffectual effort to pound on his chest, then just letting them rest there. "Damn you, Gabriel, I waited for you—I waited!"

He closed strong, callused hands around her wrists, but gently. Once again he was frowning. "I don't understand. You expected me to come to Boston?"

Annabel's tears, so valiantly withheld, would no longer be contained. They pooled in her lashes and made her vision blurry. "Yes! I wanted you to come and get us, Nicholas and me. I wanted you to say you were sorry, that you'd never be unfaithful again, with Miss Sermon or anyone else—"

Gabriel cursed and flung her hands away, turning his back on Annabel, shoving splayed fingers through his already mussed hair. Finally he faced Annabel again, and found her biting her lower lip.

"First," he said, with an obvious effort to hold his temper, "I *didn't know* you expected me to come chasing after you like that, when you'd left me of your own free will. And second, I will not defend my relationship with Julia. I made my marriage vows to you and I kept them."

"Please!" Annabel scoffed and turned to descend the porch steps in such high dudgeon that she caught one foot in her hem and would have landed headfirst on the walk if Gabriel hadn't caught her arm. She did not know whether his grasp was born of chivalry or fury, but either way, he wasn't letting her go.

"Why is it so damned hard for everybody to believe that a man and a woman can *like* each other? Julia Sermon is one of the best friends I've ever had!"

That time Annabel did slap him. It was a primitive reaction, over and done with before she had time to think that it was wrong. Gabriel had never struck her, never been rough with her at all, except in a very intimate way that she had enjoyed, and she'd had no right to raise a hand to him.

"I'm sorry," she said.

Gabriel released her and gave a sigh that seemed to come from the bottom of his soul. "Me too," he replied, somewhat cryptically. "Me too." He started past her, as if to walk away, to just walk away and leave everything unsettled, and Annabel couldn't endure that.

She hurried after him, blocked his way at the gate. "No, Gabriel," she said, looking up at him in challenge and determination. "We're going to put aside our differences, you and I, right this moment. It isn't important what I think of your friendship with Julia Sermon or what you think of my running off to Boston and leaving you. Nicholas is all that matters." He started to speak, but Annabel raised an index finger to silence him. "You weren't listening, Gabriel. Our son's future, maybe even his life, is at stake. I'm going to find a way to help him, but I need your cooperation to succeed."

"You want to declare a truce."

She nodded. "Once we know Nicholas is safe, you can say whatever you want to me. Tarnation, make a list if you're afraid you'll forget one of my many sins, but keep it to yourself until we've won this battle."

Gabriel stared at her for a long time. Then he thrust a hand through his hair again and sighed once more. "All right," he said hoarsely. "But I'll be damned if I know where to start."

Annabel could have hugged Gabriel, she was so desperately grateful for his agreement, but she didn't indulge the impulse. She just linked her arm through his. "We start by attending the Independence Day dance," she said, with shaky merriment. "We'll know what to do if we simply pay attention."

For the first time, Gabriel let his own concern for Nicholas show. "I hope that's true," he muttered. "Sommervale and his men are here to find the rustlers who've been intercepting the army's supply of beef, and they'll run everyone involved to ground if they have to link arms and crisscross the whole state."

He opened the gate, steered Annabel through ahead of him.

"I guess you and I had better find them first," she said.

The dance was held on a temporary plank floor laid out in the churchyard and rimmed in colored lanterns. The band consisted of two fiddlers and the piano player from the Samhill Saloon, who could be persuaded, on special occasions like that one, to bring out a cello and pluck a few spritely notes.

Without any particular ceremony, Gabriel took Annabel into his arms and whirled her into the stream of music and dancing. He was exceedingly graceful at this, as he was at everything—riding, shooting, making love.

Annabel felt safe in his embrace, and even though she knew it was an illusion, she allowed herself the simple pleasure of being led, even guided, through the steps. The other dancers were a haze around them, and for that blessed time out of time she thought of nothing but the man holding her. The man who had made her a woman so long ago and set her thrashing and soaring beneath him.

She wanted that again, though she knew the choice would be both unwise and impermanent. For one night she yearned to find solace and fire in Gabriel McKeige's bed.

"You are more beautiful than ever," Gabriel said matter-of-factly, at the end of the first set, and Annabel knew the compliment was genuine. It was not in him to speak pretty, frivolous words, even in the most intimate of situations.

Annabel raised her gaze to meet his. "Thank you," she murmured, just as the music took up again. They might have moved into another dance if Captain Sommervale hadn't stepped in.

"May I have the pleasure?" he asked cordially, offering a hand to Annabel. He was an attractive man, though in his late fifties and long married, and she was glad to see that the invitation, however harmless, made a muscle leap in Gabriel's jaw.

"Why certainly, Captain," Annabel said brightly, taking the offered hand. She'd seen Nicholas on the edge of the crowd, as Gabriel plainly hadn't, and she gestured toward him with a subtle motion of her eyes. "It would be a pleasure."

Gabriel spotted their son at last, excused himself,

and went to the far side of the dance floor to speak to him.

As the captain spun her deftly into the flow of music, Annabel hoped Gabriel would choose his words wisely, instead of simply confronting Nicholas straight out, in his blunt and often tactless way.

Looking over the captain's shoulder as he chattered on about what a nice town Parable was and how he'd like to bring his wife there upon his retirement from the army and settle down, Annabel noted with a sinking heart that the exchange between Nicholas and Gabriel was an angry one.

Nicholas turned, finally, and disappeared into the night. Gabriel watched him go, started after him, and then thought better of the plan and turned back, tossing Annabel a look of helpless irritation.

Annabel closed her eyes for a moment, grateful that Gabriel had not pursued Nicholas; in their state of mind, they probably would have come to blows instead of reaching any kind of accord. If she and Gabriel were going to turn Nicholas back onto the straight and narrow, they would have to win his trust first, and for her, at least, that was going to be a tall order.

So tall that she probably wouldn't have attempted it for anyone else, but this was Nicholas, her only living child, and though she had allowed him to walk away from her once, she would not make that mistake again. For him she would fight to her last breath, to the final, fluttering beat of her heart.

It was only when Annabel came back to herself, and glanced up at the captain's thoughtful and somber face, that she realized he had been watching Nicholas, too.

Five

FIREWORKS SPLASHED AND SPILLED AGAINST THE SKY like stars exploding and tumbling to earth, raising cries of delight from those onlookers who were still awake, still upright. The horses nickered and tossed their heads, were soothed only when the brief marvel had finished. Those who had fallen too soon, mostly the very young and the very old, lay sleeping upon the ground, amid the debris of their family picnics, tenderly covered with blankets brought from the wagons and buggies and traps parked some distance away.

Now, with Independence Day properly observed, men in shirtsleeves went to unhobble and hitch their nervous teams, while women in dresses stained with grass and food gathered up sticky offspring, blinking grandmothers, baskets, and blankets.

Annabel, standing beside Gabriel in the starlight, her neck aching from watching the fireworks, took in the scene and remembered yet another thing she loved about Parable. About America.

The rigors of a long and emotional day had caught up with her at last; she was utterly exhausted, but two separate and very powerful realities kept her awake and aware. The first blazed in her heart—she was that fiercest and most deadly of all creatures, a mother whose child was in danger. The second was a fire of another sort, ignited by the man who stood next to her, comfortable with silence in a way that she herself had never learned to be.

"Nicholas has gone to Jessie's," Gabriel said, with a degree of gentleness uncommon in him, taking Annabel's elbow in a light grasp and guiding her into the heart of the departing wagons. He found the McKeige rig unerringly, collected the appropriate horses, and put them quickly into harness.

Quiet good-nights flowed thick all around Annabel, a provincial chorus of men and women calling from one rig to the next. Babies fussed, and bigger children whimpered that they wanted to go home. Horses whinnied, harnesses and rigging creaked, wheels and hooves clattered softly on the summer ground, beneath its carpet of fragrant grass.

It was, Annabel thought, a wonderful mix of cozy sounds, and once again, briefly, she knew that tender illusion of belonging, being part of things.

She gave herself a little inward shake as Gabriel swung up beside her and took the reins. She had come to secure a divorce from the gloriously handsome, impossibly willful man beside her, and she dared not forget her real mission in Parable.

Granted, her plans had been altered slightly by the discovery that Nicholas was in trouble, but when her son had been turned away from his present and probably disastrous course, she would have no choice but to depart. Even if she wanted to stay, she had to remember that she would never truly find a place for herself in this town where everyone knew everybody else, and practically everything about them.

Dismayed, Annabel knotted her hands in her lap. She wasn't particularly close to anyone in Warwickshire, either, or in Boston; though she had acquaintances, she could not think of a single friend in whom she would have confided her deepest secrets. She was, it seemed, condemned to wander the earth all her days, as her father had, and her reasons for exile, she realized, were not so very different from his.

Ellery Latham, for all his nefarious shenanigans, had only been searching for a place and a people that would accept him, take him in. The objective, so simple for most human beings, had eluded him all his life.

Beneath all these gloomy conclusions flowed a deep river of desire, and as the small wagon bumped and jostled over the stony ground and onto the equally uneven road, Annabel was repeatedly thrust against Gabriel's side. He felt like a shelter of stone, and smelled pleasantly of fresh air, green grass, and man, substantial in spirit as well as person. His presence gave Annabel a certain frenzied solace.

Impulsively, and because she had felt so alone for so long, she slipped her arm through his and let her head rest lightly against his shoulder. The wish that things might have been different between them welled up in her and spilled over in the form of tears she would not let him see. Tears that burned behind her eyes but were subdued before they could flow down her cheeks.

Gabriel said nothing at all; it was enough, for that

one night, that he was beside her, that he would protect her, whatever their differences. That he knew the way home through a starry night.

The ranch house was dark when they arrived, but a man waited on the porch, smoking, the end of his cheroot glowing crimson, the tobacco scenting the heat-heavy air. He pushed away from the wall of the house as Gabriel got down from the wagon seat, was already whispering rough, tender words to the tired horses when Gabriel lifted Annabel to the ground.

The hired man got into the rig and set off toward the barn, and when he was gone, in one swift and graceful move, Gabriel swept Annabel up into his arms.

She was breathless and exhausted, exhilarated and dismayed. Only Gabriel, she suspected, could have had exactly that effect on her.

"What are you doing, Mr. McKeige?" she asked, with an effort toward primness but none toward gaining her feet.

"You didn't think I'd forgotten, did you?" Gabriel asked, carrying her across the yard, up the steps, and onto the porch.

"Gabriel—"

He silenced her with a brief, light kiss that nonetheless set off new and most improper yearnings within Annabel, in addition to the many that already plagued her. "Hush," he said. "Now, tonight, you are still my wife, whatever your intentions might be to the contrary, and I am still your husband. There is no wrong in taking our pleasure together."

Annabel could not argue, though at another time she might have made a rousing case for the opposing view. As it was, she was blessedly tired and full of wanting; she yearned to catch fire in Gabriel's bed, yearned for the delicious melting sensations that would follow, the bliss of sleeping wrapped in his arms.

All the reasons why she and Gabriel could not, should not, be together could damn well wait until tomorrow, when they would without a doubt reassert themselves.

She buried her face against Gabriel's neck, drew in the unique scent of him, and lay pliant in his arms as he opened the door and carried her inside, into the cool gloom of the entryway, up stairs draped in shadow, along the corridor to their room.

It was only when he'd set her upon the bed, that one patch of space in which Annabel had ever had full confidence in her ability to please this man, that she had second thoughts.

"What about Charlie?" she asked.

Gabriel struck a match, lifted the painted globe from the kerosene lamp on the bedside table, and lit the wick. The scent of oil and sulfur was not unpleasant but intimate, indicative of secrets. "He's got a cabin five hundred yards from the house, Annabel. He won't hear anything."

Annabel turned her face away and blushed and then thought to herself how silly she was, behaving like some missish young girl. While privacy was certainly important, it wasn't as if everyone for fifty miles around didn't know what was about to happen in the McKeige household—especially Charlie. Tarnation, he'd probably known before *she* had.

Gabriel caught a finger under her chin and made her look at him. "Stop thinking, Annabel." He slipped off his suspenders, and the act, simple and masculine, seemed incredibly sensual to her.

She watched, wide-eyed, as Gabriel began to unbutton his shirt, revealing a rancher's muscular chest, a crop of golden hair . . .

"Annabel," he said pointedly, but with a little smile, "it's customary to take your clothes off."

When she still did not move—she was entranced, like some feckless girl—Gabriel sighed, ceased his own fascinating efforts to disrobe, and reached for Annabel's foot. He pulled off both her slippers and then lifted her skirts, searching for the garters that held up her stockings.

Annabel gasped in surprised pleasure and could not find a protest anywhere inside herself, even though one was certainly called for. Her blood singed her veins and pounded in her temples and at the base of her throat when Gabriel pushed her gently back onto the pillows to roll down one stocking, then the other.

He moved with excruciating slowness, and Annabel broke out in a shimmer of perspiration that had nothing to do with the season. She felt tendrils of her hair clinging to her neck, her cheeks, her forehead.

Gabriel could have uncovered her womanly place then, could have taken her, and Annabel would have welcomed him with ferocious eagerness, but he was too skilled and too stubborn to make matters so mercifully easy. Instead, he ran a hand lightly along the length of her legs, first outside, then inside. His fingertips brushed the junction of her thighs—her pantaloons were already damp—but did not linger there.

"Annabel?" he said again, when she lay before him, already submissive, her slender body, made supple by years of riding, ever so slightly arched toward him.

She opened her eyes, fevered, her teeth sunk into her lower lip. Gabriel was tossing aside his shirt, unfastening his trousers.

"I'm having a good time here," he said, with just the faintest upward curve at one corner of his mouth. "Would you care to join me?"

She dared not answer, for fear of saying something he would taunt her with later. So she got up, forced by that very act to stand in dangerous proximity to her husband and her only lover, and began, with bumbling fingers, to open her bodice.

Gabriel chuckled, smoothed a lock of picnic-tousled hair back from her cheek. "You look as nervous as you were the first time we were together," he said. "Do you remember?"

How could she have forgotten? She'd been sixteen years old, married only a few hours, and terrified that she would not know what to do, how to begin the thing or how to finish it.

They had gone from their small wedding in Jessie's parlor, she and Gabriel, to their first home: a cabin on the site of the present ranch house. There had been a storm that day, and they'd been wet to the skin when they arrived, forced by good sense, as much as passion, to strip away their clothes.

They'd gone naked and shivering to the bed that had been Gabriel's alone and had lain down together, found their way together. Taught each other.

"You were so tender and patient," Annabel recalled.

Gabriel ran a fingertip down the length of her neck. "I was as scared as you were."

"But surely . . . ?"

Gabriel laughed softly. "No," he said. "I'd grown up on a ranch, and I understood the mechanics. But I'd never bedded a woman."

Annabel recollected the exquisite sensations she'd been introduced to that night, despite the initial pain, sensations so elemental and primitive that they'd made her writhe and cry out in ecstasy. "But I—but you—"

He grinned. "Like I said, Annabel, I had a general idea what to do. Instinct is a powerful thing." She became aware that Gabriel had taken over the task of opening the bodice of her dress, and the force of her need made her sway a little.

Gabriel smoothed her gown away from her shoulders, down over her waist and hips, and it fell with a whisper to her feet. She was not wearing a corset, only a camisole, drawers, and a cotton petticoat.

With the backs of curved fingers, he teased her breasts through the thin fabric of the camisole, causing them to harden and chafe, and Annabel heard herself groan. She tried to remember why she wanted to divorce this man, why she had not been able to live with him, but her hungry body had memories of its own, and every tiny hidden muscle, every fiber and cell, strained toward Gabriel. Toward the fulfillment only he could provide in full measure.

Recollections of other bouts of lovemaking seemed to rise from her pores rather than her mind; there had been times of great tenderness, building from a stolen caress at breakfast, or simply a glance, gaining momentum throughout the long, busy day, finally culminating in joyous cataclysm in the dark of night. On other occasions they had not been able to wait. Gabriel had lifted Annabel's skirts—she'd seldom worn drawers then—and taken her against a wall, in a chair, in the sanctuary of the deep grass.

Now, as he untied the minute ribbons that held her camisole closed, she could not recall why she'd left Gabriel. She was being consumed, devoured by a blaze that burned within her own body, her own soul, and all she knew was that she wanted him—his mouth on hers, as well as on her breasts and her belly, her thighs and the backs of her knees.

She made a low strangled sound when her breasts were bared to him at last. Gabriel cupped them in his callused hands, stroking the nipples with his thumbs, and bent to take her mouth in a kiss that was restrained at first, then more demanding. Then so deep that it was a conquest of its own, a triumph so thorough that it released the first small tremors of satisfaction far inside her, causing her to groan and whimper as the kiss went on.

She literally could not stand on her own by the time it ended; Gabriel was supporting her, one arm wrapped around her waist. With his free hand he dispensed with her drawers; she did not know whether they had been torn away or simply pushed down and off, nor did she care.

Boldly he cupped the triangle of hair between her legs, a man reclaiming what had always been his and his alone.

She cried out as his fingers burrowed through the silken tangle to find the sensitive nubbin of flesh awaiting him, awaiting his touch. He groaned, exploring her more deeply.

"Annabel," Gabriel breathed, "I don't think this can happen slowly."

"No," she agreed, capturing his quick, frantic kisses, greedy for every one.

Gasping, he set her away from him just long enough to finish removing his own clothes, and the seconds seemed like hours as he kicked off his boots and socks, shed his trousers and the trunks beneath them.

He was so spectacularly beautiful, like a statue come to life in some Grecian garden, that Annabel could not resist touching him, kissing his chest, running her hands over his belly, his hips, his chest.

Gabriel submitted, and was magnificent even in that, his eyes blazing as he held her gaze and endured, enjoyed, her torment. When she closed her hand boldly around his length and held him tightly, a cry broke from his throat; he flung his head back and held her shoulders as if he feared to fall.

Annabel stroked her husband, felt a triumph older than the stars as he swelled between her palm and fingers. When she bent and touched her tongue to him, his control snapped. She landed on her back on the bed in a motion so quick and fierce that it nearly knocked the breath out of her.

Poised over her, Gabriel put his hand between her legs, preparing her, taking revenge. She twisted and tossed beneath him, pleading senselessly, and finally, in one long, forceful thrust, he claimed her. For a few exquisite, excruciating moments, they lay still, their lips brushing but never quite making contact.

Then Gabriel withdrew and delved again, and the friction drove her quite mad. She was suddenly drenched with sweat, as was Gabriel, and their bodies were slippery as they came together, parted, and came together again, at an ever more desperate pace. The motion progressed to a tender violence in the moments ahead; she clawed at his back, giving one continuous, raspy howl as the suspense mounted, became unbearable, and went beyond that.

Just when she would have splintered into a million sparkling pieces, like one of the displays at the Fourth of July picnic, Gabriel slowed his pace, his breathing ragged and deep. He slid down her body a little way, until he was just barely inside her, to nuzzle her nipples, first one and then the other, to take awkward suckle while her fingers flexed and unflexed in his hair. While she begged shamelessly for release.

At last, grudgingly, or perhaps because he himself could bear the delay no longer, Gabriel shattered her very being with a series of short, rapid strokes. Every part of her body, down to the cells themselves, was caught up in the wondrous extremity of her response, while her spirit soared, as if set free for those few but seemingly endless moments.

As she descended, she heard Gabriel's hoarse cry, felt him stiffen upon her again and again, felt him spill inside her. She hoped, on the most private level of her being, that they had conceived a child, offered a wordless vow that no one, not even Gabriel, would take this baby from her.

As the blissful haze began to clear, as her heartbeat slowed to a bearable pace and her lungs stopped grasping for air, the contentment came. Gabriel was still inside her, still holding her close, though he had by then collapsed into the depths of the feather mattress, as spent as she was.

She wound a finger loosely in a lock of his silken hair; in a very real and important way, she liked this part of their lovemaking the most, this tender interlude that followed the ecstasy, the total surrender of self.

Gabriel lay unmoving for such a long time that she began to think he had gone to sleep. The kerosene lamp burned out, and night sounds echoed in the room: crickets and the distant bawling of cattle, the ticking of the long-case clock on the landing, the pounding of her own heart—or was it Gabriel's?

She smoothed his hair, brushed his temple with her

lips, believing herself safe in revealing such affection, because he had dropped off the edge of wakefulness into slumber.

Except that he had not.

He began to swell inside her, to grow strong and hard and commanding again. He kissed her face, her jawline, her neck and collarbone. And then he fell, with a ravenous leisure, to her breasts.

Soon she was bucking beneath Gabriel once more, scaling unscalable heights, a pilgrim seeking redemption in her own destruction, victory in her own defeat. At last there was solace, blessed surcease, found in the molten core of a final skirmish between two bodies that knew and remembered each other and would not willingly be put asunder.

Her sleep was a void where neither dreams nor nightmares could reach. She awakened as well pleased as a sultan's favorite courtesan, utterly rested and prepared for the inevitable challenges of a new day.

The bed was awash in sunlight, the sheets in pleasant disarray, but Gabriel was up and gone.

She sighed—most likely the accord they had achieved in the night would have dissipated by the time she saw him again, but that should come as no surprise. This was not a reconciliation, after all, but merely an indulgence, freely agreed to by both of them, with no further promises made.

Even as a twinge pulled at her heart, she reveled in the luxurious languor of her body. She had been wholly and shamelessly satisfied, and she had no regrets about that. In fact, she admitted to herself, with a soft smile, she would have done it again, given the opportunity.

She stretched, felt the residue of their lovemaking on her inner thighs, and brought out the secret hope she had cherished the night before—that she was with child.

A pregnancy would be infinitely inconvenient, of course, a natural impediment to any proper courtship, making it imperative to pass her confinement in relative seclusion. Perhaps a year later she might resume an active social life.

She had no plans to stay with Gabriel, no reason, for that matter, to think he would *want* her to stay, but she fully intended to secure her divorce and catch a husband nonetheless. She was not and had never been easily dissuaded from her objectives.

She daydreamed for a while about a sturdy fair-haired baby. All the while her muscles and nerves, turned to butter in the night, were awakening, knitting themselves together, resuming their normal tautness.

Gabriel had left a pitcher of fresh water on the bureau, and she poured some into the basin and washed thoroughly, then donned fresh underthings from her trunk, topped by a sateen dress, deep brown in color.

When she descended the stairs and made her way to the kitchen, she was surprised, pleased, and a little embarrassed to find Nicholas sitting at the table, drinking coffee. He was dressed for the range, and although he looked tired, there was a mischievous gleam in his eyes.

"You're up early," she said too hastily, tangled in the awareness that her skin had a translucent glow and her own eyes were shining.

Nicholas tossed her a wry grin. "It's ten-thirty, Miss Annabel. Around here, anybody still in bed past six o'clock is automatically horsewhipped." He assessed her with another quirk of his lips. "Except for you, that is."

She helped herself to coffee—it was as bad as she remembered, a penance of sorts—and set about fetching an egg and a slice of bread from the larder. "I thought you were spending the night at Jessie's," she said, when she had stoked up the fire and was standing at the stove with her back safely turned to Nicholas.

"I had to be back here to ride the fence line this morning," he said. "Didn't make sense to go to bed at all."

Her voice came out unnaturally high. "Oh," she said.

"Don't worry, Miss Annabel," Nicholas replied, with a smile in his voice. "I wasn't here."

She summoned up a disapproving frown and turned to meet her son's gaze. "You are entirely too forthright, young man," she scolded. "Lord knows, I've made mistakes aplenty, but I'm still your mother and I will be spoken to in a decent fashion."

Nicholas was silent, but his eyes were still dancing and the shadow of a grin lingered on his mouth. It came to her once again how beautiful he was, and she hoped, for the sake of innocence, that the marshal's pretty young daughter was on her toes.

She turned back to her awkward efforts to cook. She had not, in point of fact, prepared a meal more than once or twice in the twelve years she'd been gone, and she was woefully out of practice. She burned the bread, and the egg looked as though it could withstand several hard slaps against the wall.

She was startled to find Nicholas standing beside her; she had not heard him leave the table or cross the room. He laid a hand on her shoulder and spoke quietly.

"I'm sorry. I didn't mean to be disrespectful."

She looked up at Nicholas and saw that he was serious. How strange it was that he was so much taller than she, when she could still feel the echo of the child-shape of him in her arms. "And I did not mean to be quite so sharp," she said, after releasing a long breath. "If you're going to the barn, would you please ask someone to hitch up my surrey? I have business in town, and when that's done, I might call on Jessie."

Nicholas withdrew a little way, and a guarded expression came into his eyes. She had no idea what she'd said to trouble him, and small hope that he would enlighten her.

"Sure," he said. "I'll see to the surrey myself, and round up that driver of yours. Last time I saw him, Pa had given him duds fit for work and set him to digging postholes."

She smiled, imagining Mr. Hilditch, always a little full of himself, undertaking such labor. She'd be lucky if he didn't take to the hills before she was ready to leave for San Francisco, where the two of them would board a ship bound for England. "No doubt he will be relieved to drive again," she remarked, plopping the egg and the toast onto a plate and heading for the table.

Nicholas eyed the meal dubiously; surely if he'd nursed any fantasies of savory food cooked by his mother, this had cured him.

"Charlie would have been glad to scare up something for you to eat," he said.

She couldn't resist a bit of mischief. "*I* know," she cried, as if caught in the throes of bright revelation, "why don't you eat this, Nicholas, and I'll make more? You *must* be hungry, after working so hard—"

He retreated a step, swallowed. "Umm, thanks, but I'm really not—"

She laughed. "Nicholas?"

He looked even more alarmed. "What?"

"I'm teasing you."

"Oh," Nicholas said.

In that moment he so resembled the little boy she remembered that she didn't know whether to laugh again or to cry. She wanted to put her arms around him, but at the same time she did not dare to do so. He was polite, Nicholas was, but she had no illusions that their differences had been settled. He was as strong-minded as she was, as Gabriel was, and that meant he might *never* truly absolve her of her many and willful mistakes.

"I love you," she said plainly. "I have always loved you."

Nicholas looked away, swallowed again, and then worked up a smile that was as much a defense as a shield would have been, or a suit of armor.

"I'll see to that surrey," he said hoarsely, then fled the room, and her presence, so quickly that she feared he'd trip on the threshold and plunge headlong into the dooryard, where Charlie's chickens were scratching and pecking.

She stood in the doorway, watching Nicholas's escape. The hens squawked and flapped their wings as he passed among them.

Within a matter of minutes Hilditch appeared, at the reins of the surrey, wearing canvas trousers and a homespun shirt and looking pathetically grateful to be called away from his posthole-digging duties.

"Heaven will bless you for this, Mrs. McKeige," he exclaimed. "I've got calluses up on my calluses. Before God, I can barely hold these reins proper like, my hands are that sore!"

Annabel, wearing a hat and carrying a parasol,

offered no sympathy. "You've commanded a good wage these several years, Mr. Hilditch, with little required of you except that you wear fancy livery and occasionally curry the horses. It will do you good to work for a living. Now, if you'll just step down and allow me to take the reins myself—"

Mr. Hilditch looked affronted, not to mention stunned. "You can't mean to send me back to that slave driver, mum!" he protested, with considerable vigor. "Surely there is no need to remind you, with all respect, of course, that I don't work for Gabriel McKeige?"

"You won't work for me, either, if you don't stop complaining," she said sweetly.

He got down from the rig and grudgingly offered his assistance, which she took, making a great business of settling herself, arranging her skirts.

"Where are my dogs?" she asked, looking about as she took up the reins.

Hilditch plainly relished the answer. "He's got them out on the range, that man of yours, teaching them to fetch back stray cattle. You'd best have a care, mum, or you'll find yourself putting a new roof on the barn or planting a field of maize."

"True enough," she said, with an amused smile. "Gabriel puts little stock in idleness." Then she slapped the reins down pertly upon the horses' gleaming backs. "Good day, Mr. Hilditch."

Her high spirits were short-lived, as it happened, for she had barely traveled a mile from the ranch house when she encountered Captain Sommervale, accompanied by a detail of half a dozen grim-faced soldiers.

He did not seem like the same man who had, with his wife, entertained her so graciously at Fort Duffield, confiding that he found this new post a most daunting challenge, coming so late in his career.

He drew in his horse and offered a wooden smile and a touch to the dusty brim of his cavalry hat. "Good morning, Mrs. McKeige," he said. "Tell me—where might we find your son?"

Six

GABE CORRALLED NICHOLAS IN THE TACK ROOM OF THE barn, just as he was putting up his saddle and heading back toward the stalls to feed and groom his horse. It was obvious that the boy had been out all night and that he now hoped to snatch a few hours of badly needed sleep. It was equally obvious that he would have preferred not to encounter his father just then.

Fortunately Gabe was in an expansive and generous mood. He blocked Nicholas's way, there in the cool-shadowed barn, with its familiar smells of hay and leather and old rope, along with the inevitable horse manure. Took note of the .45 riding low on the boy's hip.

"Any fences down?" Gabe asked.

Nicholas shook his head. As usual, his expression gave away nothing; if he was in Dutch, he wasn't about to confide in Gabe. "None that I could see," he said. "I sent Pedro and Jimmy on to trace the boundaries, just in case." He paused and tugged at the brim of his hat, a gesture Gabe often employed himself, when he felt private.

"And?"

Nicholas sighed heavily. "And I think there are more cattle missing. Maybe as many as a hundred head."

"Were you planning to mention that to me or just wait till I heard it from somebody else?" Gabe demanded, in a low voice, folding his arms. He was a rich man, and the loss of a hundred cattle or a thousand would not cause so much as a crack in his financial situation, but business was business and thieving was thieving. He had a right, not to mention a responsibility, to protect what was his, and, as his heir, so did Nicholas.

Nicholas stood his ground, pulling off his leather gloves with angry motions of his hands and shoving them into his hip pocket. "I thought you'd gone to one of the mines—Cherry Hill, Ben said."

"Cherry Hill," Gabe mused, quietly furious and very much afraid. "The one just south of the ravine over there." He indicated the direction with a nod, arms still folded.

Nicholas flushed slightly, and his eyes blazed. Folks said his son was like him, but at that moment Gabe saw Annabel in Nicholas, plain and simple, and nothing of himself. "I know where it is, Pa," he snapped.

"Then I guess you could have ridden over there and told me about those cattle."

A muscle flexed in Nicholas's jaw. Before he could come up with an answer, though, there was a ruckus outside—five or six horsemen, Gabe figured, and a lot of clattering hardware. Soldiers.

Frowning, he turned away from Nicholas, as if to shield him, and strode outside.

Captain Sommervale had come calling, along with a few of his men. With a nod of greeting, the visitor swung down from his saddle and swept off his hat to wipe a sleeve across his brow. The detail sat impassively behind him, awaiting their orders.

"Morning, Captain," Gabe said. He hadn't dealt with this particular officer before, since he was new to Fort Duffield, but he'd sold a good share of the cattle he produced to the army over the years and he knew how they operated.

Sommervale's gaze skittered past Gabe to rest briefly on Nicholas. The old soldier replaced his hat. "Is there someplace we could talk privately?" he asked.

Gabe gestured toward the house. "Inside," he answered, with gruff and unsmiling cordiality. "Your men are welcome to stretch their legs and water their horses, if they'd like."

Sommervale nodded once more, distractedly, and muttered a simple order. The toy soldiers became real again, leather creaking as they dismounted to jaw with several ranch hands who had gathered nearby like a flock of hens, out of plain nosiness.

Nicholas kept pace with Gabe and the captain as they moved toward the house, but he walked a little apart, his jaw set, his gaze fixed straight ahead.

Charlie assessed the situation in a glance when the three men entered by the kitchen door; without a word, he stopped peeling potatoes for the midday meal and set himself to brewing fresh coffee.

Gabe smiled to himself, despite the undoubted gravity of the visit. Sommervale seemed like a good man, undeserving of the vile stuff Charlie would pour out of that old enamel pot.

In the study, Gabe indicated a chair for the captain, while Nicholas leaned a shoulder against the framing of one tall window, probably unaware of the more subtle connotations of that position. Gabe himself took a seat behind his desk.

Sommervale glanced at Nicholas before setting his cavalry hat on the floor beside his chair. "We are all busy men," he said, "so I will not waste time getting to my point." He was watching Gabe by then, but his awareness of Nicholas was almost palpable. "Mr. McKeige, the United States Army has purchased a great many cattle from you over the years. Just recently we ordered two hundred head."

Gabe took a cheroot from a jar on the desk and offered the same to Nicholas and the officer with a motion of his head. Both of them declined, in the same silent language.

"I'm aware of the army's patronage, Captain," Gabe replied, after lighting the cheroot, "and I appreciate it."

Sommervale cleared his throat, cast another look in Nicholas's direction, as though he expected him to bolt through the window. In a way, Gabe had been half prepared for the same event, which was foolish, he realized now, because Nicholas had been standing his ground ever since he could walk. He wasn't likely to change now.

"We lost those cattle, Mr. McKeige, somewhere between this ranch and Fort Duffield. The whole damn herd of them."

Gabe had known about the theft, of course. Everybody in Parable did, but he pretended it was news. "I'm sorry to hear that," he said, "but I don't see how it concerns us. We didn't send any of our men on that drive. A dozen soldiers came out from the fort to collect the cattle, if I recall." He remembered the deal perfectly; the army had deposited a sizable advance payment into one of his Virginia City bank accounts.

Sommervale cleared his throat, a clear signal of thirst. Nicholas went to the liquor cabinet without a word, poured a shallow splash of whiskey into a glass, and handed it to the army man.

"The men who collected those cattle were not soldiers of the United States Cavalry, Mr. McKeige," Sommervale confessed, red-faced, after a restorative gulp of firewater. "They had waylaid our men and taken their uniforms, as well as the papers authorizing them to act on the government's behalf."

At the edge of his vision, Gabe saw Nicholas roll his eyes, and was not reassured.

"What about your men?" Gabe asked, suddenly wishing for a drink himself. "Were any of them hurt?"

"Not seriously," Sommervale allowed, avoiding Gabe's gaze for a few moments. "They were, however, abandoned along the trail in their underwear, with no boots, no weapons, and no horses. The results might have been tragic if a patrol hadn't come across them."

Gabe suppressed an imprudent desire to laugh; while the images in his mind might have been funny, the situation wasn't. "You have my sympathy, Captain," he said, "but I still don't understand what brings you here. Unless you want to replace those cattle, of course."

Sommervale threw back the rest of his whiskey and set the glass down on Gabe's desk with an angry thump. "Damn it, McKeige, you're the only rancher within a hundred miles who can provide the volume of beef we require, and you know it," he growled. "I have no choice but to buy from you!"

Gabe raised an eyebrow, stole another look at Nicholas, who was now perched on the windowsill, one foot drawn up on his knee, arms folded.

"We'll be happy to provide whatever you need," Gabe said quietly. "Just as soon as the bank wires me that they've received the agreed price."

Sommervale flushed again; he knew then that Gabe refused to grant the army credit because they had a tendency to take their sweet time paying up. "You'll have your blasted money," he growled. "Same price as before. In the meantime, we want you to know we're going to catch those rustlers, and we're going to hang them."

The picture of Nicholas swinging at the end of a rope came to mind, and soured the contents of Gabe's stomach. Charlie chose that moment to knock and enter with that devil's brew of his, and nothing more was said until he was gone.

"I'd like an invitation to that hanging," Gabe said, pouring coffee for his guest and shoving the cup across his desk. He'd changed his mind about Sommervale deserving it. "We've been bleeding cattle ourselves."

Sommervale tasted the coffee, grimaced, and set it aside. "May I?" he said, taking up his empty whiskey glass.

Gabe gestured toward the cabinet, and the captain got up to pour himself another dose, remained standing as he drank.

"Our intelligence says you might be involved," Sommervale said, gazing directly at Nicholas.

Nicholas's grin was slight but replete with mockery. "You have described the army's 'intelligence,' Captain. Therefore, it shouldn't be surprising when I tell you they're wrong."

Gabe seethed in silence, yearning to throttle his son. Certainly this was no time for insolence; the captain was neither an idiot nor a buffoon. If Sommervale thought Nicholas had taken part in the theft of two hundred cattle, there was sound reason to believe it was so.

"I don't have any proof," Sommervale admitted, "but our information came from good sources. If you're guilty, young Mr. McKeige, we'll get you."

A chill tripped down Gabe's spine. He'd endured his share of disaster, most notably his mother's kidnapping, Susannah's death, and Annabel's running off. He'd been shot twice, once accidentally and once on purpose, bitten by a rattlesnake, nearly wiped out by droughts, blizzards, and financial panics back east. He'd been within a breath of bankruptcy more times than he cared to remember.

None of it came near the agony he would feel, seeing Nicholas mount a scaffold to die. Gabe would rather have been hanged himself, a hundred times over.

"For a man who plainly values his time," Nicholas said smoothly, his gaze steady on Sommervale's face, "you seem anxious to throw it away. I've got no reason to steal, Captain. I'm the only son of Gabriel McKeige." He favored his father with a quicksilver grin, gone the moment it appeared. "So far, that is."

Although Gabe was aware that that last was meant to nettle, to let him know that the intimate and very private events of the previous night were no secret, he was too afraid to be angry. Nicholas did not seem to understand that he was in a grievous predicament and that a simple denial would not suffice to get him out.

Gabe meant to clarify the situation once the captain was gone.

"No," Sommervale replied at length, regarding Nicholas in the somber fashion of a man who probably had sons and grandsons of his own. "You don't need to steal. But it appears that you may *want* to, which is another matter entirely." He sighed, reached for his hat. "I have made my position clear," he said, turning now to Gabe, "and I hope I have dealt with you honorably. If you would save your son from a military trial and the unfortunate results of a guilty verdict, Mr. McKeige, you had best make matters right before we are forced to do it."

With that, Sommervale nodded politely and went out.

Gabe and Nicholas remained in the study, glaring at each other, the doors still ajar.

"What the hell is going on here?" Gabe demanded, after a long and sizzling silence.

Nicholas leaned forward slightly, and in that moment he resembled Annabel more than he ever had. "Someone is stealing cattle," he drawled, widening his eyes.

"Damn it, Nicholas, if you know anything about this, you'd better tell me right now!"

Nicholas put on his hat, pulled the brim low. "I've got work to do," he said, and Gabe in no way missed the meaning of that cool dismissal—he'd used those same words himself so often that they came to his lips unsummoned, like a prayer learned in earliest childhood.

"Nicholas—"

The boy strode out of the room, slammed the front door behind him.

Gabe, frozen until that moment, started around the

desk in belated pursuit, but Charlie appeared from the hallway and spoke quietly.

"Let him go," he said. "There'll be no reasoning with him until he's cooled off. He's too much like you, God help him."

Gabe brought a fist crashing down onto the desktop, but he didn't go after Nicholas. "Christ, Charlie," he rasped, after a few moments spent catching his breath. "The army is after him. They think he's been stealing their cattle."

Charlie didn't react. He seldom did. "What do *you* think?" he asked quietly.

Gabe sighed. He hadn't felt so much like weeping since he'd come home from that long-ago cattle drive, bone-tired and set on making things right between him and Annabel, only to find her gone.

"I can't believe he's a thief," he said.

Charlie nodded, serenely solemn, as usual. "Then I guess we'd better find out who *is,*" he said. "Most likely we're dealing with some of your own men. Seems like it's only your cattle that are wandering off. None of the other ranchers have been complaining of losses, and the army doesn't buy from anybody else."

"Were you listening at the door?"

Charlie grinned. "Yes," he said, without hesitation.

Arriving in town, Annabel headed straight for Parable's one bank. The president, a round and boisterous little man named Oldmixen, had been appointed by Jessie to run her late husband's enterprise.

He greeted Annabel a bit eagerly, perhaps aware that Gabriel had always been generous with her financially. She had, in fact, accumulated a modest fortune of her own over the years, having invested wisely both in England and in the United States. In fact, if she never received another penny from her husband, she could still live comfortably for the rest of her life.

If Mr. Oldmixen cherished the hope that Annabel would trust more than pin money to his frontier bank, however, he was quite mistaken. Such institutions were robbed on an almost monotonous basis, and their depositors left without recourse.

"Good morning, Mrs. McKeige," Oldmixen trilled merrily, and then consulted his pocket watch.

"Good morning," Annabel replied crisply.

He cleared his throat. "What can I do for you today?" he asked, swinging open the little gate that set his office apart from the teller's cage and the vault.

Annabel swept through the gateway and into Mr. Oldmixen's tiny and cluttered quarters. At his gesture of invitation, she primly took a seat, planting the tip of her parasol on the floor and curving her fingers around the handle as one might grip a cane.

"I have little or no need of banking services," she announced, and felt mildly guilty when she saw the degree of his disappointment. "Instead, I have come to ask your aid in another matter, since you are undoubtedly one of the most knowledgeable and important citizens in Parable."

Oldmixen beamed, as pleased as if she'd likened him to Alexander the Great or Constantine. His nod, given as he sank into his own chair, was deferential. "Surely," he blustered. "What do you require, Mrs. McKeige?"

Her answer, she knew, would spawn as much gossip as her arrival in Parable undoubtedly had, not that it mattered. "I should like to acquire a small house," she said. "It is my hope that you might know of one, either for sale or to let."

The banker opened his mouth, shut it again, harrumphed and interwove his fingers across his plump belly. "A house," he ruminated aloud, as though unfamiliar with the word. No doubt he had presumed, along with almost everyone else in Parable, that she and Gabriel had reconciled.

She suppressed a sigh and waited patiently. Despite the pleasures of the past night, nothing could have been further from the truth. Gabriel had not really changed, and neither had she. She wished to stay in Parable, for a while, at least; that was true. Because of Nicholas.

"There is the Jennings place," Oldmixen mused, raising his bushy eyebrows, apparently surprised to find the memory lurking in his mind. "It wants a lot of work, though. No one's lived there since the murder."

Annabel squirmed, but her resolution was unwavering. "The murder?" Nicholas had not mentioned such an incident in any of his letters.

"Mrs. Jennings shot her husband there, two years back."

"That's terrible!"

"There were those who said he deserved it," Mr. Oldmixen said, with a world-weary sigh.

"Did he beat her?"

Oldmixen reddened. "No, ma'am. She found out he was—er—philandering. Keeping a mistress."

There was an awkward silence. Annabel couldn't help thinking of Julia Sermon, and no doubt Mr. Oldmixen's thoughts had taken a similar course.

"I can understand her position," Annabel said at last.

Mr. Oldmixen cleared his throat again and looked away. "Well, then," he said. "Well, then."

"I will take the house," Annabel decided aloud. "Where is it, and to whom should I direct my inquiry?"

"To me," Mr. Oldmixen said, plainly flustered. "There was a mortgage, and after Mr. Jennings's unfortunate demise, we were forced to foreclose. Naturally we should prefer to sell the place and recoup our investment, if that is possible."

Annabel rose, her business completed, as far as she was concerned. "Very well, then. I shall have a look at the house and advise you of the price I am willing to pay. If you would kindly direct me to the property?"

The banker was breathless with the scramble to keep up; the speed at which Annabel made decisions and pronouncements very often had that effect on people. "I—er—well, the house is unlocked. I'll be happy to escort you there."

She merely nodded, and they left the bank, after going through the whole ritual of door and gate opening, this time in reverse.

The house proved to be quite substantial, a two-story frame structure perched at the edge of town. It had a temporary look about it, as though uncertain whether to throw in its lot with Parable or sidle farther out into the countryside.

To Annabel's great relief, there were no bloodstains on the wallpaper or the floors—the gravity with which Mr. Oldmixen had spoken of the murder had led her to expect some lingering sign of gore—and the general air of the house was benevolent. No unhappy ghosts, then, bent on clomping across the attic floor at all hours or rattling pots and pans in the cupboard.

"How much?" Annabel asked, when she had completed her tour of the property.

Mr. Oldmixen named a figure and had the good grace to look shamefaced when he did so.

"Preposterous," she said and stated what she was willing to pay.

The banker shuffled his feet and coughed a few times. "I'm sure that will be satisfactory," he allowed, and when Annabel offered him her gloved hand, to seal the agreement, he looked downright confounded.

"I shall require servants," she said, sweeping past him. "A cook and a maid, at the very least. If you should hear of anyone seeking employment, please contact me immediately."

"Wh-where will you be?" Mr. Oldmixen ventured to ask.

"Why, right here in Parable, of course," Annabel replied. *Here, out of temptation's reach.* "You will have my draft first thing in the morning. I shall move in then."

With his mouth moving, but no words coming out, Mr. Oldmixen watched Annabel descend the steps to the walk, mentally dusting her hands together.

She made a stop at the general store to place an order for goods and supplies. Then, after reclaiming the team and surrey from in front of the bank, she proceeded to Jessie's house, which stood at the opposite end of town from her newly acquired one.

Jessie was surprised but not inhospitable when she opened her front door and saw her estranged sister-in-law standing on the stoop, parasol in hand.

"I am sorry for just appearing this way," Annabel said, "but I've not brought along a single calling card—otherwise I'd have sent Hilditch by with one and given you warning."

Jessie pushed open the screen door. "Good heavens, Annabel, we don't use such fripperies as calling cards in Parable. Surely you remember that."

Feeling a little set back, Annabel accepted Jessie's implied invitation and entered the house, surrendering her gloves and parasol in the modest foyer. Perhaps her motions might have been a bit brisk.

"Now, Annabel," Jessie said, "don't work yourself into a tizzy. I meant to put you at ease, not get your feathers up. Come in and settle yourself comfortably in the parlor, and I'll make some tea and sandwiches."

Annabel had not eaten since her own attempt at making breakfast that morning—the results had not been noteworthy—and she was starving. She longed for tea as well; Charlie did not seem to stock the stuff in his plain kitchen.

"Thank you," she murmured.

Once Jessie had seen Annabel to a chair, she vanished, returning some minutes later bearing a silver tray. At least some of the graces survived in Parable, Annabel thought, as Gabriel's sister served tea, delicate sandwiches, and cookies.

Annabel ate ravenously, could not help herself, for while she was a woman of great energy and stamina, she was also a woman of great appetite. Gabriel had ungraciously remarked, when they were younger, that she ate more than he did.

Jessie watched her with a half smile. "I see that Charlie's cooking has not changed," she observed.

Embarrassed color stung Annabel's cheeks. "I fear I have forgotten my manners," she said, dabbing at her mouth with a linen napkin. "And fairness compels me to admit that it is not Charlie's cooking but my own that has left me wanting nourishment."

That produced a soft laugh from Jessie. "I have

missed you, Annabel—even though there were times, I confess, when I wanted to travel to England and personally snatch you bald-headed."

The remark required no explanation, and Annabel did not demand one. Jessie was Gabriel's sister, his only living relative, besides Nicholas, and they had always been close. It was natural enough that Jessie would have taken Gabriel's part and paid little or no mind to the fact that Annabel had not been entirely to blame for all that had happened.

"I have purchased a house," she said.

Jessie leaned forward in her chair, nearly upsetting her teacup. "What? Here—in Parable?"

"Yes," Annabel said, perhaps a bit defensively.

"I don't understand."

Annabel fidgeted with her tea napkin. "I cannot impose upon Gabriel's hospitality any further," she said, in a voice that barely qualified as a murmur. "It isn't proper."

"You *are* his wife, and Nicholas's mother."

"Jessie," Annabel said, speaking more directly now and much more firmly, "you know full well that Gabriel and I do not have a genuine marriage. I should like to spend time in Parable—specifically, with Nicholas—but I have not changed my mind about divorcing his father."

"I don't think Gabriel has changed his mind about the divorce, either," Jessie pointed out helpfully. It could only be concluded that she had taken notice of Annabel's translucent skin and bright eyes and that she understood what those things meant. "I know my brother, Annabel—he'll throw four kinds of fit when he finds out about this."

"He will be pleased to have me out from underfoot."

Jessie shook her head. "Quite the contrary, Annabel. The whole of Parable will see what's happening, just like before, and Gabriel will be mortified by that. Have you no sense of a man's pride?"

Annabel sprang to her feet and paced along the length of the hearthrug, wringing her hands. She had not undertaken this course to embarrass Gabriel—she was merely trying to protect herself from her own vulnerability. If she stayed at the ranch much longer, she would be little better than a harlot.

Wife or none, Annabel did not intend to stay in Parable any longer than necessary, and to continue to share Gabriel's bed would be deceitful. And yet she was sure she would not be able to resist. Her wanton behavior the night before was proof enough of that.

"I don't want to hurt Gabriel or anyone else," Annabel maintained miserably.

"I know," Jessie said. "Do sit down. You are making me dizzy, sweeping back and forth like that."

Tears sprang into Annabel's eyes, and she blinked them back. "No matter what I do, it does not seem to be right. I was a terrible mother, a terrible wife—"

"Sit *down,*" Jessie pleaded.

Annabel sank back into her chair with more despair than grace. "Why must everything be so complicated?" she cried.

Jessie's smile was sad. "How I miss those sorts of complications," she said.

The distraction, however momentary, was a welcome one. "You've surely had a hundred chances to remarry, Jessie. Why did you never take another husband?"

"I've had suitors since Franklin died, it's true," Jessie confessed, pouring herself a second cup of tea and stirring busily. "But I've never felt what I felt with Frank. I couldn't accept anything less."

Annabel averted her eyes. "I understand."

"Do you, Annabel?" Jessie asked, reaching across the narrow space between their chairs to touch Annabel's hand. "Then maybe you've considered the possibility that no other man is ever going to make you feel the range and depth of emotion you've known with Gabriel. Not the joy, not the passion, not the exasperation or the pain. Annabel, you and my brother built that ranch together. You made Nicholas together. And it doesn't take a Pinkerton man to see that you spent last night in Gabriel's bed. You've been walking an inch off the floor ever since you stepped into this house, and you shine as if you'd swallowed a piece of the moon. Surely you know you can never be happy with anything less."

Annabel could not reply.

Seven

CHARLIE BUSTLED ABOUT THE KITCHEN THAT SECOND evening after Annabel's descent upon the otherwise peaceful community, excited to prove her cooking skills to a likely suitor. It was rare enough, Gabe reflected, sipping a pre-supper cup of coffee, for him and Nicholas to take a meal together; for Annabel to be there, too, was a phenomenon of historic proportions.

It was a happy scene, and yet Gabe had an uneasy feeling, centered in no particular part of him, a feeling that had nothing to do with the bind Nicholas had gotten himself into. He and Annabel had been apart for many years, but that didn't mean he couldn't tell when she was scheming.

Like as not, Annabel had planned this little gathering—it would be so ordinary in any other house—to make some grand announcement, and the possibilities were downright disquieting. Maybe she'd decided to take up residence right there on the ranch, for instance. Or, worse still, decided to leave.

Gabe thrust an anxious hand through his hair and garnered a knowing grin from Charlie for his trouble. The Indian set a china tureen, brimming with venison stew, in the center of the table.

"That food smells so good," Gabe grumbled, "that a man has to wonder if somebody else did the cooking."

Charlie was unflappable, as always. "You don't like my meals, boss," he said, "you can always take over the job yourself."

What Gabe intended as a grin felt more like a grimace when it finally got to his mouth. He was tired; Annabel had taken all the starch out of him in the night, and he'd spent most of the day at one of the mines, with that disturbing visit from the U.S. Cavalry as the only real break.

He heard Annabel approaching, humming as she crossed the dining room, and looked down at his clothes, suddenly self-conscious. He'd taken a dip in the spring, Nicholas-fashion, and put on a clean shirt, but now, for a reason he wouldn't have allowed himself to examine, he felt as rustic and unpolished as the greenest of his ranch hands.

Annabel didn't simply walk into the kitchen; her arrival was an occasion, almost biblical in scale.

She was wearing a divided riding skirt that evening, along with a white cotton shirtwaist and boots, noted Gabe, who rarely cared what women wore. Her plentiful red-brown hair, like silk between his fingers and against his face the night before, was not bound up in the usual fashion, but braided into a single plait.

Annabel looked like a girl, Gabe thought, sweetly stricken, and the subtle scent of her perfume teased his senses, even from a distance. It did not seem possible that some twenty years had gone by since he'd taken her for a bride, that they had a grown son, that they had spent better than a decade apart.

He wanted nothing so much, in that moment of unwelcome epiphany, as to lift her in his arms and carry her back upstairs to their bed.

She smiled, as if she'd guessed his thoughts. "Hello, Gabriel," she said.

Nicholas came in just behind her, decently dressed, for once, in a crisply pressed shirt, black trousers, and polished boots. He looked at Gabe and his mother in turn. Then, with that private grin that was as much a part of his nature as the stubborn set of his will, he claimed a bowl from the table, ladled a generous portion of stew into it, and went out.

Charlie had already gone.

"Sit down, Gabriel," Annabel said, as though she were the hostess in this house she had fled so long ago. "The food will get cold."

Awkwardly, Gabe sat. He wondered why Annabel had ordered this meal served in the kitchen; she had always fussed that it was more civilized to take sustenance in the dining room. But then, she would have worn a fancy dress for that.

She smiled and took a seat on the bench across from him.

"Where do you suppose Nicholas got to?" she asked, filling her bowl from the tureen. "I meant this to be a family meal."

Gabe took a thick slice of bread and buttered it with as much care as an ancient priest inscribing commandments onto a stone tablet. Every word that came to his mind was mundane, and this didn't seem like the time for chitchat.

"He won't starve," he said at last, because that was all he could come up with right then.

Annabel smiled in acknowledgment, but she seemed troubled now, maybe a bit distracted.

Here it comes, Gabe thought helplessly.

"I have purchased a house in Parable," she said, very quickly. Annabel's grand proclamations usually struck with all the force of a flash flood, even when you thought you were expecting them. This one was no exception.

Gabe laid down his bread, staring at Annabel while she reached for his bowl and filled it to brimming with Charlie's stew. He didn't know what he felt—anger or relief, or both—but he sure as wretched hell felt *something.*

Annabel hastened to explain—a bad omen, since Annabel had never believed in explaining much of anything. "It will be best for both of us," she said quickly, nearly dumping the bowl of stew into Gabe's lap as she strained to set it down in front of him. "My being in town, I mean. Instead of here."

"What house?" Gabe asked. With Annabel, he always felt as though he'd been left standing on the station platform, clutching a ticket and watching the last train pull out.

"The Jennings place," she answered, with breathless good cheer. "You know, where the murder happened."

Gabe glared at her. Couldn't help it, she was so damned exasperating. "*This* is a perfectly good house," he said, sincerely trying, as he spoke, to unclench his jaw. "And there hasn't been a killing here." He leaned forward slightly. "Yet."

Annabel looked deflated but not entirely surprised. "Don't you see, Gabriel, that this will provide a sort of neutral ground until we can all get some perspective?"

Gabe did not want perspective; he wanted Annabel. Cooking in that kitchen, going over the books and investments in the study, warm and receptive in their bed.

"What you mean, Annabel, is that you don't want to sleep with me," he said, in an undertone. "And that's confusing, after what happened last night."

Annabel flushed in that fetching way that always irritated Gabe and excited him at one and the same damn time. "Gabriel McKeige, the supper table is no place to discuss such intimate matters," she informed him. Of course she had intended for Nicholas to be there and, by his presence, to protect her from just this topic of discussion.

Too bad.

"Annabel," Gabe went on, "it won't matter if you're in Parable or Boston or Timbuktu. Something happened last night, something more than a roll in the hay. Things are different between you and me."

She looked away, plainly uncomfortable—a sure sign that she knew he was right, that she was frightened by the shift that had occurred between them. Gabe likened the change, figuratively, to the setting of a bone or the flawless restoration of something shattered, though it was a thing of the soul rather than the flesh.

"I can't bear it, Gabriel," Annabel blurted softly, at long last, her sherry-colored eyes pleading with him for something he did not understand.

He put his hand out, closed his fingers around hers, found that she was trembling. "What?" he said. "Tell me what you're afraid of, Annabel."

Tears filled her eyes, and Gabe was moved, for it was an uncommon thing for Annabel to cry. "I'm afraid of myself, Gabriel, and of you," she answered finally, in a miserable whisper. "I cared so much before—so very much—and it wasn't enough. That's what I can't bear—not being enough!"

Gabe drew a deep breath and let it out slowly, in a bid to bridle emotions he wasn't used to feeling. Or acknowledging. Annabel was referring to Julia, of course, and God knew it was true that he was close to the other woman. While he had never made love to Julia—not physically, at least—the friendship had too much texture and substance to be dismissed as an innocent one. There were a thousand other kinds of intimacy besides the joining of two bodies.

Gabe had lain beside Julia many a night. He had confided things to her that he was unable to share with anyone else, and on one memorable occasion, when copious amounts of whiskey had failed to dull the pain that plagued him almost incessantly, he had wept in Julia's arms like a disconsolate child.

For twelve years she had been his only solace.

"Are you in love with Julia Sermon?" Annabel asked, more calmly. When she got like that, Gabe found himself mourning that Olympian temper of hers.

"No," he answered without hesitation. Loving Julia, in the manner Annabel meant, would have been as foreign to him as loving Jessie in anything but a brotherly way. But that didn't mean he could just walk away from either of them, Jessie *or* Julia, and he despaired of ever making Annabel understand.

Hell, he couldn't comprehend it himself most of the time.

"But you'll continue to see her." Annabel made the words a statement rather than a question.

"Right now," Gabe answered frankly, his food forgotten before him, "she won't allow me to come anywhere near her."

Annabel lowered her eyes, blinked several times, and then fixed him with that intrepid gaze he had come to know so well. "But you'd call on her if she would allow it?"

Gabe had never been a liar, despite what Annabel thought. "Yes," he said. Julia was levelheaded and practical; she would have helped him sort out what he was feeling. Helped him make sense of things.

"It seems we have reached an impasse, Mr. McKeige. You will not give up your mistress, and I will not share my life with a man who keeps one."

A sense of crushing hopelessness swept over Gabe; the distance between him and Annabel was more than the width of a table; it was a chasm as unbridgeable as the breach between heaven and hell, and just as nebulous.

"I don't recall asking you to share my life," he said, with a coldness that was more a matter of self-defense than anything else. "Not recently, anyway. But while we're on the subject, *Mrs.* McKeige, may I say that I have no need of a wife who runs to the other side of the country—hell, the other side of the *world*—whenever things get too tough?"

Annabel flung down her napkin and shot to her feet. "I don't know why I ever try to talk to you—it would be easier to have a reasonable conversation with your bloody horse!"

Gabe shrugged. "I rest my case," he said, with an ease as false as George Washington's teeth. "Go on, Annabel. You don't like what's happening here, what's being said here. So run away."

For a moment he thought she was going to upend

the soup tureen over his head or burst with the effort to contain her fury. Watching Annabel was fascinating, in the same alarming way watching the approach of a tornado or a tidal wave might be.

She sat down again. With force. "Bloody hell!" she muttered.

Gabe remembered his food and, now that his stomach had unknotted a little, began to eat. The stew was cold, and despite its savory aroma, it was Charlie's concoction, all right. Charlie's cooking, he often thought, was more than it seemed—a sacred trust of revenge, red man against white.

"Relax and eat your supper," he said presently. "I'll sleep in the spare room tonight, and your virtue will be safe."

Annabel glowered at him, then took up her spoon.

Out back, Nicholas set his stew bowl down on the ground and chuckled when Miss Annabel's dogs gave it a sniff, then walked away without so much as a taste. Proceeding to the bunkhouse, he changed his clothes, strapped on his gun belt, and made up a bedroll. That done, he went to the barn, saddled his horse, and headed for the foothills.

He'd made camp by sunset, in a copse of birch trees next to a stream, and was crouched by the fire, frying a mess of trout for his supper, when a half dozen men rode in. They all looked as grim as the parlor of purgatory, and they were all armed.

Nicholas rose easily to his feet and folded his arms, the .45 a solid, reassuring weight against his thigh. He offered no greeting, but simply waited while Jack Horncastle dismounted and strode toward him. The other riders remained in the saddle.

"McKeige," Jack said with a nod.

Nicholas said nothing, but simply waited.

Horncastle smiled with about as much charm as a corpse, reached into his vest pocket, and drew out an envelope. "Here it is," he said, "like we agreed."

Nicholas accepted the packet, opened it, ran his thumb over the edge of the bills in a shuffling motion. "Thanks." He tucked the money into his shirt, went back to the fire, and took the trout off the heat.

"Aren't you going to invite us to stay for supper?" Jack asked. He considered himself a humorist, though he was about as funny as barbwire long johns.

"No," Nicholas said quietly. "I'm not."

"That army captain is telling everybody in town how your pa's going to send another two hundred head of beef to Fort Duffield. It's almost like he's trying to bait a trap."

Nicholas bit the inside of his lip, squinted a little in the bright crimson dazzle of the sunset as he looked up at Horncastle. "Only a fool would try the same trick twice," he said. "We'll wait for the silver shipment to go out, late next week."

Jack wasn't too bright, for a college man, and he was plainly getting skittish. "I don't like it," he said. "Us helping you rob your own pa, I mean."

Nicholas popped a piece of fish into his mouth, chewed, and spat out a couple of small bones, his manner as cool as the pebbles in the creek bed behind him. "Fine," he replied. "You don't need to trouble yourself. I'll handle everything myself."

Jack spat a curse. There was a lot of money to be made, and he was plainly reluctant to turn his back on it. "Damn it, it just seems suspicious, that's all."

"Like I said," Nicholas reiterated, reaching for another succulent morsel, "I'll take care of it."

"All right," Jack bit out, after a few moments of

frustrated silence. "All right. Let us know when you need us, and where."

Nicholas assessed Horncastle in silence for an interval calculated to unsettle him further. "I'll send word," he said. "Now get out of here, before somebody sees you."

Horncastle lingered, uncertain again, then turned on his heel, strode over to his horse, and vaulted into the saddle. Like Nicholas, he had been raised on horseback. Unlike Nicholas, he found it nearly impossible to wait for things he wanted.

When Horncastle and the others were gone, Nicholas took the packet of bills from his shirt and tucked it into his saddlebag. Then he finished his supper, spread his bedroll on the ground, and stretched out to watch the first pale stars appear in the sky.

He'd dozed off before he realized he was tired.

Full dark had fallen when Nicholas awakened, prompted by the chilly weight of a shotgun barrel resting at the base of his throat.

"Shit," he said.

His visitor laughed. "Up to your eyeballs, boy," he said. "Any of that fish left?"

Annabel was up even earlier than usual the next morning, for she had not slept well, lying alone in the bed she and Gabriel had shared so pleasurably before. She had been haunted by mirages of his touch, his kisses, the weight of his body upon hers, the sweet, searing force of his conquering—all empty memories, now that Gabriel had gone to sleep in another room, at the opposite end of the hall.

Only distance could cure what ailed her, Annabel decided. Therefore, once she was absolutely certain that Gabriel had left the house for the day, she ordered her surrey hitched up and brought around, summoned her fickle dogs with an unladylike whistle, and then allowed a pitiably grateful Mr. Hilditch to drive her into Parable to the general store.

She had made a mental list during the long, dark hours just past, in a largely unsuccessful bid to distract herself from Gabriel's absence—ludicrous, she thought, in view of the fact that she had been apart from the man for more than a decade and enjoyed perfect slumber. But there it was; Gabriel had awakened the old hunger in her body, and she was bound to suffer until the malaise subsided again.

Annabel was, in any case, able to make her purchases with some dispatch—a hammer and nails, paint, a broom, an apron and a scarf, soap and a mop and a bucket, the accoutrements for brewing tea, and a copy of Sir Walter Scott's *Lady of the Lake,* her favorite, to occupy her mind when her work was through.

Furniture, mattresses, linens, and rugs could not be had at the Parable store, but Annabel placed an order by mail, and was promised that her purchases would arrive soon, by freight wagon, from San Francisco. In the meantime she intended to borrow what she could from Jessie, and she suspected that Charlie might be able to purloin a few necessities from the ranch house without Gabriel's knowing.

She was be-scarfed and aproned, quite industriously engaged in sweeping the cobwebs down from the parlor ceiling of her house, when she heard a great commotion on the main street, which was just around the corner.

Mr. Hilditch, perched on an upturned crate scrubbing a window, was delighted. "Look there, Mrs. McKeige," he cried. "It's the stagecoach arriving."

This was indeed an event, since the coach only passed through Parable in alternate weeks, and nobody knew exactly when it would arrive. That was why Annabel had traveled to the capital by train, carrying Mr. Hilditch, her team, and the surrey with her in a hired railroad car, and progressed from Carson City to Parable under her own power. Passing by Fort Duffield, she had acquired a military escort, since Captain Sommervale was bound that way anyway.

Annabel recalled meeting the captain on his way to the ranch earlier that day—she had been too busy until now—and her fear for Nicholas was redoubled.

She joined Mr. Hilditch at the window.

The stage had drawn up in front of the general store, and a fury of dust and noises—the driver's shouts, the horses' neighing, the creaks and groans of wood and leather—still filled the weighted summer air. For a few seconds the whole scene was cloaked in a giant plume of dirt, and when the coach itself became visible again, the passengers were alighting.

Annabel stared in horrified disbelief as Jeffrey Braithewait stepped down, then turned to aid a lady in very plain and serviceable clothes. As if he felt her gaze, Jeffrey actually looked in Annabel's direction.

Mr. Hilditch was squinting. "Isn't that Braithewait?" he asked, dashing her fleeting hope that she'd been mistaken.

Annabel let her forehead rest against the window frame for a moment, in pure dismay.

Jeffrey was a wealthy Londoner with social connections others only dreamed about. He had long been Annabel's admirer, sending her flowers and small gifts, all of which she had immediately returned, and love notes that had made her blush. On more than one occasion Jeffrey had offered to buy Evanwood and install her there, as wife or mistress, whichever she chose.

For all her desire to remarry, establish a home, and bear more children—it had not eluded her that this last, at least in part, sprang from a need to make amends for her failure with Nicholas—Annabel had never had any intention of accepting Braithewait's suit. He was, for all his charm, his money, his good looks, an adventurer and an absolute scoundrel, a more fortunate version of her father, Ellery Latham.

Outrage replaced Annabel's shock in short order; she flung the broom to the floor with a crash and reached back to untie her apron. It was no coincidence that Jeffrey—who spent most of his time in England or on the Continent—had come to Parable, Nevada. The West was a big place, and Parable wasn't exactly a crossroads. He had followed her here, damn his eyes.

"Mrs. McKeige," Hilditch said quickly, bravely, when she would have stormed out to confront Jeffrey and send him packing. "Don't. If there's another scene like the one when we got here, nobody around here will ever remember anything else about you. That'll be what they think of when your name is raised." He paused to take a tremulous breath. "Like as not, the gossip won't trouble you much—you'll be going back to England one day—but what about your son? This is his home, and he's likely to marry in Parable and raise his children here."

The speech was long for Mr. Hilditch, not to mention forward, but his reasoning was sound. She had caused more than her share of scandal already; she would bide her time, and if—when—Braithewait sought her out, she could give him a piece of her mind. In private.

"Thank you," she said, with all possible dignity, and retied her apron.

Barely half an hour later Jessie appeared, dressed for calling. Entering Annabel's house, in mid-restoration as it was, she dabbed at her nose with a dainty handkerchief against the miasma of dust and mice and mildew, but her smile of greeting was friendly, if rueful.

"I hoped, I confess, that Gabriel would have changed your mind before now," she said, pulling off her gloves and looking around the forlorn little parlor. Unlike Jessie's stately residence and Gabriel's sprawling ranch house, Annabel's new home was too small to boast an entryway. There were two quite spacious rooms downstairs, a parlor and a kitchen, and two less commodious bedrooms upstairs. "I see I was wrong."

Annabel was glad to see Jessie. Nonetheless, she responded as might have been expected. "I had never heard that McKeiges were *capable* of being wrong," she said.

Jessie took no offense, since none had been intended, and laughed softly. "Perhaps I was hasty," she countered. "My guess is that Gabriel doesn't know you're here. We'll see what happens when he finds out."

Annabel rolled her eyes. "Come in," she said, "and sit down. You have your choice of seats—either an apple crate or an apple crate. While you settle yourself, I'll brew a pot of tea."

Jessie was strolling idly about the parlor when Annabel headed for the kitchen.

When she returned, her sister-in-law had taken up a post at the window. She looked like an elegant Norse goddess, standing there, rimmed in sunlight. Hearing Annabel, she turned, smiled, but the shadows of private worries lingered upon her face.

"I think you are a fool, taking this place, when you could live on the ranch," she said briskly, "but I suppose this is an improvement over your lighting out for England. You need to be near Nicholas."

Annabel looked about in vain for a place to set the two ungainly mugs of tea she'd carried in from the kitchen. There were no delicate china cups in that house, or in the general store to be bought, for that matter. No pretty teapots, no gleaming silver trays, no linen napkins edged in lace.

In Warwickshire, Annabel served tea in grand style. Here, it was just as well to abandon all pretense of grace and refinement.

"Yes," Annabel said, at some length, grateful when Jessie simply reached out and took one of the mugs. She sighed wistfully. "I wish I could persuade Nicholas to return to England with me, if only for a year or two. That would solve so many problems."

Jessie arched one delicate eyebrow. "Would it? Gabriel is unlikely to grant you a divorce in any case, but if you do not plague him constantly, and at close range, you'll have no chance whatever of success."

"Nicholas is more important," Annabel said with a little sigh. She took a thoughtful sip of her tea. "If only he would confide in someone. I know that Nicholas does not—perhaps *cannot*—feel close to me. But why won't he talk to you, Jessie, or to his father?" A flood of misery swamped her. "God in heaven, have I scarred my son so badly that he trusts no one at all?"

"Nicholas has always kept his own counsel. I'm not certain he would have been any different if you'd been in that ranch house every day of his life."

Annabel considered Jessie's words for a few moments before replying. "He was a little boy when we went to Boston. I was his mother, and ostensibly in charge. Perhaps I should not have permitted Nicholas to return to Parable." Her eyes stung at the memory of putting her small son on a westbound train that long ago day, accompanied by a woman traveling to Fort Duffield to join her husband.

"Don't torture yourself, Annabel," Jessie said. "Nicholas *would* have run away, just as he warned you, and heaven only knows what might have happened to him then." She looked about the room with bright eyes, calculating eyes. "I believe I have a few things stored in my attic that would improve the appearance of this place. I'll borrow one of Gabriel's wagons and a couple of his men to help."

Annabel was touched, not just by Jessie's generosity but by the friendliness of her gesture. Gabriel's sister had been furiously angry, that long-ago day, when Annabel had boarded the stagecoach with Nicholas, leaving Parable, and Gabriel, behind. "I had not expected such kindness from you," she said in her straightforward way.

Jessie patted Annabel's work-reddened hand. "I'm sorry if you've counted me as an enemy all this time," she replied, "but it's really your own fault if you have. You must learn, darling Annabel, that people can be angry with you and still love you very much. Gabriel, for instance. And Nicholas."

Annabel did not know what to say in response, so she took a sip of tea as a tactic of delay. In her mind's eye she saw her drunken father, shirttails out, hair mussed, looming over her, impossibly powerful, furious because she'd interrupted some tryst. "I should have put you into a foundling home," he'd said. "It would have been better if you'd died with your wretched, whining mother. Don't think there are no ways to be rid of you, my girl, for there are. There are."

Annabel shivered, brought herself firmly back to the present. Ellery Latham was long dead; unfortunately, however, his influence was not.

"I have decided to hold a tea party in your honor," Jessie said, "this Saturday afternoon at four o'clock. The invitations have already gone out."

Annabel gaped at her, both delighted and fearful. She yearned for acceptance, for belonging, and yet she knew the good women of Parable considered her a harlot. "Jessie, no one will come!"

"Of course they will," Jessie said, plucking at the crisp fabric of her skirts. "They will have to, if they want to meet the new schoolteacher. She's boarding with me, you know. She arrived on today's stagecoach, so everyone in town knows she's here. Her name is Olivia Drummond and she is quite lovely, in her own particular way." Jessie leaned forward, lowering her voice to a confidential whisper. "Thirty if she's a day, and no sign of a wedding ring. The ideal wife for Marshal Swingler. We must make sure they meet on Sunday morning after church."

Annabel laughed with quiet joy. So many things were wrong in her life, she could barely count them. But Jessie had befriended her, and that made up for a great deal.

Eight

GABRIEL WAS LOWERED INTO THE MINE SHAFT ON A small plank platform, a mechanism operated by a system of ropes and pulleys. He held a kerosene lantern over his head and peered uneasily into the gloom. He'd made a bank full of money out of that hole, and several others like it, but he avoided the place whenever he could. To his way of thinking, a man shouldn't have to spend time underground before he was buried.

Knute Gilchrist, his foreman, materialized beside him, like some kind of ghost. "Follow me, boss," he said. He was as surefooted and confident in this anteroom of hell as Gabe was in the Samhill Saloon. "The new vein's back a ways."

Gabe followed. Through the darkness, he heard the muted, rhythmic ring of picks striking stone, the low murmur of the men talking as they worked. The pit was cold, even though it was July, and smelled dank and raw, like a newly dug grave.

The blended light of his own lantern and Gilchrist's

blinded Gabe, though he knew the other man could see like a cat. They moved deeper and deeper into the bowels of the shaft, through a snarl of catacombs, and it occurred to Gabe that if Gilchrist abandoned him, he might never find his way back to the sunlight. Back to Annabel.

"Here it is," Gilchrist said, at long last, when Gabe figured they must surely be somewhere under Montana Territory. The foreman laid a hand to the wall of stone and held his lantern high. "This vein looks like it runs from here to Carson City," he announced. "We'll have to blast to get to her, though, and that's probably going to bring down a lot of dirt and rock."

Gabriel sighed. He had more money than his grandchildren could spend—provided Nicholas stayed alive long enough to give him some, that is—but there were other considerations. Parable thrived on the work these mines provided; families depended upon the wages drawn by the specter-men laboring behind him in the shadows. He could not simply throw up his hands and quit.

Hell, he didn't even know *how* to quit.

"What do you think?" Gilchrist prompted, when Gabe didn't speak right away. The foreman was a middle-aged widower with three plain but lively daughters, all of whom had pursued Nicholas at one time or another. This job was everything to Gilchrist.

"If you're sure it's worth closing down the rest of the mine," Gabe concluded wearily, "then go ahead and blast."

Gilchrist's crooked, horselike teeth gleamed in the lamplight as he smiled. "You won't be sorry, boss," he said, caressing the stone as though it were a woman's flesh. "Hell, you'll be able to open your own bank once we start bringing this ore to the surface."

Gabe sighed. "Yeah," he said. He hadn't slept well the night before, knowing Annabel was lying just down the hall in their bed, and his mood was as dark and complex as the web of mine shafts around him. His desire for her was so strong, so all-pervasive, that it clouded his brain, ached in his groin, weakened his knees.

If he had any sense, he'd give Annabel her divorce, let her go back to England and marry some tenderfoot. That prospect was painful, and the reality would be like cauterizing a wound, but once she was gone, the healing could begin.

"Boss?"

Gabe jumped slightly. He'd let himself get distracted again, and that wasn't smart—especially fifty feet underground. "Did you say something?"

Gilchrist chuckled. "Yes, sir. I said we'd have a batch of ore ready for transport in just a few days. We'd better bring along a few extra guards this time, I figure. Considering the trick that was played on the army, I mean, over them cattle."

Gabe thrust a hand through his hair, relieved that Gilchrist was headed back toward the main shaft. He could think more clearly in the light of day, and he had a lot on his mind, between Annabel, Nicholas, and the coming cattle drive to Fort Duffield.

The ore would be sold to a smelter in Carson City—if it ever arrived there.

"I'm heading up the drive to Fort Duffield myself," Gabe said. "Hire as many men as you can get to ride with the ore. Nicholas will go along for good measure."

They had reached the central shaft; Gabe could make out the platform that would carry him back up to the surface of the ground. He was light-headed with relief, but he didn't miss the little silence that preceded Gilchrist's too-hearty answer.

"Good," he blustered. "That's good."

Mounting the platform, Gabe wondered how eager the mine foreman would have been to marry off one of his daughters to Nicholas these days, the talk being what it was.

Gabe called to the man waiting on the surface to hoist him up. "Let me know when you're ready to move the ore," he said, in parting, "and make sure you issue some kind of warning before you blast. Last time, every cow within a ten mile radius either ran off or gave cottage cheese for a month. I got nothing done for counting out silver dollars to sodbusters."

The pulleys creaked; the platform jiggled violently and began to rise.

Gilchrist laughed and waved a hand in farewell.

On the surface, Gabe drew in several deep, hungry breaths and secretly reveled in the bright warmth of the sun.

"Where is Nicholas?" he asked twenty minutes later, when he arrived at the barn. He would outline his orders to his son first, Gabe decided, then find Annabel and try to reason with her. If that failed—and it probably would—he'd be left with only two choices: seducing her or jumping into the spring to cool himself off.

"Town, I guess," one of the cowboys answered. "He rode in here this morning, but he ain't in the bunkhouse or at the corral."

Gabe suppressed his irritation. Nicholas drew a salary, like the other hands, but he wasn't around half the time. It was no wonder folks thought he was an outlaw, the way he vanished whenever he got a fancy to, and the other men had a right to resent him, since they worked hard for every penny of their pay.

"If you see Nicholas, tell him I want a word with him." Gabe swung down from the saddle, tethered his horse where it could drink from the water trough.

"Yes, sir," said the cowhand. "Should I go lookin' for him?"

"I'll do that myself," Gabe said, and started toward the house.

He found Charlie in the kitchen, mixing what looked like dumpling or biscuit batter. Tossing his old friend a curt nod for a greeting, Gabe pumped water into a bucket at the sink, then started back to the porch, where the wash bench stood.

"You seen Nicholas?" he asked, from the threshold.

Charlie shook his head. "Not since last night, when he left one of my good dishes in the yard," he said. The Indian's expression hadn't changed—it never did—but he sounded like an indignant housewife. "Fed my stew to the dogs, that's what he did."

Gabe quickly subdued the grin that flashed onto his mouth. He didn't dare comment; maybe Charlie's cooking wasn't memorable, but it filled the stomach, and there wasn't another man on the ranch willing to take over the task. "Remind me to tie Nicholas to a fence post and horsewhip him," he said. "What about Annabel? Is she up and about?"

Charlie looked amused now, as well as testy, like somebody who has just gotten the upper hand after a series of affronts. "Up and about? She's been gone since half an hour after you left the house. Wouldn't even let me make her breakfast."

Gabe set his jaw, went outside with the bucket, and

took the enamel basin down from its nail on the wall. He shrugged out of his shirt and flung it over a railing. Then, slamming the basin down onto the bench, he splashed the water in, reached for a bar of yellow soap stout enough to take the hide off a wild pig, and lathered his face and torso in swift, almost violent motions.

Annabel's dogs came to his sides, snuffling and whining.

"Go on, scat!" Gabe snapped, feeling uncharitable. Damn it, he should have known better than to think he and Annabel had settled their disagreement over her living in town.

The dogs whimpered and rubbed their sides along his thighs, like giant cats.

Gabe got soap in his eyes, looking to see what they were carrying on about, then sent them skulking away on their stomachs with a resounding bellow. An instant later the contents of the water bucket flew into his face, followed by those of the basin.

Gabe shook his head, flinging a soapy spray in all directions, and when he could finally see, he was confronted with Charlie.

"Somebody here to see you," the Indian said, the bucket in one hand, the basin under his arm. When he was pissed off, he had a way of letting it be known without mincing words. "'Round front, on the porch."

The man stood in the shadows, wearing a broad smile and the kind of clothes that marked him off immediately as a friend of Annabel's.

"Mr. McKeige?" he asked, beaming.

Gabe's mind was still on Charlie. He was dripping water like a baptized hound and in no mood for social calls. He figured his expression would have set Geronimo back on his heels, but he nodded, in grudging admission that he was indeed Mr. McKeige. "And you would be . . . ?"

The dandy beamed. "Jeffrey Braithewait. I wonder, is Annabel about?"

Gabe remembered the towel around his neck and used it. "My wife is occupied elsewhere," he said, putting only the slightest emphasis on the first two words. "Maybe I can help you."

"I don't think so," Braithewait said. He looked troubled now, and, for Gabe, that was a source of some satisfaction, however small. "Fancy that. I came all this way believing Annabel—Mrs. McKeige—had surely secured a divorce by now. She's talked of nothing else for years."

Charlie appeared in the doorway, sporting his apron and looking annoyed. Gabe knew he was there to protect the stranger, not him.

"I'm afraid there won't be a divorce," Gabe said evenly. Was it possible that Annabel wanted to marry this greenhorn? Did she expect to get the babies she claimed to want from such a puny specimen?

Braithewait rocked back on his heels, looking smug. Gabe decided that anybody who'd dare to confront a man twice his size—and one he didn't know, at that—on such a subject, should not be underestimated. This fellow was either crazy, criminal, or brave beyond all good sense.

"I'd like to hear those words directly from Annabel, if you don't mind," said the banty rooster. He had deer-brown slicked-down hair and ears like the handles on a sugar bowl, and Gabe could not imagine what his wife or any other woman saw in him.

Charlie came outside and handed Gabe a clean shirt. His brown eyes held a solemn warning. The dogs, having followed Gabe around the side of the house, were crouched nearby, growling at the visitor.

Braithewait flashed a toothy and wholly unfriendly smile at them. "Worthless hounds," he said cheerfully, "you'll soon see your end, whether Annabel likes it or not."

Gabe frowned, honestly puzzled. "Are we talking about the same woman?" he asked.

Charlie chortled at that—Charlie, who rarely laughed. Gabe did not succumb to the illusion that his friend was over his snit, whatever it was. The Indian's ways, like those of the Almighty, were oftentimes beyond comprehension.

"Annabel Latham McKeige," Braithewait said. "Soon to be my wife and the mistress of my estates."

Gabe took an unwilling step toward the Englishman, but Charlie stopped him in midstride with a pointed glance.

"Sit yourself down, Mr. Braithewait," said the Indian, as formal as a butler in one of those fancy houses Annabel seemed to set so much store by, indicating the porch swing. "I'll brew some tea."

"I'd rather have brandy, thank you," Braithewait said, accepting the offered seat with a sigh. His gaze met Gabe's squarely. "I don't suppose you'd be needing a ranch hand? Just temporarily, I mean? I seem to find myself short of funds, and being out of touch with my own bank . . ."

So, Gabe thought, it was like that. The little weasel was after Annabel's money. He wasn't entirely displeased by the discovery, although it did nothing to raise his opinion of Jeffrey Braithewait.

"You'll find I'm a fair horseman," Braithewait pressed, when Gabe didn't speak. "A sporting man, if you will. I can shoot, too."

It wouldn't be a bad idea, Gabe reflected, to keep the skunk in plain sight, and the alliance was bound to offend Annabel's delicate social sensibilities. He smiled and offered his hand. "Go find the foreman when you've had your brandy," he said. "You're hired."

Jeffrey looked mildly surprised, but the bargain was sealed in the time-honored way.

When Charlie emerged with the brandy moments later, Gabe tossed him the towel in a way calculated to irritate, then turned without another word and headed toward the barn, there to collect his horse. He swung up into the saddle, hardly aware that his shirt was still halfway unbuttoned and his hair was slicked back from his face. His one aim was to find Annabel, and he had a pretty good idea where to look.

Jessie had gone, and Mr. Hilditch was off somewhere, probably patronizing the Samhill Saloon, when the crashing knock sounded at the front door.

Annabel, who had been scouring the floor in the main bedroom upstairs, closed her eyes against the sound. Gabriel, of course. No one else in the world cared enough to be so angry.

With a sigh, she got to her feet, looked with despair at her soiled dress and apron, and descended the staircase as regally as if she were the mistress of a grand country manor.

Gabriel appeared ready to break down the door when she swung it open. His clothes were askew, and his fair hair, usually in charming disarray, looked as though he'd tried to face down a hurricane. His skin was streaked, part clean and part dirty, as though he'd bathed in a mud puddle.

Annabel put a hand to her breast. "Gabriel, what on earth?"

He stormed past her and pushed the door shut with a crash, using the sole of one boot.

"I won't ask what you're doing here, Annabel," he growled, through his magnificent teeth, "because I know you're going to say you're setting up housekeeping. I guess there's nothing I can do to stop you, short of dragging you back home by your hair, but *by God,* if you try to entertain men here, I'll—"

Gabriel had backed Annabel up until the newel-post at the base of the stairs was pressing into her back and his nose was maybe a quarter of an inch from hers.

"You'll what?" she demanded, putting her hands on her hips. With Gabriel, there was no taking the defensive—only the *offensive* offered any hope of success. "*What* will you do, Gabriel McKeige?"

His blood was running so hot that she could feel an echoing burn in her own. His blue eyes flashed like clear sapphires catching the midday sun, and she saw that his right temple was throbbing, as though the pulse would break through the skin.

"I'll—" he began fiercely, then stopped again. In the next instant he'd taken Annabel by the shoulders and raised her up on tiptoe. His mouth descended upon hers like the unholy vengeance of some greater realm, had already claimed and conquered her before she could manage a protest.

She whimpered, but she did not try to break away. Indeed, the possibility didn't even occur to her. She'd always been helpless against Gabriel's kisses, no matter how outrageous they were or how inappropriate the circumstances.

When Gabriel finally released her, he was gasping for breath.

Annabel herself would have slipped to the floor, so useless were her knees, if he hadn't still been grasping her by the shoulders.

"Gabriel," she whispered, and the name was both a plea and a protest.

He lifted her into his arms and started up the stairs, his gaze holding hers as surely as if they'd somehow been fused. That Gabriel had encountered Jeffrey Braithewait, that he was staking a primitive claim on her, the way a wolf or a wild stallion would mark its mate as a warning to others, Annabel was certain. She also knew she would not stop him.

The upper landing was shadowy and cool. Private.

Gabriel pressed his lips to hers once again; her tongue sparred with his.

"There—there are no beds," she murmured, her mouth swollen with the sweet pressure of his kisses, when he drew back to take a raspy breath.

"We don't need a bed," he said, raising her skirts to lay his hands on her waist.

"No," she agreed miserably, joyously. Her body felt hot, and ached on every plane and in every curve and crevice. She put her arms around Gabriel's neck, knowing she would curse him—and herself—later, and stood on tiptoe to kiss him as ravenously, and with as much demand, as he had kissed her.

He groaned and pressed her against the wall of the tiny corridor, and she felt the heat and power of his erection through her dress, and was utterly lost in that moment.

"Gabriel," she whispered, pleading. "Gabriel—"

He raised her skirts, pushed down her drawers, and put his hand boldly between her legs, wringing a cry of despairing pleasure from her as he stroked that most intimate place.

"Tell me, Annabel," Gabriel demanded, as he plied her with expert fingers. "Tell me what you want."

It was an old ritual, Gabriel's insistence that she invite him into her body before he took her, reserved for times when desire flared suddenly between them. Times when the power of his wanting was such that he knew he could not contain it without her help.

She nuzzled his neck, breathed her answer against his ear. "I want you to have me, Gabriel."

He opened his trousers and raised her off the floor by the waist. His first thrust pushed her hard against the wall.

She kicked away her hobbling drawers and, with a low cry, flung her legs around Gabriel's hips. He kissed her mouth, her jawline, her eyelids, the hollow beneath her ears, but the coupling was not a gentle one. The movements of their bodies grew more violent, more reckless, with every stroke.

Finally the storm broke with shattering force; Gabriel plunged deep into her, with a low, ragged shout of triumph and surrender, while she flung her head back, her fingers threaded through his hair, and buckled helplessly, fiercely against him.

They slid bonelessly to the floor, in one motion, still joined and clinging together as if to keep from slipping into the yawning mouth of hell.

Gabriel knelt, Annabel astraddle of his thighs. Her lips grazed his neck; his face was buried in her hair, his hands still clasping her bare buttocks, still holding her closer than close.

Annabel was just starting to get her breath back and

assemble a train of sensible thoughts in her head when she felt Gabriel growing hard inside her again. She moaned as he drew back to open her bodice and the camisole beneath, freeing her eager breasts. Covering them with his palms.

"I'm not through with you yet, Mrs. McKeige," he warned, just before he lowered his head to take greedy suckle at her nipples, first one and then the other.

Her hips were already moving slowly, steadily, against his. She was moaning and arching her back, to give Gabriel greater access to the breasts he was already plundering. No more, she thought, than I am through with you.

When Nicholas arrived on his mother's front porch, just after sunset, with a mess of fish in one hand and a skillet stolen from Jessie's kitchen in the other, she was glowing like the western sky. He might have turned around and left, out of simple decency, if she hadn't been so overjoyed to see him.

"Nicholas!" she cried, pulling him over the threshold. "Come in—please."

He frowned, glancing toward the stairs. "Is Pa here?"

Miss Annabel's color heightened a little, and her eyes were bright. "He paid a call a few hours ago," she said and, too late, looked away.

"I wouldn't want to intrude," he said, hiding a grin. He guessed it was naive to hope for a reconciliation, but somewhere inside him that angry, desperate little boy still lived, clamoring to have his mother and father back together. He wouldn't have minded a baby brother or sister, either; that way, if things didn't work out according to plan, there would have been somebody to replace him.

"You aren't intruding," Miss Annabel insisted. "I would love to have company." Her gaze fell to the trout. "And I'm starving."

"This old place has a cookstove, I assume," he teased, closing the door behind him.

"That's about *all* it has," Miss Annabel admitted, with a laugh.

Maybe it was a trick of the light, but in that old dress, with her sleeves pushed up and her hair hanging down her back, his mother didn't look any older than sixteen.

"I think I'm going to have to swallow my pride and drive back out to the ranch after we eat," she said. "I thought I could sleep on the floor, but I fear I might find myself eye to eye with a rat."

"You could probably bed down over at Aunt Jessie's," he suggested, as they entered the kitchen. He didn't want to push Miss Annabel toward his pa; they were both stubborn, and too much pressure might make them take the bit in their teeth.

Parents, he concluded, needed careful handling, like wounded porcupines and hibernating rattlesnakes. He'd just leave them alone, put them in each other's way as often as possible, and let them think it was all their idea.

The borrowed skillet made a pleasant clanging sound as he set it on the stove. Miss Annabel had been brewing tea, so there was a fire in the grate; it just needed a little building up.

Expertly, he added leftover kindling from the cobweb-draped box on the back stoop, then wood. The blaze caught and was soon crackling away, and crimson rims of light gleamed around the stove lids.

Miss Annabel looked happy. "You never said a

word in your letters about cooking," she said. She was turning up the lamps, rummaging through a box of goods until she came up with a package of lard.

"I would have been lying if I had, Miss Annabel. The only thing I can cook is trout."

She drew a little closer, gazing nervously up at the shadows draping the ceilings. "You didn't mention the murder in this house, either," she said.

He grinned, smearing lard in the skillet and watching it melt down to a clear, gleaming oil. "It was pretty sensational," he said. "Not fit for a lady to read about."

Miss Annabel shivered. "Nicholas McKeige, you tell me what happened here. Right now!"

He chuckled. "Mrs. Jennings's husband came in late one night, and she shot him with a double-barrel shotgun, right there by that door." He pointed with Jessie's spatula, snitched when he borrowed the frying pan. "Died on the threshold, old J.T. did, face down in his own—well, face down."

Miss Annabel gasped, plainly horrified. The idea of spending the night safe on the ranch had to be gaining new appeal with every passing moment. "Why did she shoot him?"

He shrugged. "She testified that she thought he was a bandit, come to steal her jewelry. It was dark as the devil's heart outside, so I guess she could have been telling the truth."

"What happened to her?"

He took his time answering. It was a story he loved telling, and he liked to spin out the suspense as long as possible. Later he would admit that he'd made up practically every word.

He rinsed off the trout under the rusty pump in the

sink, then tossed them into the pan. "She was found guilty and hanged—from that big oak tree in the churchyard."

Miss Annabel's eyes were as round as the skillet. "No!"

He nodded solemnly. "Yes." He spoke in a low voice, but carefully. His mother was not a stupid woman, but she was tired, it was especially dark that night, and once he'd gone, she'd be alone in a strange and largely empty house. "There are those who say they've seen a figure dangling from a limb of that oak, of an evening, and heard a terrible wailing sound."

Miss Annabel punched him hard in the arm. "You rascal!" she cried, looking more like a girl than ever. "You're *trying* to scare me."

Impulsively, he kissed her forehead. "I might be pulling your leg a little," he confessed. "Either way, you don't need to worry. If anybody haunted this house, it would be poor old J.T. After all, he was the injured party."

"You are a wretch," she said, but her eyes were gleaming and her skin was translucent in the dim light. She was beautiful, his mother, and he, Nicholas the boy and Nicholas the man, begrudged every day they'd spent apart.

Eventually they would have to sit down and talk, he and Miss Annabel, about those years between his leaving Boston and her return to Parable, but that night, in her bare kitchen, with the ancient paint peeling and the trout sizzling, fragrant, in the skillet, was not the time.

I love you, he thought, but he wasn't sure when, if ever, he'd be able to say those words aloud.

"I hope you have some dishes in this place," he said

instead. "Otherwise, Miss Annabel, we'll have to eat with our fingers."

She went to plunder the supply box again, came up with two enamel plates of the kind he carried in his saddlebag when he was on the trail, along with some equally elegant forks.

Presently, when the fish was cooked to crispy perfection, he dished up the meal and they sat on the front step to eat, watching the stars, their plates balanced on their knees. The faint, cheeky music of the piano in the Samhill Saloon chimed in their ears, along with the sounds of hooves and wagon wheels on the dry, hard-packed dirt of the main street. There were cowboys out and about, and soldiers, but all the ladies of Parable were tucked safely away in their kitchens and parlors, and so were their children.

"Your aunt Jessie is holding a tea party for me on Saturday," Miss Annabel said. She'd finished her supper by then and set the plate aside. "I'm looking forward to it . . ." Her voice fell away into silence, and her expression was pensive.

"But?" he prompted.

"But at the same time, I'm afraid."

"Why?"

Miss Annabel rested her head against his shoulder, just for a moment, and he liked the feeling it gave him. "Women can be unkind," she said. "Not to mention unforgiving."

He stiffened at the idea that the people of Parable thought they had the right to be *forgiving* Miss Annabel for anything. Her leaving was a family matter, her business and his father's. And, in another way, his own.

"Jessie will stand by you," he said. He relaxed a

little. "Don't worry. Every woman in town will want an invitation to that shindig, if only because they're curious." He took Miss Annabel's plate, stacked it on top of his own, and rose to carry them back to that dismal kitchen. Looking down upon his mother's upturned face, he spoke gently. "You gather up your things now, and I'll fetch that surrey of yours from the livery stable and drive you home."

For a moment, he thought Miss Annabel would give him an argument. In the end, though, she just nodded, and when he brought the surrey around, fifteen minutes later, she was ready and waiting.

Nine

ANNABEL HALF EXPECTED TO ENCOUNTER GABRIEL when she entered the ranch house that night, exhausted and grubby, yearning for a hot bath and a long, oblivious sleep. She did *not* expect to meet Jeffrey Braithewait, clad in a silk smoking jacket and trousers that looked alarmingly like pajama bottoms, a snifter of brandy cradled between his hands.

He was crossing the dining room as she went to ask Charlie to heat water for her tub, and he stopped in his footprints, as abruptly as Annabel stopped, plainly stunned.

"My dear!" he cried, horrified, taking in her soiled clothes and mussed hair. "Have you reverted to the pioneer life so soon?"

Annabel was in no mood for Jeffrey's snobbery or his insolence. Because of his noble birth, he seemed to think he had the right to address other people in any fashion or tone he chose. It was time he learned otherwise.

"What are you doing here, of all places?" she

demanded. Last she'd heard, he was off in Australia, harrying the Aborigines.

Jeffrey swirled the brandy in his snifter and watched it languidly while he considered his answer. "Mr. McKeige was kind enough to offer me employment, and, well, after a look at the bunkhouse, I brought myself straight back here and threw myself on the mercies of the native cook—what's his name? Charlie, that's it." He paused, rounding his eyes and shaking his head. "I daresay Mr. McKeige wouldn't have been so hospitable as the native. Doubtless he'll throw me out when he finds out I'm here."

Annabel's exhaustion was exceeded only by her exasperation, not only with Jeffrey, for following her, uninvited and certainly unencouraged, halfway around the world, but with Gabriel, for hiring him, and with Charlie, for inviting him to sleep in the house. Speech was beyond her.

Jeffrey rocked back onto the heels of his costly house slippers. "Well, if you'll excuse me, my dear, I am quite weary. The journey has been *grueling*, as I'm sure you know. Good night."

Annabel watched, open-mouthed, as Jeffrey Braithewait walked by her, probably on his way to the downstairs bedroom, humming a romantic tune under his breath. When shock permitted, she proceeded into the kitchen and was almost more surprised to find Gabriel there than she had been to meet Jeffrey in the dining room.

He was working at the table, ledgers and papers spread before him, within the golden circle of a single kerosene lantern. Annabel's uneasiness was tempered by a stab of abject tenderness, for he wore spectacles. She had not known that, not known so many things. Had missed so many small transitions.

Gabriel raised his eyes, removed his spindly wire-framed glasses, and set them on the table. His attitude was reserved, almost remote; one would never have guessed that he had made love to Annabel against a wall only hours before.

"You look a sight," he said, noting her disheveled state in a sweeping glance but, unlike Jeffrey, without apparent judgment.

He didn't rise, and that irritated Annabel, but she could not find the stamina to make an issue of etiquette. Without replying, she went to the sink, bent to collect the stacked buckets beneath, and began pumping water into the first one.

Gabriel must have moved as silently as the missing Charlie would have done, for he was beside Annabel in a moment, elbowing her aside to take over the pumping of water himself.

"Build up the fire," he said. "Charlie's already banked it for the night."

Listlessly, Annabel obeyed. Then she got out the largest kettles and set them on the stove for Gabriel to fill.

He did so efficiently.

"Why," Annabel asked, when she could trust herself to speak, "would you permit Jeffrey Braithewait to spend the night in this house?" She did not look at Gabriel, but was painfully aware of him, standing so close beside her. "He claims he wheedled an invitation out of Charlie, behind your back, but you must know he's here."

Gabriel smiled. "I'll toss him out in the morning," he said easily. "Why be so unneighborly, Annabel? Braithewait's a friend of yours, isn't he?"

She turned to look fiercely up into Gabriel's eyes. He had bathed since their encounter in the Jennings house that day; his hair was clean and well brushed, and it glistened like Asian silk in the lantern light.

"Mr. Braithewait is not my friend," she said. "He is, to the contrary, an obnoxious, self-important woodchuck with an exaggerated sense of his own charms. Had I known he was here, I would have passed the night at Jessie's or, failing that, in a horse stall at the livery stable!"

Gabriel grinned despicably, and Annabel was reminded of Nicholas, though the comparison was quickly gone. "But he's come all this way to win your hand, Lady Annabel. Here's your chance for a husband and a whole family of simpering nippers in velvet knee pants and caps with tassels."

Annabel's cheeks ached with color. If she hadn't been so desperate for a bath, she would have turned on her heel and walked out right then. "I can hardly marry Jeffrey or anyone else," she said, with defiant reason, "when I already have a husband. One who has refused to release me from an untenable union, I might add."

"Untenable? Is that what you were thinking today, when you reached inside my shirt and clawed off a band of hide from my spine to my belly? When you said—"

"Stop it!" Annabel hissed, telling herself that the passion of her answer stemmed from indignation and not from the reawakening of scandalous feelings. She turned her head, but Gabriel grasped her chin, very gently, and made her look at him.

"I'm sorry, Annabel," he said, with apparent sincerity and a sort of gruff tenderness. "I can see that you're tuckered out, and I shouldn't be baiting you. Go and sit down, and I'll throw together a pot of that tea you like so much."

Annabel was flabbergasted; dealing with Gabriel was a confusing matter indeed. One moment he was behaving like a rascal and an oaf, the next he was a gentleman, caring and calm. Wearing spectacles to read.

She stumbled to the table and collapsed onto a bench.

"Have you eaten?" Gabriel filled the teakettle and then made a place for it on the crowded stove top.

"Nicholas brought a mess of trout to the house," Annabel said, cheered by the recollection. "We had supper together."

Gabriel looked back over his shoulder. "Ah, the elusive Nicholas. I've been looking for him on and off all day long. Do you know where he is now?"

"In the barn or the bunkhouse, I would imagine. He drove me out here in the surrey."

A tea canister appeared from a shelf, along with a chipped crockery pot, a cup, and a sugar bowl. Gabriel seemed to have a remarkable grasp on the process of making tea, for a rancher who'd lived much of his life as a figurative bachelor, and Annabel wondered with a pang if he'd done this for Julia, in her private quarters above the Samhill Saloon.

Gabriel offered no comment. While the kettle was heating, there among the giant pots of soon-to-be bathwater, he went out onto the back porch and returned in a few moments with a round copper washtub. He set it in front of the stove and tested one of the pots of water with the swirl of an index finger.

Annabel's eyes widened. "You can't think I'm going to bathe *here,*" she protested, "with all the kingdoms of the earth parading in and out?"

A corner of Gabriel's mouth quirked upward in a semblance of a smile. "And you can't think, Mrs.

McKeige, that I'm going to lug all these buckets up the stairs, only to have you complaining that your bath is cold."

Annabel swallowed. "Gabriel, you know how busy this kitchen is."

He went to the back door and braced a chair under the latch. Then he set a second one in front of the entrance to the dining room.

"I'll stand guard myself," he said.

Annabel groaned and laid her head down on folded arms. There would be no talking Gabriel out of this unsuitable plan, she could see that, and she was simply too tired to carry the tub and the buckets of water upstairs herself.

"You *want* to torment me!" she accused, looking up.

"No," Gabriel answered, with a scoundrel's grin. "I want to see you naked."

Annabel had no reply at hand. She wasn't even sure she *minded* that Gabriel would indeed see her unclothed. She just sat there at the table, befuddled with fatigue, watching Gabriel brew the tea and tend his kettles, like some splendid magician in his cave, mixing potions and casting spells.

Steam was rising in tantalizing curls from the great cauldrons by the time Annabel had received her tea, holding the glass mug in both hands like a beggar given a share of broth. It contained a generous portion of whiskey.

"Why don't you put your spectacles back on?" she asked tipsily, after a few bracing gulps, while Gabriel poured priceless hot water into the washtub. "I like the way they make you look. All studious and wise."

Gabriel laughed, a low and delectably masculine sound, and made a beckoning gesture with one hand.

"Would that it were so easy to be wise," he said. "Hurry, Annabel—your bath will be cold."

During the seemingly interminable time it took Annabel to cross that not overlarge kitchen, yawning and shedding her clothes as she went, Gabriel turned down the lantern at the table, until there was almost no light. Just the faintest, gentlest glow of gold, catching in his hair, sparking in his eyes. His face, and with it his expression, of course, was draped in shadow.

He handed Annabel a bar of soap and a cloth, without a word, and then took up his post in the chair barring the dining room door.

Annabel sank into the water with a rapturous sigh. She might have dozed off and slept straight through till morning if Gabriel hadn't been there to look after her. *That* would have flapped the unflappable Charlie, she thought, with a chuckle.

"You put something in my tea," she pointed out belatedly.

"Maybe," Gabriel admitted. She could see that his arms were folded and that his left ankle was resting upon his right knee.

"You mustn't do that," Annabel said, trying in vain to catch the soap as it skittered away from her and struck the side of the tub with a resounding clunk. "Suppose we had conceived a baby, you and I? Surely strong spirits cannot be good for so small a person."

Gabriel was silent for a few moments, and when he spoke, his voice was hoarse. "What if we have made another child together, Annabel—what will you do?"

Annabel was trying to wash her hair, but the tub was not large enough. "What any woman does when she carries a babe within her, Gabriel," she said reasonably. "Eat too much. Put my feet up whenever I get the chance. Dream a thousand dreams and whisper twice that many prayers."

"You were uncommonly beautiful when you were carrying Nicholas. Susannah too."

She smiled in the relative privacy of the darkness. "Both times I felt marvelous every waking hour. Well, except for the mornings and the last little while before the births, that is. Gabriel, help me wash my hair. I can't seem to manage, and I know it's full of dust and spiderwebs."

He crossed the room, got a pitcher from somewhere, and knelt beside the tub. Annabel relaxed with a happy sigh while he poured water over her hair, lathered it, scrubbed at her scalp with strong fingers, and then rinsed the soap away. After that, he took up the washcloth and bathed her as tenderly as if she were made of rose petals.

The experience was eminently sensual. Gabriel was as thorough in this task as in any other he might undertake—but he made no attempt to arouse Annabel. He was simply looking after her, something only a few people had ever done in the whole of her life. Before she and her father had stumbled upon the town of Parable, when she was fifteen, and she'd met Gabriel, there had been no one who cared enough, and because of that, Annabel had developed a deep-seated and violent sort of independence, rendering her all but unable to accept ordinary tenderness from anyone.

"Annabel," Gabriel said presently, standing her on her feet and toweling her dry, "you didn't answer my question."

"What question?" She allowed her head to rest against his shoulder, allowed him to scoop her up into his arms. He had wrapped her loosely in her own petticoat, since there was nothing else at hand that would serve the purpose.

"If you were carrying our child, would you go back to England?"

Annabel looked up at Gabriel's face, still largely invisible in that poor light. A lump formed in her throat, and she felt the potent sting of tears behind her eyes. "No, Gabriel," she said softly. "You have my word—I will not do that to you again."

He kissed her temple, a mere brush of his lips across her flesh. "Fair enough," he said, and carried her not through the dining room but up the narrow and seldom-used rear stairway that led from the kitchen to the second floor.

In their room he laid her on the bed but did not trouble to light a lamp.

He rummaged through the drawers in the side of the armoire until he found a nightdress, then came back and put it on her with quick, competent motions.

"Will you stay with me?" she murmured, her eyelids already fluttering as she struggled to resist sleep.

Gabriel bent and kissed her forehead. "Yes," he said, tucking the covers around her. "I'll be back after I empty the bathtub and put away the pots and pans. Get some rest, Annabel. You've had a hell of a day."

She smiled and snuggled down into the blessedly soft feather mattress. "At times like this, I find it hard to remember exactly why you and I have such problems getting along with each other."

He laughed. "It'll come back to you," he assured her. Then he touched her mouth with his and was gone.

When Annabel awakened, deep in the night, Gabriel was indeed in bed beside her, and he was gloriously naked. He was also sitting up, with a book in his hands and pillows piled at his back, reading by the light of the bedside lamp. His spectacles glistened appealingly.

Annabel tried to sit up and was overcome by the sheer, lush comfort of the bed itself. Of having Gabriel there beside her.

"How long until morning?" she asked, with a yawn.

Gabriel closed the book—not a treatise on animal husbandry or mining, as she would have expected, but a volume of epic poetry—and set it aside. Then he turned down the wick until the glow was dimmed, and Annabel heard him set his spectacles on the table. "Three or four hours," he said, and put his arms around her.

Annabel was caught up like flotsam on a swell of sleepy joy. "Plenty of time," she said, nibbling at Gabriel's shoulder.

He chuckled. "Wanton," he said. Then he covered her mouth with his own, kissing her in an unhurried, quietly passionate way.

Their joining that night was neither frenzied nor fierce; Gabriel took Annabel at his leisure and brought her very slowly and very gently to a climax that reverberated within her like the tolling of a great bell. When it was over, they clung together, Gabriel's leg still sprawled across Annabel's thighs, breathing deeply and in rhythm with each other.

"My God," Gabriel whispered, at length. "Every time I think you can't possibly surprise me, you take me to some part of myself where I've never been before."

Annabel stretched, sated to the very marrow of her bones, and eased her arms around his neck. "You are a fraud, Gabriel McKeige—pretending to be a hard-bitten rancher when, inside that Grecian body of yours, you have the heart and mind and spirit of a bard."

He brushed her lips with his; she caught her own musky scent on them. "What about my tongue?" he teased. "Is it better fitted to a frontier ruffian or a man of letters?"

She laughed softly. "You are incorrigible."

Gabriel raised his head, and even though Annabel could not see his features, she knew by the sudden if nearly imperceptible tension in his limbs and chest and shoulders that his mood had changed. "Why is it, Annabel, that we are in such accord in moments like this, and at each other's throats in the light of day?"

She traced the length of his patrician nose with a light finger. "I don't know," she said sadly. "But let's not think about what will happen tomorrow. Doesn't it make more sense to enjoy our happiness to the fullest, where and when we find it?"

"It does," Gabriel agreed in a low voice. "Provided you find that happiness with me."

Annabel smoothed her fingers through his hair. "Shh," she said. "There is no one else."

"Not even Jeffrey?"

She laughed aloud. "*Especially* not Jeffrey," she replied merrily, but she found that a note of seriousness had crept into her voice when she went on. "If we discuss loyalty now, Gabriel, we shall spoil everything."

Gabriel gave a great sigh, whether of frustration or despair, or both, Annabel could not guess, and allowed his forehead to rest against hers. "If only we could go back, Annabel, like pawns to their original squares on a chessboard, and begin again."

Annabel stroked his powerful tapered back, the very back where she had indeed left the marks of her fingernails earlier in the day. "Now that, Mr. McKeige, is a pretty dream. What would you do differently?"

He raised his head, and in the cozy gloom she saw that a stray beam of light had caught in his eyes. "I guess I would say what I felt, straight out, instead of expecting you to know it from the way I worked to give you this house, those pretty gowns, and all that jewelry." He paused, and when he spoke again, his voice caught. "I would have been more patient after we lost Susannah."

She caressed his strong jaw with a soft motion of her hand. "You had your own grief to deal with, Gabriel, and you were kind to me. Do you still think about her? Susannah, I mean?"

"Every day."

She nodded. "Me too," she said, and steered the conversation onto firmer ground. "If I had another chance, I would try not to be so prideful and so stubborn, so caught up in my own sorrow. But there are many things I *wouldn't* change. That day we found a maple tree growing all by itself in the middle of nowhere, and we huddled beneath it for two hours while the rain pounded down all around us. Our wedding night, when it seemed there was no one else on earth but us, that we were the new Adam and Eve, with a deed to paradise. And most of all, I would never change the fact that together, out of fire and love and fury, we made Nicholas and Susannah."

Gabriel kissed her lightly and yet with a certain reverence. Then he stretched out beside Annabel and gathered her close against him, and they slept.

* * *

When Nicholas came into the ranch house kitchen from the bunkhouse, preferring even Charlie's cooking to that of the cowboy whose turn had come up, he was startled to find a stranger sitting at the table. The man was small, almost puny, and his hair looked as though he'd dipped it in a vat of pomade and then smoothed it flat against his head with the edge of a trowel. His clothes were natty, and at his throat he wore a neckcloth so white that it made Nicholas squint.

"Mornin'," Nicholas said, exchanging a look with Charlie as he went to the stove and helped himself to coffee.

"You must be Annabel's son," the newcomer concluded, somewhat doubtfully.

Nicholas couldn't decide what it was that troubled the fellow—his lack of resemblance to Miss Annabel, his rough clothes and the empty but well-worn holster on his hip, since Charlie didn't allow irons in his kitchen, or his size and age. Maybe it was all those things.

"That's right," Nicholas said, pausing for a critical inspection of the pan of hash Charlie was tending on the stove, then crossing to the table and straddling the bench opposite the houseguest. "And who would you be?"

The cheerful sojourner offered a hand, which Nicholas shook.

"Forgive me for not introducing myself," he said. "My name is Jeffrey Braithewait, and I've come to accompany your mother back to England. It's neither safe nor wise for a woman to travel alone, and across an ocean and a continent the size of this one, no less! Lord knows, I tried to warn Annabel, but she can be quite inflexible. . . ."

In all his prattle, Jeffrey must have missed the slight but eloquent *thunk* when Nicholas set his coffee down on the tabletop. Before he could get a word in edgewise, Charlie had shoved a plate of food at him, and in almost the same instant Miss Annabel swept into the room.

She was wearing riding clothes—a split skirt, boots, and a loose-fitting blouse—and her hair was plaited into one thick braid. Once again Nicholas was struck by her youth—it seemed impossible that she could have carried him in her womb twenty years before.

"I am not going back to England," Miss Annabel announced, with a smile and nod at Charlie for an aside. "At least, not yet. And certainly not with you, Jeffrey. If you must have an American adventure, why not go on to San Francisco? You will find the accommodations and the society far more to your liking."

Nicholas suppressed a grin. He'd been prepared to take Miss Annabel's part, but it was plain enough that she could take care of herself.

Now, if only his pa would walk in. That would make this scene even more interesting.

As if on cue, Gabe came down the back stairway, dressed for work. Nicholas didn't miss the fact that it was late for him; his father was usually on the range before sunrise. Nicholas didn't think much about his parents making love, and when he did, he concentrated on theory, not practice. For all of that, he noticed an unmistakable easy litheness in the set of Gabe's broad shoulders and a certain glint in his eye. Nicholas, for one, was not fooled by the fact that the two of them had entered the room from different directions, nor was Charlie, who was making an elaborate point of not noticing. The vote was still out on Braithewait.

"Mornin'," Gabe said, to everyone in general and no one in particular, and got himself a cup of coffee and a plateful of hash.

Miss Annabel took a seat beside Nicholas, who swung his leg over the bench to sit properly, while Gabe settled in across the table, next to Jeffrey. Charlie served the lady of the house with an air of elegance.

The Englishman looked as befuddled as Nicholas felt, but Gabe and Miss Annabel acted as though that were a perfectly ordinary moment.

After he'd eaten half of the food on his plate—Gabe was a man of legendary appetite—the master of the manor saw fit to address the bewildered visitor.

"We expect everyone to earn his keep around here," he said. "If you care to stay on, Nicholas will give you a horse and gear and show you where to sleep."

Braithewait cast a plaintive glance at Miss Annabel, but she was busy buttering a piece of toasted bread, and didn't see. "My accommodations are perfectly suitable," he sputtered.

Nicholas suppressed a grin and mentally stood back.

"This is a working ranch, Mr. Braithewait," Gabe said directly, fork suspended between his plate and his mouth. "While I might permit a lady to loll about in the spare room, able-bodied men are another matter." There was a brief, eloquent pause. "You are able-bodied, I presume? Or at least you claimed so yesterday."

Jeffrey flushed to a rich shade of crimson. "Of course I am," he snapped, wadding up his cloth napkin and tossing it down beside his plate. He looked to Miss Annabel for support once again and found her still fascinated by her bread. "May I say that I was wholly unprepared to meet with such a reception?"

Charlie handed Gabe a folded newspaper—Nicholas knew for a fact that it was a week old and his pa could have recited the headlines from memory—and Gabe furrowed his brow in pretended concentration as he read. "Nicholas," he said, "see that Mr. Braithewait is settled in and introduced to the other men."

For once in his life Nicholas jumped to obey.

"This way," he said and started toward the outside door. On the back porch, he reclaimed his .45 from the shelf where he'd laid it and slipped it easily into its holster. Miss Annabel's dogs, docile when Nicholas had entered the house, hunkered down and growled when they saw Braithewait.

"Quite outrageous," Braithewait muttered, hurrying to keep pace with Nicholas.

Nicholas grinned. Maybe the new man could interest some of the boys in a rousing game of croquet, he thought.

"If I didn't know better," Annabel muttered, snatching up the newspaper the moment Gabriel laid it down on the table, "I would think you were trying to keep Jeffrey on this ranch."

Charlie refilled her coffeecup, pointedly overlooking Gabriel's, then went outside, ostensibly to feed his chickens.

Gabriel's smile was downright unchristian. "On the contrary," he said, "if I boot him out, he'll just come slithering back. This way, he'll either make himself useful or get fed up and leave."

Annabel perused the outdated headlines with interest. "Do not underestimate Jeffrey," she warned. "He is very clever, and he has a great deal of experience as a houseguest."

Gabriel laughed and got up to carry his plate, utensils, and mug to the sink. "Claims he's a good hand with a horse," he said, with surprising goodwill, "even if he does look like he'd blow away in a spring breeze."

"We could not be so fortunate," she said, without looking away from the newspaper article she was reading. "Jeffrey has been known to haunt his victims for years. He moves in the best circles and appears to have money, at least intermittently, though no one seems to know where he gets his funds. His family, though titled, has been bankrupt for as long as anyone can remember."

He came to stand behind her, Gabriel did, and she was so conscious of his presence and his proximity that she drew in a sharp breath and braced herself, her prattle falling off into uneasy silence.

Morning had come, after all, and the truce of the night was over.

Gabriel bent and kissed the top of her head then, brushing aside the heavy braid from her neck. "At least I don't have to worry about competition," he said. "Not from him, anyway."

Annabel turned on the bench and looked up into her husband's face. "Nor do I," she replied. "Because I've decided to shoot you, Gabriel McKeige, if you so much as look at another woman."

Julia's name rose between them, acrid as smoke, and then dissipated.

"Don't start, Annabel," Gabriel warned.

"Gabriel," she replied evenly, "I have hardly begun."

He sighed and straightened, thrusting a hand through his hair. "All right," he said. "If you need space between us, except when we're both naked and the house is dark, so be it."

Annabel felt color pulse in her neck and beneath her cheekbones, perhaps because Gabriel had struck so painfully close to the truth. When they were intimate, when he held her, she trusted him completely. In the daylight, with the real world operating at full tilt all around them like some gigantic, uncontrollable and wholly unpredictable mechanism, she was less confident.

As Gabriel, without a backward glance, left the house by the same route Nicholas and Jeffrey had taken, Annabel watched him go, unwilling—no, *unable*—to call him back.

Ten

ANNABEL PUT HER HANDS ON HER HIPS AND SURVEYED the selection of ponies in the corral, while Nicholas leaned, braced by one shoulder, against the high rail fence, awaiting her choice. These were working animals, not the sleek jumpers she rode in England, but sturdy-looking and surefooted.

She finally chose a small dapple-gray mare, and Nicholas nodded to one of the men, who threw a halter over the horse's neck and led it into the barn.

"Jessie sent a kid out with word that she wants some wagons and half a dozen men to move furniture from her place to yours," he said. "Have you changed your plans?"

Annabel shook her head, embarrassed because Nicholas had every right to think she'd decided to remain on the ranch, and not just because she was going to spend the day riding instead of setting her town house in order.

"No," she said miserably. "Nothing is different."

And yet so much had changed, or simply made itself apparent.

Still, Annabel intended to keep the house in Parable and to outfit it as a comfortable refuge. Without it, she would have felt as much adrift as Jeffrey, here in the great and undeniably wild West.

"That's all right, Miss Annabel," Nicholas told her, laying a hand briefly, gently, upon her shoulder. "We all need someplace to run to once in a while."

Annabel's temper was nettled, or perhaps it was her conscience. She followed after Nicholas with brisk strides when he headed into the barn, where the spotted mare was being saddled and fitted with a bridle. "Is that what you think?" she demanded in a whisper. "That I'm some sort of coward—that I mean to *hide* in that house?"

Nicholas smiled and raised gloved hands in a mock gesture of self-defense. "Whoa, Miss Annabel. There's nothing wrong with wanting to be by yourself now and again. I like to ride up into the foothills sometimes, just to put my thoughts in order."

Annabel felt foolish and laid one hand to her throat. "I'm sorry. I shouldn't have snapped at you that way. It's just that I . . . well—"

"No need to explain," Nicholas interrupted charitably, one side of his mouth quirked upward into that grin that Annabel found both endearing and consummately annoying. "Was there something else you wanted to say? I'd like to take a look at that surcingle; make sure it's good and tight."

He had given her the opening she wanted, though perhaps unwittingly, and Annabel had always subscribed to the axiom that there is no time like the present. She glanced to one side and then the other, and while the barnyard and the corral were bustling with their usual noisy, dust-raising, and faintly profane activity, there was no one within earshot. "Is that truly where you go, Nicholas—to the foothills?"

He faced her squarely, arms akimbo, as her own had been only moments ago. Just beyond Nicholas's left shoulder she caught a glimpse of Jeffrey, looking forlorn in ill-fitting cowboy duds, steaming toward them like a train, and wished him away. Far, far away.

"What kind of question is that, Miss Annabel?" Nicholas asked, in a tone of reason, but with his eyes narrowed and his jaw clamped down hard, he looked angry indeed. And so much like Gabriel that it took her breath away.

Annabel's reply was necessarily indirect. "Saddle your horse," she said, instead of what she wanted to say, taking one step forward to let Nicholas know, diversions notwithstanding, that she wouldn't be buffaloed, sidetracked, or otherwise flimflammed. "I want to talk to you, and it's plain we aren't going to get any privacy around here."

Nicholas, again like his father, was plainly used to getting his way. He looked bewildered by Annabel's purposeful advance, and after a brief hesitation he flung out his hands, let them slap against his thighs, then turned and strode away to do as he was told. He was muttering as he went, and Annabel indulged in a secret smile.

"You might have taken my part this morning, you know!" Jeffrey thundered, having reached her side at last. "What kind of friend are you, letting a *guest* be forced into work fit only for these—these tobacco-chewing barbarians?"

"Come now, Jeffrey," Annabel said, with acid sweetness. "If you don't like the way you're being treated, you have only to leave. Furthermore, this is

Gabriel's ranch, not mine. Speak to *him* if you don't think the hospitality is up to your standards. And kindly remember, if you will, that you asked to be hired."

Jeffrey was undaunted—no surprise there. "You know perfectly well that it would be a waste of time and breath. McKeige may be a yokel, but he understands that I am a rival for your affections and as such—"

"Wait," Annabel said, holding up one hand. "Wait just one moment, Jeffrey. You are not a rival for anything, where I am concerned, particularly my affections. If that is truly why you've come all this way, I'm sorry, but it's your own fault that you made the journey in vain. You never *listen* to anyone."

Jeffrey's neck had turned a dull red beneath his pertly tied bandanna, and his eyes bulged. "What do you mean, I never listen?" he demanded. "I've been fawning at your feet for ten years, Annabel, fetching punch at parties, chasing after your lost croquet balls through hedges and thickets, sending you flowers whenever you're in town—"

"And I have been telling you, for those same ten years, to stop," Annabel pointed out.

"Are you bothering the lady?" Nicholas inquired. Annabel hadn't seen him approaching, but there he was, leading her mare and his own sinewy, impatient gelding. "I hope not, Mr. Braithewait, because if you are, I'll have to pick you up by your skinny ankles and dunk your head in the horse trough."

"Ruffian!" Jeffrey sputtered, but he seemed to know, as Annabel did, that Nicholas had meant every word of his threat and was capable of carrying it out with a humiliating lack of effort. He stormed away.

Nicholas watched him go, grinning that Nicholas

grin. "I hope that fella stays around for a while. He's downright entertaining."

Annabel laughed and swatted her son's arm lightly with the back of one hand. "Where is your father? We'd better tell him that I've led you off the path of diligence or he'll be wondering why your work isn't done."

"Pa's gone to one of the mines," Nicholas said, and helped her up onto her mare, out of good manners, even though she was an accomplished horsewoman and required no assistance. "I was supposed to meet him there—something about a shipment of ore."

"Lead the way," Annabel said.

She had yearned to ride ever since leaving Warwickshire behind, and it was glorious to urge the little mare to trot and then gallop and then race over the sweet grass. With her son riding beside her, Annabel knew moments of utter joy. Her son, whom she had so foolishly allowed to leave her, and subsequently missed with all the desperation there was to feel.

In time they slowed their mounts to a smooth canter, and Nicholas pushed his hat to the back of his head, then tugged it into place again. Where he'd shown a flash of temper before, when Annabel had asked him about his trips into the mountains, he was whistling softly through his teeth now, and his Gabriel-blue eyes were bright with enjoyment.

Annabel saw, with heartrending clarity, how important the land was to Nicholas, how he fit into it like a vital organ or the last piece of a puzzle, how the overarching cloud-smudged blue of the sky, the snowy permanence of the mountains, and even the minerals of the earth below were his heartbeat, the breath in his lungs, the food of his spirit. He belonged here, riding over the broad, rolling rivers of grass where his father's cattle gazed by the hundreds, like a prince surveying the kingdom that would one day be his.

How, Annabel wondered, could I have carried Nicholas inside my body, raised him to the age of seven, and read his letters until they fell apart, for all these long and bitter years, and still understood so little of who he is?

Nicholas stopped whistling. No doubt he had noticed the expression on her face. "I guess you want to take up that conversation we started back at the corral," he said, and there was a faintly martyrlike slant to his shoulders.

Annabel might have been amused if the situation hadn't been so serious. If even half of what she had heard was true, Nicholas's very life was at stake.

She leaned forward to pat the mare's glistening neck, giving herself time to find and frame the right words. No inspiration rewarded the tactic, however. There probably *were* no right words—only plain ones, direct and certain to raise his hackles.

"There are rumors, Nicholas." Annabel paused. Surely it was all a mistake, what people said and thought about her son, she reflected. And yet Nicholas's fate was on the line, and she dared not risk being wrong. She had lost one child; she would not, could not, lose another.

He raised an eyebrow, but said nothing, simply waiting, easy in his saddle, his attitude faintly defiant, for her to go on.

Annabel held her son's gaze steadily, though she felt shaken inside and a little sick. Worry had that effect on her, especially when Nicholas was the cause of it; he, even more than Gabriel, was her Achilles' heel, the soft spot in her armor. "Is Captain Sommervale right in believing that you were involved in the theft of those cattle?" she asked at last.

Nicholas lifted his eyes unto the hills, like the psalmist; his profile was rigid. A long while passed before he looked at Annabel again, and his response, when it came, pierced her like the point of a sword. "What do you care?" he countered.

Annabel flinched—she was unable to help that—but she would not back down. Nicholas had not gotten *all* his strength of will from Gabriel, after all; no, a more than ample measure had come from her.

"I care, Nicholas," she said evenly. "I am your mother, and I love you very much."

"I won't stoop to the obvious answer."

"That is wise of you, young man. It means I won't be compelled to smack you with my riding crop."

"You aren't carrying a riding crop."

"I'm speaking figuratively, Nicholas. An ordinary stick will do."

Suddenly all the fury he had been suppressing, for all the years they'd been apart, was plainly visible in his face. Annabel realized that she had not known the true Nicholas in even the hundredth part, and she was aggrieved and ashamed.

"Why didn't you come back?" he demanded. He didn't raise his voice. He didn't need to, for the question seemed to strike the furthest points in all directions, like thunder, reverberating, charging the air, then returning to surround Annabel like an echo. "Why?"

Annabel closed her eyes for a moment, summoned all her powers, wrapped herself in composure. "There were problems, Nicholas. Things you couldn't have understood."

"Oh, I understood, all right," he shot back. "You

were hurting over Susie. Well, so was Pa, and God knows, so was I." A sheen of tears appeared in his eyes; he blinked them away. "You thought Pa had a mistress in Julia Sermon; maybe you still do. And the hell of it is, you were wrong then and you're wrong now. But I paid the price for your stubborn pride, and for Pa's. *I* paid it, Mother."

Annabel had longed to hear Nicholas call her Mother, but not in this way. Not in contempt, in outrage, in sorrow. Yet she had heard all those things in his voice, and she marveled that he had hidden them so well and treated her with civility and even kindness since her return.

When he spurred his gelding to a faster pace, no doubt hoping to outdistance her for a while, Annabel kept up easily. Her mare was no match for his mount, however; if he'd decided to ride away, she would soon have fallen behind. She had to talk fast.

"You are right, Nicholas," she said clearly. "At least in blaming your father and me for thinking too much about our own concerns and too little about yours—pride is my besetting sin, and Gabriel's as well. Please, Nicholas, don't let it be yours, too."

Nicholas reigned in his gelding, but it was an unwilling concession, and one that obviously cost him dearly. "Let this lie, Miss Annabel," he said hoarsely. "It's too late."

"Too late?" Annabel scoffed, impatient and fitful in her pain. "Nicholas, you are nineteen years old. However advanced that age might seem from your perspective, you are hardly out of short pants. You still have choices—so many choices! Don't be a fool and throw them away."

Nicholas chewed on her remarks for a while in

irritated silence, then lashed out again. "Like you did?"

Tears smarted behind Annabel's eyes, but she was determined not to shed them—at least not where Nicholas or anyone else would see. "Like I did," she confirmed. "Listen, I know you don't believe this, but maybe one day you will, if you're lucky enough to have a child of your own. I would rather be sent to prison or even hanged than see those things happen to you. And I will fight, Nicholas, to my last breath, to save you. I will fight the United States Cavalry, I will fight the outlaws you run with, I will fight every angel in heaven and every demon in hell, win or lose, with or without your blessing. Think what you like about me, I'm just too desperate to care."

Nicholas bit his lower lip briefly, his gaze fixed straight ahead, and Annabel would have given everything she possessed to know what thoughts he harbored in his heart and head just then.

"Where was all this passion when I was eight—and nine and ten?" he asked presently, and with less venom than before.

"Oh, it was there, all right. I wanted to raise you. I wanted to be there for every day, every moment, of your life. But you insisted on coming back here, remember?"

"I thought you would follow," he said. The simple statement lay stark between them, an utterance so painfully honest that Annabel wondered if Nicholas had ever said it before, even to himself.

"I wish I had," Annabel replied, "but I had devils of my own. I wanted your father to put Julia Sermon aside and come to Boston to fetch me."

Nicholas adjusted his hat again. The mine was visible now, in the near distance, a scar on the otherwise pristine land. Their time was limited, and they had accomplished so little.

"Pa will never turn his back on Julia," Nicholas said bluntly. "If anybody busts up that partnership, it will be Miss Sermon."

If he had been trying to wound Annabel, he'd certainly succeeded.

He glared at her, not in anger, it seemed, but some other intense emotion, one he perhaps had no name for. "You think I said that to hurt you," he said.

Annabel nodded, unable, for the moment, to respond.

"Maybe I did, at least partly. But there's something you need to understand, Miss Annabel: Julia isn't like her girls. She's a lady."

Annabel stiffened at this. "If you say so, Nicholas," she said.

"Ask Pa about it."

She shook her head. "I can't. Not if I want to preserve any semblance of peace—and, God help me, I do." *Even at the expense of my legendary pride.*

"All right, then," Nicholas replied, "pay a call on Miss Sermon. She'll give you a straight answer."

Annabel reeled. "I am impressed, Nicholas. We were talking about you. Now suddenly the local madam—and by the way, the word 'madam,' in this context at least, and the word 'lady' are mutually exclusive—is the topic of conversation. Do you really think for one second that I am going to walk into the Samhill Saloon and ask to see Julia Sermon?"

"You will if you want to know the truth," Nicholas said. And then the discussion was over, because the mine was before them, with its noisy steam-powered machinery.

Gabriel came toward them, and as Annabel

watched him, she felt a fierce sense of proprietorship, something primitive and territorial, more elemental than jealousy, more animal than human.

She tried to put the overwhelming emotion aside but could not.

There was a brief exchange between father and son, and then Nicholas touched the brim of his hat to Annabel and proceeded to the mine.

Gabriel remained, watching Annabel, seeing too much. "What did he say to you?" he asked. "You look ready to fidget right out of your hide."

Annabel's throat felt thick, as though she were coming down with the grippe. She sighed; if she'd caught anything, it was a case of despair, for she was never ill. "He's angry," she admitted. "Of course."

Gabriel's response surprised her mightily. "I'm sorry, Annabel," he said quietly. "Do you want someone to see you back to the ranch?"

She smiled and shook her head, dangerously close to tears. "No—I know my way."

He drew nearer, laid a leather-gloved hand to her thigh. "Annabel, don't suffer so much. Nicholas is a kid. Maybe he's got his nose out of joint—God knows, he has the right to be furious with both of us—but you're his mother and he loves you. Give him some time."

Annabel nodded, reined the little mare blindly around, and rode off.

Nicholas would not have attended Aunt Jessie's tea party, let alone put on a collar and coat for the occasion, except for two things. First, he wanted to show support for Miss Annabel, whatever his own differences with her might be, and second, Jessie had issued one of her commands.

So there he was, holding a silly-looking cup with some kind of fruit juice in it and wishing he were anyplace but where he was, wedged in at one end of Jessie's piano, with the frond of a potted palm tickling the back of his neck.

The get-together looked like a success, though, and that was some comfort. Miss Annabel was the center of attention, wearing a bright green dress and glowing as she chatted with the good women of Parable, who had turned out in a herd.

Nicholas took a sip of the fruit juice and scanned the room, hoping to catch his father's eye and let somebody know just how much he was suffering. Gabe was engaged in a conversation with Marshal Swingler, though, and the two of them made their way out onto the front porch.

Nicholas felt deserted, and pulled at his collar with one curved finger. How long, he wondered dismally, could a thing like this last?

He heaved a rueful sigh. Probably a good three days, like the tent revivals that occasionally passed through Parable for the salvation of sinners.

So intent on his misery was he that when Jessie materialized at his side, he started and nearly dropped his juice.

"Olivia," she said, "this is my nephew, Nicholas McKeige. Nicholas, Olivia Drummond, the new teacher."

Miss Drummond's eyes were a deep shade of gray, like thunderclouds gathering on the horizon, and her hair was dark and glossy. Nicholas had a strange sensation, as he looked down into that beguiling face, of tumbling end over end into some chasm of the soul.

Mentally he scrambled to catch himself, to break his fall, but it was already too late. Before the new schoolteacher spoke, certainly before she smiled, Nicholas was profoundly in love.

This incredible realization caught him so far off guard that for a few moments he couldn't breathe, couldn't think.

"Nicholas?" Jessie prompted. She took the cup out of his hands and set it aside, and for that he would be forever grateful.

"Hello," he said, blurting out the word as though prodded from behind with a sharp stick.

Olivia Drummond smiled, and Nicholas was sent reeling all over again. He had heard about the schoolmarm, of course—heard that she was a spinster, just on the shy side of thirty. But this woman was ageless, and it was only by the rarest good fortune, in his opinion, that she had not been married off long before.

"Hello, Mr. McKeige," she said, and offered him her hand. It felt slender and cool in his grasp, but strong, too. Capable and unhesitating.

Jessie was frowning. "Are you quite well, Nicholas?" To his mortification, his aunt reached up to test his forehead for fever. "You seem very flushed all of a sudden."

Olivia's gray eyes danced, and she watched Nicholas over the brim of her cup as she sipped from it.

"It is a little warm in here," Nicholas said, tugging at his collar again and immediately feeling like a complete hayseed.

Miss Drummond lowered her magical eyes, not out of shyness, Nicholas suspected, but out of mercy, because she knew he was squirming. "It is hot," she agreed demurely, "even for the height of summer."

Nicholas took Olivia's arm, touching her as gently as if she had no more substance than a butterfly's wing, and steered her toward the front door. She made no protest as he squired her across the front porch, passing his pa and the marshal without a glance for either of them, let alone a word of explanation or greeting.

In Jessie's shady side yard, next to the screened veranda where Nicholas had often slept on summer nights, stood a gnarled maple tree, planted by his late uncle. A swing dangled from a sturdy branch, and Nicholas took off his coat, without thinking of the implications of that, and spread it on the splintery seat.

Olivia sat down, cup in hand, looking as delicate as a flower.

Standing behind her, Nicholas took a tight hold of the dusty ropes of the swing and gave her an easy push. A breeze rose like a blessing, soothing his skin through the moist cotton of his shirt.

"Your mother is a lovely woman," Olivia said, without looking back at him. Her dress was simple and shabby by comparison to the things his mother and aunt wore, and yet he was stricken to the quick by her beauty.

"Thank you," Nicholas answered, and immediately felt foolish. As if he could take credit for Miss Annabel's appearance.

Olivia looked back at him, over one slender shoulder. Her eyelashes were as thick as brushes, and it came to Nicholas that he had never noticed a thing like that about a woman before. "Did you go to school here in Parable, Mr. McKeige?"

"Nicholas," he corrected. "Yes. Yes, I did."

"Mr. McKeige," Olivia insisted pleasantly. "I was born in San Francisco."

"You've come a long way, then." Nicholas was

calming down, breathing evenly. Regularly. "Won't you be homesick?"

She averted her eyes. "No," she said. "No, I don't think so. Would you be homesick, if you ever left Parable?"

Nicholas had no trouble admitting the truth. "Yes, ma'am," he said. "I'm not much for traveling."

"That surprises me a little," Olivia confided. "You look like an adventurous sort of man. Slightly wild, probably."

Slightly wild. He smiled, almost himself again—except, of course, that his life had been irrevocably altered, five minutes before, in his aunt Jessie's parlor. "I've seen the error of my ways," he said.

Olivia turned her head to look at him again. "How old are you, Mr. McKeige?"

"Just short of twenty," Nicholas answered. "But you make me feel like my own grandfather, calling me Mr. McKeige like that."

"I am the schoolteacher," she reminded him, and her lips quivered just a little, making Nicholas want to kiss her then and there, in front of God and creation. "I must behave with absolute propriety if I want to keep my post." Olivia paused. "I turned twenty-nine last March."

I don't care, Nicholas thought, but he didn't say the words aloud, because it was too soon. Because meeting Olivia Drummond was the most important thing that had ever happened to him, and he didn't want to botch it up.

"You'll be boarding here, with my aunt?" he asked, standing beside the swing now, holding the rope steady with one hand and gazing straight down into Miss Drummond's remarkable eyes.

Olivia nodded.

"Good," Nicholas said. Maybe that was too forward, but he wouldn't have taken it back. He didn't want to scare Olivia off, but at the same time, he meant to have her, one way or the other, and the clearer that was, the better.

She wet her lips with the tip of her tongue and stood, a little shakily, and so suddenly that she nearly caught Nicholas under the chin with the top of her head. "Nicholas—Mr. McKeige—"

It was absolutely all he could do not to kiss her.

"What?" he asked, and much of what he felt must have been audible in the roughness of his voice.

She was fidgety now, and flushed. "I really—I really should go inside."

Nicholas grinned, nodded, and offered her his arm. "Tell me, Miss Drummond," he asked, in a whisper hardly more forceful than the breeze that ruffled the dark, moist tendrils of hair at her cheeks and along the nape of her neck. "Are you usually so concerned about what people think?"

"Nearly always, yes," she admitted, still flustered. "I have my way to make, Mr. McKeige."

"Nicholas," he said.

"Nicholas," she conceded, with a little sigh.

"She's too old for you," Jessie scolded, two hours later, taking care to speak softly. She had finally managed to corner Nicholas in the kitchen, where he was helping himself to leftover tea cakes. All the guests were gone, including his parents, and Olivia was upstairs, doing whatever women did when they had just left a crowded, stuffy party.

"I don't care if she's a hundred," Nicholas said blithely, licking powdered sugar from his thumb. "I'm going to have her."

Jessie was well on her way to a tizzy. She walked over, stood toe to toe with Nicholas, and shook a finger in his face. "Now you listen to me, Nicholas McKeige. Miss Drummond is no one to be trifled with. If you seduce her, you will answer to me!"

"Seduce her?" Nicholas uttered the words with an air of wounded innocence, even though he'd spent most of the afternoon plotting ways and means of getting Olivia Drummond into his bed. He spread the splayed fingers of one hand over his heart. "You misjudge me cruelly, Aunt Jessie."

"I wish that were true," Jessie retorted. "Do you think I don't know what you're up to? I've seen that look in your eyes before."

"I swear this is different." He raised a hand, as if making an oath.

Jessie merely looked at him, but her skepticism was plain enough.

"You'll see," Nicholas said. He leaned back against the counter, folded his arms, and grinned. "You'd better start looking for a new schoolmarm, Aunt Jessie," he said. "I mean to marry this one."

Eleven

"I WILL GO WITH YOU," ANNABEL ANNOUNCED, UPON Gabriel's somewhat tentative announcement, following Jessie's tea party, that he intended to take two hundred head of cattle to Fort Duffield. He had escorted her back to the ranch, even stooping to drive the surrey personally, and opened the front door for her like a gentleman.

Next thing, she decided, a little wryly, he'd be taking tea of an afternoon.

"No, Annabel," he replied, as quietly adamant as ever. He did not even trouble himself to add an explanation; on that ranch, his word was law, and he expected her to obey him as readily as any one of the hands.

Inside, she unpinned her favorite feathered hat and set it aside, noting with no little satisfaction that Gabriel's gaze followed the rise and fall of her breasts as she lifted and lowered her arms in the process. "I shall not be dissuaded," she said, tugging off her gloves. "I have business in Fort Duffield."

Gabriel arched an eyebrow. "What business?"

Annabel smiled remotely. She had not been at all certain that anyone in Parable, or on the ranch, for that matter, would offer her shelter, and she had left several trunks at the fort as a result. Now, of course, she had taken a house, and no one could refuse her shelter. More importantly, she wished to speak privately with the fort's commander.

"Just things I want to do," she said.

"Annabel, this is not a pleasure outing. We're driving two hundred head of beef over some very rough country, and we're expecting trouble."

She turned to face him, leaning back against the narrow table beneath the hall mirror, the one where Gabriel usually tossed his hat and thin leather gloves. Next to the looking glass was a peg where he hung his gun belt.

"You can't be expecting Nicholas to steal that herd—"

Gabriel moved in close to set his hat on the table; he had not worn his holster, Jessie's tea party being a social occasion, although Annabel knew there was a rifle tucked neatly beneath the seat of the surrey.

She was damnably aware of his body, of his strength, and leaned back in a fruitless effort to avoid the almost overwhelming substance of the man, an attribute that was, conversely, more a mental and spiritual quality than a physical one. Color stole into her cheeks as Gabriel's breath warmed her lips and made them tingle, causing Annabel to forget what she'd been concerned about in the first place.

"Nicholas is no thief, whatever Sommervale thinks," Gabriel said, ruining everything with a brisk and breath-stealing splash of reality: Nicholas was in over his head, whether they believed him to be guilty or not. "No, Annabel, I'm looking for someone else to make a move. Someone else entirely. And that's why you are not going along. I have enough to think about without a woman to tend to."

Annabel did not know whether to be pleased that Gabriel did not think their son culpable, or furious that he saw her as too helpless to take care of herself on a simple cattle drive. While some of these journeys involved traversing hundreds of miles in the most difficult and treacherous of conditions, Fort Duffield was not so very far away. "I would kick you," she said, "if I weren't so grateful for your faith in Nicholas."

Gabriel smiled—for a moment she thought he would kiss her, right there in the entryway—then drew back with a sigh and shrugged out of his Sunday coat. "Go ahead and kick me, Annabel," he said. "You're still not going on the cattle drive." With that, he turned and headed toward his study, looking unbelievably splendid in his good trousers, white shirt, and brocade vest.

Annabel followed posthaste. "You are being unreasonable," she argued, hurrying to keep pace, "not to mention patriarchal and downright silly. Can you possibly have forgotten that I made the same trip by surrey just a few days ago?"

A few days ago. Dear Lord, so much had happened that it seemed more like a year.

In the study, Gabriel closed the doors, then gestured for Annabel to take a seat. She did so, but not out of any sort of docility; she'd awakened with a slight headache that morning and a certain queasiness that had left her oddly weary.

Gabriel poured himself a glass of brandy, but, out of concern for any child they might have conceived, did not offer Annabel a drink.

"We will not be traveling by surrey," he said, upon turning to face her, and she saw just the faintest quiver of amusement, quickly subdued, at one corner of his mouth.

Annabel's temper flared, but she conquered it by force of will. "Do not patronize me, Gabriel," she warned evenly. "I had thought to take a horse, and I am as good a rider as you or any man on this ranch, as you well know."

"I'll concede that," Gabriel said, swirling the brandy in the bottom of his glass and causing Annabel to feel a little thrill of triumph. And, perhaps, something else. "But the trip will take two days, if not longer—cattle are slow-moving creatures—and we just lost a sizable herd to rustlers. I don't want you there if they try it again."

"And at the same time, you are hoping they will—whoever they are?"

"Of course I am," Gabriel said, as though surprised that there could have been any question. He was behind his desk now, in his creaky leather chair, looking like what he was: one of the most powerful ranchers in Nevada. There had been talk, Jessie had told Annabel, of nominating him for public office.

A horrible image unfolded in her mind—one far worse than that of Gabriel bossing around a whole state instead of just a town and a flock of ranch hands and miners. And her.

"You could be shot," she murmured.

Gabriel had reached for his spectacles—Annabel once again felt a feather's brush against the vulnerable underside of her heart at the sight of them—and opened one of the ledger books. "That," he said, sounding distracted now, and distant, "has always been a possibility." He did not look up from whatever figures he was studying. "None of us will live forever, Annabel."

"Exactly," Annabel said, after catching her breath. What was it about those glasses of Gabriel's that made her react like a witless girl? "You have just made the perfect argument for my presence on the cattle drive."

Gabriel looked up. "No, Annabel," he said. "And that's final."

"You know me better than to make such a proclamation, Gabriel."

"Don't make this into a contest, Mrs. McKeige. I assure you, I will win it."

"This is America. If I want to travel between Parable and Fort Duffield under my own power, I can certainly do so. I am not, after all, a prisoner."

Gabriel looked at her speculatively for a few unnerving moments. "Maybe that's the solution. Locking you up somewhere."

Annabel moved to the edge of her chair. "If you so much as attempt such a thing, Gabriel, I shall personally see that you regret it until the end of your days! I have a vital errand at Fort Duffield, and I mean to attend to it." She planned to speak with Captain Sommervale, reason with him, as the father of sons, convince him that Nicholas was not his cattle thief, but she wasn't about to reveal her mission to Gabriel or anyone else. If necessary, she would reimburse the army for the missing beef out of her own funds.

Gabriel heaved a sigh and sat back in the chair.

Early evening was settling over the countryside, shadow seeping into the light, a shade at a time. Charlie could be heard in the kitchen, clattering supper pans and skillets, and an orchestra of crickets had taken up an eager symphony just outside the window.

"We'd do better, I think, to change the subject," he said.

Annabel agreed. "Did you see Nicholas with that new schoolteacher?" she asked.

Gabriel smiled. "Oh, yes," he answered. "I saw."

"What did you think?"

"That he appreciates a pretty woman."

Annabel sighed. "It's more than that, Gabriel. I think he's smitten."

Gabriel chuckled. " 'Smitten'? Somehow that word just doesn't seem to fit Nicholas."

"Nonsense," Annabel said, with some impatience. "I was watching when Jessie introduced the two of them. He practically stepped on his tongue."

"What is your point, Annabel?"

"What do we know about her?" Annabel countered, with quiet intensity.

Again Gabriel chuckled. "Hell, Annabel, what do we know about Nicholas? Besides, that boy is your son and mine—meaning he's obstinate to the bone, among other sterling qualities. If he wants to court Miss Olivia Drummond or anyone else, he'll do it, and the devil take anybody else's opinion."

"She's nearly thirty," Annabel protested, but with less insistence than before. Gabriel was right, of course, and she could not quite bring herself to state the reason Nicholas might be drawn to a woman ten years older than he was.

Gabriel regarded her over the rim of his spectacles, a

slight smile playing on his mouth. "Are you thinking, by chance, that Nicholas is looking for a mother in this young woman?"

"No," Annabel said vehemently, fidgeting. "Well, yes. Maybe."

Gabriel laughed, a throaty and wholly pleasant sound. "Nicholas has pursued numerous women in his short lifetime, many of whom are older than he is." He paused, as if considering the wisdom of venturing onward, into a territory fraught with singular perils. Being Gabriel, he didn't hesitate long. "Isn't it possible that he simply prefers them? They generally have more sense, not to mention greater experience and intellect."

Annabel blushed, but just slightly, so there was hope that Gabriel hadn't noticed. She did not like to think of her son in that context, of course, and yet she could not help feeling gratified to hear Gabriel express a preference, however indirectly, for women of a certain maturity. She herself was thirty-seven, after all.

"Perhaps you're right," Annabel allowed. "But wouldn't such a woman find a boy of Nicholas's age—well . . . shallow?"

Gabriel cupped his hands behind his head and pondered the question. "No," he finally concluded. "Nicholas has read every book in this study and in Jessie's library as well—everything from *Gulliver's Travels* and *Robinson Crusoe* to treatises on the political structure of the Roman Empire. He knows the atlas from front to back, and even though he seems to have no desire to leave this ranch for any considerable length of time, his mind ranges far beyond any limits you or I might ascribe to it."

Annabel merely nodded; she could not say, without

being ungracious, how the depth and breadth of Gabriel's own intelligence constantly surprised her. Not that she had ever deemed him stupid; anyone exposed to the searing heat of Gabriel's mind for long quickly realized that he consumed knowledge with the voraciousness other men reserved for water and air.

She wondered, with another pang, what he and Julia had talked about when they were together. Was Julia as well read and insightful as he was?

Suddenly the answer to that question mattered to Annabel, and mattered deeply. She had always yearned to be more attractive to Gabriel, more charming, than the other woman. Now it seemed even more important to engage his mind than his body.

"What are you thinking?" Gabriel asked, catching her off guard, as he so often did, hopelessly entangled in the vast net woven of her doubts and certainties, dreams and fears, triumphs and humiliations.

She was understandably flustered, and still struggling a little. Perhaps that was why she did not choose her words more carefully. "I was wondering what you see when you look at me," she confessed, bluntly and with no apology.

Gabriel leisurely assessed Annabel, still perched on the edge of her chair like a schoolgirl waiting to flee the headmaster's office. Then he met her gaze squarely. "You are without doubt the most beautiful woman I have ever seen," he said, with equal forthrightness. "And you affect me like some diabolical opiate. When we are apart long enough, I can at least function without you. When you are nearby, I think of almost nothing and no one else."

Annabel was taken aback by his words and required a few moments to absorb them, to assign them a proper place in her mind. She hadn't the faintest idea just then whether she should be insulted or honored, wounded or mended in all her many broken places.

"But what about me, Gabriel? What of my mind, my spirit? Do you find me dull or interesting? Smart or stupid? Deep or shallow?"

He considered her in pensive silence for a disturbing length of time. Finally, his expression solemn, he replied, "You are a complex woman, Annabel, despite the fact that you sometimes behave like an impulsive child. If you ever stop trying to outrun that frightened, desperately lonely little girl inside you, and put your roots down in earnest, be it here or in England, you will be fathomless. As it is, you have to keep the whole world at arm's length and rush hither and yon to avoid becoming too close to anyone, including your own husband and son. You are a ghost, Annabel, cloaked in evasion and temper and injured pride."

"I did not avoid Nicholas," Annabel felt compelled to point out, in an anguished whisper. "He left me!"

Gabriel leaned forward, resting both forearms on the desk. "He was seven years old, Annabel. You were an adult. You didn't have to let him go."

Annabel swallowed. "He would have run away!"

"So he said, and maybe he meant it at the time. On the other hand, maybe he just wanted to know he could trust your grip. Kids need to find out where the boundaries are, Annabel. They want to be sure you'll make rules and enforce them. Otherwise they don't feel safe."

Annabel's eyes filled with tears; she blinked them back. "Damn you, Gabriel," she whispered. "Must you make everything out to be my fault?"

He rounded the desk, drew her gently onto her feet

and into his arms. She was trembling and could not hide the fact, and there was nothing for it.

"I wasn't trying to place blame," Gabriel told her, his breath soft and warm against her temple. He hooked a finger under her chin and made her look up at him. His eyes searched hers, somber and fretful and excruciatingly tender—so tender that Annabel would have dodged his gaze if he'd allowed it. "Don't run anymore, Annabel. The demons will always follow, wherever you go. Stand your ground and fight. I'll be right beside you."

With a little sob, Annabel let her forehead rest against Gabriel's sturdy chest. He took her shoulders in his hands, kneaded them lightly with his fingers.

"I will never be able to make up for my failure with Nicholas," she grieved.

Gabriel kissed the top of her head. "Perhaps you failed," he agreed. "And perhaps you were the mother Nicholas needed to meet his destiny. Only God can know for certain."

She tilted her head back to look up at him. "When did you become a philosopher, Gabriel McKeige?"

He smiled slightly, sadly. "A few moments ago, when I realized how much you must have tortured yourself over the years. Whether you did wrong or right—most likely it was something in between—the little boy Nicholas used to be is gone forever. Let go, Annabel, before you drive yourself insane."

"I have so many regrets."

Gabriel smoothed gossamer tendrils of red-brown hair back from her forehead and cheeks. "So do I, Mrs. McKeige. So do I."

"What?" she asked, ever so softly, ever so cautiously, watching his face intently. All of her being was focused suddenly on that one question.

"I wish I'd come after you, Annabel. I wish I hadn't been so muleheaded."

Annabel was touched by these admissions, even though they didn't quite clear up all her doubts. "What about Julia? Do you regret your friendship with her?"

"No," Gabriel said, without hesitation, and when she would have pulled away, he held her shoulders fast and went determinedly on. "No, Annabel. I have no reason for remorse where Julia is concerned, except that I deliberately allowed you to misunderstand the situation. For that I truly am sorry."

She stared at him, baffled, trembling, flushed. For once, Annabel could not speak.

"Annabel," Gabriel said, "I have always loved you. You were the first woman I slept with and the last. There has never been anyone else."

The words struck Annabel somewhere deep and private, and resonated there in a way that only the purest truth could have done. She had, in fact, never felt any conviction so deeply as she did that one: that she had indeed been Gabriel's only lover, just as he had been hers.

Yet how could that be? How could a man of such expertise and such appetite be celibate for twelve years?

"But you and Julia—"

"We were children together, Annabel—you knew that. After—after my mother was taken, my father went crazy. Jessie was older, and she had a husband of her own, a home to look after. I didn't have anybody besides Julia, and she had no one besides me.

"She kept me from drinking myself to death after you left, or getting killed in a gunfight or a brawl. Julia has a gift for listening and for talking sense. Hell, for just *being* there. Sometimes that's all a person needs."

Annabel was still jealous, wildly so, for while she believed that Gabriel and Julia had not been physically intimate, she hated knowing that her husband had turned to another woman for solace. Solace she had been unable to provide.

"What about you, Gabriel—what was your part in the bargain?"

"Because of me, Julia never had to deal with men who wanted to share her bed."

"Never had to deal with . . . but she's a prostitute!"

Gabriel shook his head. "No," he said.

"What do you mean, no? Julia Sermon runs a brothel!"

"Yes. And she's accountable for that, just as the rest of us are for the things we do. Julia has a past—that's all I'll say about it, because it's her business, Annabel, not yours or mine—and everything she is now is rooted in that time before she came to Parable."

"You won't tell me what happened?"

"No," Gabriel answered. "If you want to know, you'll have to ask Julia directly. The fact is, it doesn't matter anyway. I've never made love to her, Annabel. I've passed a night or two on her bed, I'll admit to that, and I've wept in her arms a time or two as well."

Annabel put her hand to her heart and turned away from Gabriel's embrace. She supposed she should have been jubilant to know she'd been wrong about him all these years, but there were other emotions to be dealt with, and they were all but overwhelming.

She'd wasted so much time.

And while Gabriel had been faithful to her, in the strictest physical sense of the word, he and Julia had shared a very deep and private affection that was perhaps more profound for its innocence, rather than less.

"I need to be alone for a little while," she whispered.

"I'll bring your supper upstairs, when it's ready," Gabriel responded.

Annabel offered no reply, nor did she look back. A great deal had been said, and she would require time and solitude in which to sort it through.

Olivia Drummond had never met anyone like Nicholas McKeige, and, she reflected, sitting at the dressing table in her hostess's guest chamber, she had no business furthering the acquaintance.

She had led a spinster's sheltered existence in San Francisco, taking care of her widowed brother, Caleb, and his daughter, Eleanor, teaching the odd piano lesson for pin money, tutoring her niece and several of her schoolmates in Latin and mathematics. Going to church on Sundays and sacred holidays, diligent in her housekeeping duties during the week.

Nothing more was ever required of her. From earliest childhood, people had made a point of observing that she wasn't the least bit pretty—no, indeed, nothing like her dear sainted mother. Except for the occasional vague and embarrassing yearning, the odd daydream, Olivia had been resigned to her fate.

Then, suddenly, just a few months before, Caleb had remarried, accepted a post with a banking concern in Hong Kong, and sailed away from San Francisco, taking his new wife, Bella, her two young sons, and Eleanor along with him. There had been, of course, no place for Olivia in this newly made family.

Olivia had not precisely been abandoned. Certainly Caleb had not left her homeless, or penniless, but during the hectic weeks before the wedding, she had come to an understanding with herself. It was time she made her own way in the world, she'd concluded, and that decision had led her to seek employment.

She had answered a newspaper advertisement for a teaching position in Parable, Nevada, and now here she was.

And there Nicholas was. Downstairs at this very moment.

Olivia gazed at her reflection in the vanity mirror. Her complexion, usually pale, was blooming with delicate color. Her eyes were overly bright, and her heart thundered away inside her chest like a spring foal trying to kick down a stall door.

It had all begun when Nicholas offered her his arm during the tea party and suggested that they step outside.

Olivia propped her elbows on the table and dropped her forehead into her palms. It was impossible, she told herself, to be feeling what she was feeling. Utterly impossible!

His eyes were so blue, so audacious. Wise in a way that betrayed both formidable intelligence and pain that was often nearly beyond bearing. The shape of his mouth incorporated a little boy's propensity for mischief and a man's forthright sensuality. His hair, if unbound, would brush his shoulders, like the tresses of some Norse god, a golden savage accustomed to conquest.

Olivia trembled. She had sometimes imagined being conquered, but the whole process had been rather nebulous and dreamy, a fantasy that, like an exotic flower, bloomed only in the night and closed in upon itself in the harsh light of day. A wish with no more substance than a scent wafting by on a breeze.

Nicholas was quite real, however, and there could be no doubting his substance. Olivia's hand was unsteady as she laid her silver-backed brush aside, having done all she could with her hair.

Nicholas McKeige, she reminded herself sternly, was nineteen. Barely older, surely, than some of her students. Why, it was scandalous to think the things she was thinking—how it would feel to walk with him beneath a summer moon, her hand tucked safely into his. What his lips would feel like, touching hers . . .

There was a firm rap at the bedroom door.

"Yes?" Olivia called.

Nicholas's voice came to her, like a gruff caress. "Supper's ready, Miss Drummond," he said.

That was all, and yet the words affected Olivia in varied and disturbing ways—her flesh was warm, and there was an aching heaviness in her middle, so pervasive that she wasn't sure it would ever lift.

"Yes . . . thank you," she said, her tone faltering and timorous, the murmuring of a vain girl, not a woman grown.

Olivia went to the wash table and splashed her face with tepid water, but it did nothing to cool her raging senses. All wit and common sense had deserted her, it appeared, and there was no telling when or if she would recover them.

Miss McKeige had set the table in the dining room with a pretty cloth, edged in lace, and what must surely have been her best china and silver. The chamber was lit by flickering candles, lending a magical and festive air to an otherwise ordinary evening.

Ordinary, except for Nicholas. He was freshly washed, his hair still damp, his youthful skin glowing.

He was wearing his suit coat, and as Olivia approached the table, he smiled and drew back her chair, having already seated his aunt.

"I see I have not wasted my efforts to make a gentleman of you, Nicholas," the older woman said, and though her tone was merry, she wore a strained expression.

Had Olivia been anything but a realist, she would have concluded, quite happily, that Miss McKeige was merely tired after a busy day spent preparing for a tea party, then entertaining what must surely have been half the town. Rather, Olivia knew that her hostess had noticed the flirtation between her nephew and the spinster schoolteacher, and she did not approve.

Olivia took her seat and spread a linen napkin in her lap, keeping her eyes down until she had bolstered her composure. When she looked up, it was to see Nicholas grinning at her from across the table.

She had known he was in the room, of course, and yet the meeting of their gazes was a physical shock to her, like taking hold of a thunderbolt with both hands.

"Have you been to see the schoolhouse yet, Miss Drummond?" Nicholas asked. He was the image of eastern etiquette, but the spark of sheer knavery in his eyes gave the lie to his attitude of propriety.

"I'm afraid there hasn't been time," his aunt interjected.

Olivia wondered if she would be sent away from Parable before she ever had a chance to teach. It would be a pity if she was, for if she had a gift, it was for working with children. She had learned that while tutoring and serving as a surrogate mother to Eleanor, her niece.

"Then I think we should remedy that, directly after

supper," Nicholas announced, with the air of a man who wasn't used to differing opinions and was therefore unlikely to suffer them graciously. "We'll be wanting a walk anyway."

Olivia concentrated on her plate, which Nicholas had filled to overflowing with sliced meat, potatoes, green beans, and biscuits. She had wanted few things in her life with the same sore desperation as that simple tour of a one-room schoolhouse, and yet she did not see how she could agree.

"A good idea," Jessie said, and Olivia's gaze flew to her face in startled disbelief. Jessie was watching Nicholas. "I understand from your father that you will be working tomorrow," she added.

Olivia was aware of an undercurrent; some sort of sparring match was going on between aunt and nephew while she sat on the sidelines, unenlightened and plainly an outsider. The realization filled her with a sudden and poignant sorrow, for she was aware of her aloneness in that moment as she had not been before.

I love this man, she thought, dumbstruck, watching Nicholas out of the corner of her eye, memorizing everything about him. He will never be mine, and I shall never cease to care for him.

Olivia overcame a desire to lay her head down and weep disconsolately. From that moment on, she could not swallow another bite of food.

Nicholas noticed, although he had the good grace not to comment, and when the torturous meal ended at last and Olivia made a bumbling attempt to help clear the table, he interceded. Jessie took over the task with brisk dispatch, cheerfully promising to save the washing up for her nephew.

Olivia was mortified, for it was plain in Nicholas's

eyes that he knew her feelings, her fears, and perhaps her secrets as well.

He led her as far as the entryway, where the first shadows of evening fell through leaded-glass windows, and there he took her into his arms, with both infinite tenderness and contained passion, and kissed her soundly.

Twelve

If Annabel wanted to eat the dust of two hundred cattle, Gabriel concluded, as he and a dozen men set out on the drive at dawn the following morning, so be it. He had spent the night making love to the woman; he had no strength to spare for arguing with her. Besides, he knew she had an agenda, some wild plan to save Nicholas no doubt. It was a hell of a lot safer, by his reasoning, to keep her where he could see her.

He smiled to himself even as he scanned the perimeters of the bawling herd before him. Damn if Annabel didn't look a grand sight, dressed for rough country in a riding skirt and boots and perched alongside the cook in the box of the chuck wagon. A bright pink parasol, brought along out of practicality rather than guile, rested on her shoulder. The dogs, ever faithful, trotted along on either side, occasionally snuffling the ground with their long snouts, as though trying to pick up a scent.

It bothered Gabriel only slightly that Jeffrey Braithewait had joined the drive and had so far stuck pretty close to Annabel's side. He looked incongruous in his western clothes, stiff-backed on the skinny horse he'd been assigned, like some inadequate sentinel, bravely attempting to guard his queen. Still, Gabriel allowed, he had to give the man credit for perseverance, and that was a quality he valued almost as highly as courage.

When he was certain that the drive was well under way and the drovers were doing their job, Gabriel wheeled his horse around and rode back to fall in beside the chuck wagon, on Annabel's side. She looked about sixteen years old and determined enough to fight the whole U.S. Army on her own, if that was what she had to do.

She was already covered with dust from the point of her parasol to the toes of her boots, but she sat up straight on the seat, and the expression in her whiskey-colored eyes dared Gabriel to comment on her presence. He considered rising to the challenge, thought better of it, and backed down with a grin.

It was sincere, that grin. It was also meant to remind Annabel of how she'd carried on in their bed the night before. That was the only time she ever let him have the upper hand, unless he fought for it—when they were making love. The rest of the time, Annabel seemed to regard him as some sort of treacherous adversary who wanted watching.

He tugged at the brim of his hat. "Mornin'," he said.

Annabel knew what he was thinking—she often did—and blushed to the roots of her hair. "Good morning, Mr. McKeige," she said, as though she hadn't awakened in his arms barely an hour before, her legs entangled with his, her hair spilling over his chest like some glimmering silken garment carelessly tossed aside.

Gabriel couldn't help chuckling at her stiff response to his greeting. "So far, it has been," he replied.

She glared at him in a plain warning that if he pursued that intimate subject any further, she would exact solemn revenge.

Since Annabel was not without the means to do just that, Gabriel took another, slightly less dangerous tack. "I hope you aren't expecting to enjoy yourself," he said. "As I believe I've mentioned before, Mrs. McKeige, this is not a Sunday-afternoon outing."

"Gabriel," she said, "I can ride as well as you and shoot a little better. Early on, when we could not afford drovers, I helped with the cattle. Kindly do not patronize me."

The old cook, at the reins beside Annabel, hawked up something and spit. She winced, and Gabe swallowed another grin, which faded when he noticed that Braithewait had drawn closer.

"You have been away from ranching for some years," Gabriel pointed out smoothly. "And you will not be required to shoot." He touched his hat brim again, this time in parting. "Don't overextend yourself."

With that, Gabriel turned and rode toward the large, noisy herd, in search of his foreman.

Nicholas surveyed the small train of ore wagons lined up in front of the mine. He'd assigned two men to each rig, one in the box and one riding alongside, both armed with rifles as well as the handguns they normally carried. An anxious sensation had coiled itself in the pit of his belly, despite the daylight logic that said he'd worked the situation through and was ready for anything.

All well and good, he thought, except that he had hardly slept for lying there in his bed at Aunt Jessie's place with his hands behind his head, brewing schemes for winning Miss Olivia Drummond as his own.

It wasn't that she didn't want him—he knew from her timid but eager kiss and from the way she looked at him that she felt much the same as he did—but the ten-year difference in their ages lay between them like a mountain chasm. Time didn't matter to him, only substance, but he knew Olivia felt differently. And so, most likely, did the town.

If Nicholas had been a spitting man, he would have spit. As it was, he'd never taken it up, so he just muttered a curse under his breath. To hell with Parable and everyone in it, if the townspeople didn't approve. He didn't give a holy damn what they thought.

The trouble was, Olivia did. Though shy, she clearly wanted to be accepted, to join the community as a respected member, and that meant propriety mattered to her. Once she found out a little more about his reputation, that alone would probably be enough to put her off forever.

"Morning, McKeige," Jack Horncastle said, falling in beside Nicholas as he raised his arm and shouted a signal to start the wagons rolling. The trip would take a week, if things went according to plan.

Which, of course, they wouldn't.

Nicholas grumbled an answer, scanning the hills with a quick but well-practiced gaze.

Horncastle was in high spirits. "The ladies of

Parable are stirred up fit to sting like bees, and so are their mamas," he said gleefully. "Seems you showed an obvious preference for the new schoolteacher yesterday at your aunt's get-together."

Nicholas glared at Horncastle but offered no other response. Jack had to be there—that was part of the plan—and Nicholas himself had hired him on. But he didn't have to like it.

"Know who's really got herself in a pretty little snit? The marshal's daughter. I hope you didn't tell Callie anything incriminating during a romantic moment, McKeige, because she might just be aggravated enough to pass a confidence or two on to her dear old daddy."

"Is there a point to all this?" Nicholas asked, his eyes roaming constantly. That there would be trouble he knew for certain, and the prospect loomed on the inner horizon like a storm. What he didn't know was when it would break.

Horncastle grinned, but there was malice in his eyes and in the set of his mouth. No surprise there—he and Nicholas had fallen in together as bad companions, but they had never been friends.

"Yeah," Jack answered. "I'd like to know that your mind is on your business, McKeige, and not on what's under the schoolmarm's petticoats. We have a lot at stake here—our necks, for instance."

Nicholas drew close alongside Horncastle and backhanded him across the mouth. The movement was so quick that it was over and done with before Nicholas had considered any of the consequences.

It wouldn't have mattered, he supposed, if he had.

Blood trickled from a split in Horncastle's lower lip, and fury blazed in his eyes like fire, but he didn't retaliate. A wise choice, Nicholas thought, with no little disappointment. He would have liked to take Jack Horncastle apart piece by piece. Had been awaiting the chance for months—hell, for years.

"What the devil—" Horncastle sputtered, furious and a little pale as he wiped his mouth on a sleeve.

"If you have opinions about Miss Drummond," Nicholas said coldly, quietly, "kindly keep them to yourself. That way, I won't have to make you eat your teeth."

Horncastle whistled, low and shrill. "I'll be damned," he said. "It's finally happened."

"Get to work," Nicholas snapped. "You're paid to guard these wagons, not to chatter like some old woman."

Horncastle grinned at the reference to spinsterhood, an unfortunate slip on Nicholas's part, and then reined his horse around to ride behind the train and take up a position on the other side.

Nicholas swore again, under his breath, and then swept off his hat and wiped his brow with a hard pass of his forearm. By the time he'd replaced the hat, Charlie had materialized beside him, riding his ancient dun-colored mule. Because there was no one at the ranch house to take care of, the Indian had appointed himself as trail cook, saddled up, and come along. All without a by-your-leave from anybody.

For reasons that had nothing to do with Charlie's wretched coffee and hard biscuits, Nicholas wished his old friend had gone with the cattle drive instead. Charlie saw him too clearly, knew him too well, and under the circumstances, that could be deadly.

When all hell broke loose—and it would—Nicholas didn't want Charlie to be there, caught in the crossfire.

"This trip is bad enough without your cooking to

make it worse," he said, instead of all that he was thinking.

Charlie, dressed for travel in rough clothes and a spotless black bowler, a long-ago gift from Miss Annabel, sent all the way from England, allowed himself the merest flicker of a smile.

"Somebody's got to look after you," he retorted. It was a deliberate jab, though a good-natured one, and Nicholas felt it in the tenderest part of his temper. "Damn fool kid."

"Nobody appointed you my guardian Indian," Nicholas answered, somewhat bitterly, keeping his gaze forward. If you let Charlie catch your eye in a vulnerable moment, that was the end of any secret. The old man could look right into a man's soul, if he chose to, and read whatever happened to be scribbled on the walls.

"You're in trouble, Nicholas," Charlie said, with quiet seriousness. "I want to help you."

"You can't," Nicholas told him flatly. "Nobody can."

Charlie sighed. "That's what you said the time you went off into the hills to hide out because of that party at the schoolhouse. Everybody was supposed to bring their mother, remember? You were about nine, I think, and you took to your heels. Gabe and I found you two days later, and he asked what the hell you thought you were doing, heading for the high country like that, without a word to anybody. You said he couldn't understand, that nobody could, so there was no point in your explaining. Gabe wanted to whale the tar out of you then and there, you'd put such a scare into him. I wouldn't let him—put you in front of me in the saddle, and on the way back down to the ranch, I got you to tell me what was chewing on you.

And I suggested that you invite your aunt Jessie to the party."

"This is different," Nicholas said patiently, but his throat was thick at the memory. He'd wanted Miss Annabel to be there at the schoolhouse shindig, so he could prove he had a mother, but Jessie had been pleased to fill the breach, and she'd done him proud.

"Maybe it's different," Charlie agreed ponderously. "And maybe it's not."

Nicholas wished he could confide in his friend—the burden he carried was a heavy one—but that might have ruined everything. He hadn't told Jessie what he was doing, though he'd wanted to a thousand times, or even his father; he hadn't dared.

"Look, Charlie," he said now. "Go back. Catch up with the drive. I don't need you here."

Charlie was silent for a long time. Like Nicholas, he was watching the hillsides all the while, except for the occasional glance backward. "I prefer to stay," he said at long last. "Miss Annabel's there to look after the drive."

Nicholas surprised himself by laughing at the image of his elegant mother undergoing the singular rigors of a cattle drive. Next thing he knew, she'd be wanting to wield a branding iron and break broncs in the corral. "She's just trying to make sure my pa doesn't have a peaceful moment between now and doomsday," he said.

The Indian's eyes were bright with amusement. "No doubt she will succeed, then."

Nicholas swept off his hat, tilted his head back in a vain attempt to ease the crick in his neck. The sky was of some comfort, hot and clear and painfully blue. Permanent in a way that human beings couldn't be.

"I think they're in love," he said, in a low voice, not

meant to carry to anyone besides Charlie. "Pa and Miss Annabel, I mean."

"There is hope, then, for your powers of observation."

The mockery in Charlie's voice caused Nicholas to glance in his direction. "You think she'll stay this time?" He meant Miss Annabel, of course. He still couldn't bring himself to refer to her as Mother. It wasn't exactly a matter of blame; he'd been the one to leave her behind in Boston all those years before, not the other way around. No, it was more that he didn't feel he knew her well enough to use a term that intimate.

Charlie sighed. "I don't know."

Suddenly Nicholas felt like a seven-year-old again. "But if she loves my pa?"

"Love is a good thing," Charlie said, "but it isn't always enough to hold two people together—especially a pair as strong-willed as the boss and Mrs. McKeige. They remind me of a wild stallion and mare. When they mate, it's a passionate thing. When they fight, it's downright dangerous to get too close. And both of them need to have their head once in a while, and run free."

"You're talking about Julia now."

Charlie shook his head. "No, Nicholas. Might be better if things were that simple, but they aren't. No, what drives your pa is inside him, and nothing to do with any woman. The same applies to your mother. They're not to be tamed, either one of them."

The thought made Nicholas weary. "I don't understand."

Charlie smiled at last. "Neither do they," he said. "And that's all right."

* * *

Throughout the day, Annabel breathed dirt. She tasted grit on her tongue and absorbed it into every pore, but she uttered not a single word of complaint. Indeed, she would gladly have smothered beneath a grave full of the stuff before admitting that she was miserable.

When the drovers had corralled the herd in a shallow ravine for the night, Annabel happily ordered Mr. Hilditch to pitch her tent alongside the cook wagon. Gabriel and the drovers had arrived at the campsite well ahead of them; a large fire was blazing, and cowboys milled about, waiting for coffee and food. Supper, such as it was, would be taking shape as soon as the cook got himself squared away.

Gabriel, damn his arrogant hide, stood waiting when Annabel got there. He was covered with trail dust from head to foot, but he might have spent the day in a rocking chair for all the fatigue he showed. He touched his hat brim with one hand and helped Annabel down with the other.

She closed her parasol with a snap and barely resisted the temptation to whack Gabriel with it. She would have sold her soul for a hot bath, a clean nightgown, and a bed. Oblivion, at that point, was her only aspiration.

"I'm sorry I can't offer you tea," Gabriel said easily, "but we'll soon have coffee."

Annabel dismissed both Jeffrey and her driver, who had converged upon her, with a gesture, and, wisely, they busied themselves elsewhere, Mr. Hilditch with the tent, Mr. Braithewait heading for the creek that flowed past the site.

Annabel gazed longingly at the water for a few moments, knowing all the while that she could not avail herself of its comfort, being the only woman in a camp crowded with men. Then she turned back to Gabriel.

"I should like coffee very much," she said, without inflection. "Provided Charlie doesn't brew it."

Gabriel laughed. "Charlie's with Nicholas, so you're safe."

Moving through the camp beside Gabriel, Annabel felt exhausted in the extreme. Every muscle in her body ached, but she wouldn't have confessed it to Saint Peter himself, if that had been her dying day. She would be damned if she would have Gabriel or anyone else thinking that the rigors of ranch life were too much for her.

When a little time had passed, Gabriel selected a metal cup from a row set up along the surface of an old wagon tongue, long since abandoned by some unfortunate traveler, and carried the mug to the fire. Dropping easily to his haunches, he took up a grubby bit of cloth, meant to serve as a potholder, and lifted a massive coffeepot from the embers.

The coffee, when he presented it to her, now seated on an upended crate provided by the cook, was hot and fresh and entirely delicious. She could not help giving a little sigh of pleasure when she took the first bracing sip.

Gabriel dragged up another crate and sat beside her. "You can still go back to the ranch, Annabel," he said quietly. "Hilditch will ride with you, and I'll send two or three of the men for good measure, to make sure you get there safely."

The offer was kindly phrased, and Annabel knew by Gabriel's tone that he was trying to help her save face—not to mention her aching limbs. For all of that, she could not persuade herself to take the easy path and simply leave. Too much depended on her coming interview with Captain Sommervale.

"I would prefer to stay," she said, with a certain confused resignation.

Gabriel pushed back his hat and scratched his head. "All right," he answered, sighing. He looked at the tent, a pink-and-white striped affair that he had tucked away in the barn after a party years before, and shook his head. "I'd advise you to turn in early, though, because tomorrow will be a long day."

"We'll reach the fort before sunset, surely?"

Gabriel shrugged. "I'm not sure. It depends on whether or not we run into any trouble."

Annabel made her eyes widen. "Rustlers?" she trilled, and batted her eyelashes. "Surely you would save me."

He laughed. "Maybe. And stop making fun of me. This is no foxhunt, Annabel. About a thousand things can happen on the trail, and nine hundred and ninety-five of them are bad."

She leaned forward slightly, and when she spoke, she was quite serious. "Like what?"

"Stampedes," Gabriel replied obligingly. "Renegade Indians, lightning storms, broken wagon wheels or axles, spoiled food, bad water, outlaws, injured cowboys, rattlesnakes, wolves . . ."

Annabel's fatigue suddenly seemed overwhelming, and it carried just the faintest tinge of nausea. Her time of the month, always regular to a fault, was due; she put the malaise down to that. "Wolves?" she whispered. Her childhood fear of the animals came back, unaccountably, and she scanned the twilight horizon uneasily.

Her dogs had found her and lay at her feet, chewing

on soup bones the cook had apparently brought along for them. Annabel rarely saw the ungrateful beasts anymore; they had become a part of the ranch, with lives wholly unrelated to her own.

"Don't worry, Mrs. McKeige," Gabriel said in a confidential tone, leaning close. "I'll look after you."

Annabel blushed and averted her gaze. Gabriel would surely keep her safe from wolves and outlaws and food poisoning, but who was going to protect her from him? If Gabriel decided to take her that night, she would be unable, as always, to resist him. And unless she gagged herself with a dish towel or a stocking, everyone in camp would know exactly what was happening.

He caught her chin in his hand and made her look at him. She saw that his eyes were dancing with mischief, and his mouth quivered on the very brink of a smile. "We'll go downstream, after it's dark, and you can bathe. In the meantime, I'll see if I can rustle you up some liniment for those sore muscles of yours."

"You are not going to watch me bathe," Annabel said in a hasty whisper, and her tone was completely at variance with the relief she felt at the prospect of being clean again. "And what makes you think I'm sore?"

"You limp. And I mean to do more than watch you bathe, Mrs. McKeige," Gabriel responded smoothly. "I'll be taking the soap to you myself."

With that, he rose easily to his feet and walked away to confer with his men, a cluster here, a cluster there. The dogs, traitors that they were, trotted after him, as though he were their master.

Annabel gave a little groan at the thought of Gabriel's hands moving over her flesh, even in so seemingly innocent and practical a task as lathering away a day's accumulation of trail dirt. Threaded through her anxiety was a thrumming strand of pure anticipation.

Dinner was salt pork, fried black, and more coffee. The cowboys ate in relays, while others rode herd on the restless cattle and still others stretched out on the ground to catch a wink of sleep. They made a point of ignoring Annabel, these mostly youthful men, but neither did they shun her. The stories they swapped were less ribald, she suspected, than they might otherwise have been, and when one of the hands produced a mouth harp and began to play a sad, sweet tune, Annabel felt very much a part of the group.

Night settled softly over the harsh land, like a gossamer mantle floating down from the sky, and Annabel began to look for Gabriel, even though she knew he'd eaten a hasty meal and taken the first watch.

She was at peace, sitting there watching the cheerful fire and listening to the music and to the cowboys talking in quiet voices. She could admit, if only to herself, that, at least in part, she'd wanted to make this journey simply to be near Gabriel, to take part in some aspect of his day-to-day life.

She was about to nod off when, after several hours, he returned as suddenly as he had gone, and collected Annabel from her seat by the fire without a word, simply by taking her hand and leading her into the moon-washed darkness.

He was carrying a saddlebag over one shoulder as he walked determinedly away from the camp, leaving behind the sound, the music, the dancing light of the fire.

The stars played another kind of song, however, one that only the spirit could hear, and narrow strands of silver, shed by the moon, spangled each blade of the tall grass.

Presently they came to a place where the creek widened into a pool. It was sheltered by large rocks and probably half a mile from the camp.

Gabriel slung the saddlebags over one of the boulders, tossed aside his hat, and methodically kicked off his right boot, then his left. He unbuckled his gun belt and set it aside—but where he could get to it quickly, Annabel noticed—and peeled off his stockings. Then he hauled his shirt over his head, never troubling himself to unfasten the buttons, and rumpled his glorious hair in the process.

A lump rose in Annabel's throat, because Gabriel was so beautiful to look upon. She knew he never thought of himself in that way; for all his intelligence, wit, money, and power, he was in some ways as naive and ingenuous as a little boy.

"If you try to bathe in that skirt," he said reasonably, but with a spark in his eyes to indicate that he was teasing, "you'll probably be dragged under and drowned." With that, he opened his trousers, pushed them down, and kicked them away, then strode, as naked and splendid as Michelangelo's *David,* into the water. He gave a muffled curse at the cold but was soon out in the middle, sudsing himself with a bar of yellow soap. The starlight caught in his golden hair and emphasized the rugged but still aristocratic planes of his face, the wondrous width of his shoulders, the sculpted perfection of his chest and belly.

Annabel admired him for a time, then slowly removed her own clothes. Gabriel fell still, watching her without apology as she followed him into the pool.

Her teeth chattered with the chill, and when she

reached him, he took her into his arms, and warmed her against him, holding her close, stroking her back and her arms with his strong, callused hands. Soon, the pool seemed as warm as a bath by the kitchen stove and, although Annabel shivered, it was not because she was cold.

Gabriel kissed her, cautiously at first, then greedily, and with his usual air of command. He aroused her easily, but without haste, and Annabel sagged against him, helpless, as he soaped her entire body, including her hair, and gave her the bath he had promised.

By the time it was over, she was whimpering, dazed with the need of him.

"Make love to me," she whispered, because she knew he would never take her without an invitation.

He cupped her femininity in his hand, and she felt his fingers move deep inside, teasing, making matters worse rather than better. Oh, deliciously worse.

"Not now, Annabel," he said, in a hoarse rasp.

"Why not?"

"Because I want you to want me."

Annabel's frustration was exceeded only by her passion. "But I do want you," she cried, between frantic nibbles at his shoulder, his brown, flat nipples.

Gabriel entangled his free hand in her hair, though gently, and drew her head back so that he could look into her face. In the meantime, his fingers continued their sweet torment. He had found, unerringly, that particularly sensitive place inside her, where delicate nerves rioted just beneath the surface of smooth, slippery flesh.

"Not enough," he said.

Annabel uttered a soft wail, followed by a gasp. "Oh, God—Gabriel—"

The water of the pool splashed gently around them

as Annabel began to move helplessly, desperately, against Gabriel. He bent his head and took ravenous suckle at one of her breasts; the nipple was chilled and turgid and far more sensitive than it might otherwise have been.

Annabel made a small sobbing sound that bore no relation whatsoever to grief or sorrow, but was instead akin to rapture. "Please," she begged. "Please—"

Gabriel would bring her to climax, there was no doubting that. But when he used his fingers or his mouth to appease her, the satisfaction, though fierce enough to send her body into violent convulsions of pleasure and wring raw shouts from her throat, was temporary. Only his taking her completely, with hard and repeated thrusts of his hips, would truly release her. Any other sort of loving merely made her need him more.

And he knew that, of course.

She buried her fingers in his wet hair, kissed him all over, murmuring senseless pleas as she did so, but Gabriel would not be moved. He went on about his scandalous work, stroking that secret place, tickling and teasing, and suddenly Annabel stiffened and flung back her head, calling in strangled gasps to the stars. Her legs were clenched around Gabriel's waist now, her breasts brushing his chest, and even as the seemingly relentless inner explosions racked her, he did not slacken his efforts but instead drove her higher and higher. She finally fell against him, exhausted and spent, her head on his shoulder.

And knowing, all the while, that within the hour the desire would return, hotter and stronger and more compelling than ever.

Gabriel shifted Annabel, murmuring soothing,

senseless words all the while, until she lay across his arms, limp as an angel, shorn of its wings and sent crashing to earth.

He bent to her and again took suckle at her breasts, and Annabel could do no more than offer herself, with a slight arching of her back. An almost inaudible whimper came steadily from her throat, for in this she had no will, no strength, no pride or shame. Gabriel was utterly dominant, and she would not have made things different, even if she could.

She felt his erection against her side, hard and imposing, despite the coolness of the water, and took some solace in knowing that he wanted her as desperately as she wanted him. It was only that, in matters of intimacy, he had more self-control than she did, and infinitely more patience.

Annabel's hair floated around her head like the fronds of some tropical water flower while Gabriel took his pleasure at her nipples, first one and then the other.

"I will have vengeance for this," she told him, between little cries of pure and ever-rising ecstasy.

Gabriel chuckled, and the sound reverberated pleasantly through the plump flesh of the breast he happened to be enjoying at the time. He said nothing, but slid his fingers downward, to find their way through the thicket of curls at the apex of Annabel's thighs, and dally there.

She bit her lower lip in an effort to hold back an utterance of joyous despair.

Have her vengeance she would . . . in time.

Thirteen

BECAUSE THE NEW TERM WOULD NOT BEGIN UNTIL THE end of August, Olivia had plenty of time to make lesson plans and, thanks to a private donation from Mr. Gabriel McKeige, an ample budget for supplies, including new maps and textbooks.

These last, Olivia reflected, as she stood in the small schoolhouse on that quiet July morning, after her private world had been changed forever, were badly needed. The old reading primers were soiled and tattered, with many of the pages missing, and most of the arithmetic books had long since shed their covers.

Olivia moved along the aisles, between two rows of small desks. She loved the smell of the schoolroom—the residue of last year's chalk, the distinctive scent of aging paper, even the inevitable dust. Cleaning would be her job, as well as teaching and providing whatever guidance and encouragement might be indicated for each particular pupil, but she didn't mind. It made the little structure her province—and the children's.

Ever practical and thrifty, Olivia went back to her

own desk, in front of the small chalkboard, where she had stacked the school's pitiful collection of books, intending to go through them just once more, in the hope of salvaging one or two. Most were suited only for kindling a fire in the squat stove huddled in a far corner of the room, but Olivia would not consign them to such a fate, for they were still books, however crippled and decrepit.

She would take the volumes to church, she decided. There they might find new homes with various parishioners—homes where they would surely be appreciated and even treasured, for all their bedraggled state.

The childish scrawl inside the loose cover of a reading primer took Olivia unprepared and made a sudden thickness in her throat. "Nicholas McKeige," a small hand had written in slanted, not-so-careful letters. "McKeige Ranch, Parable, Nevada, 1869."

Olivia closed her eyes, wounded in some sweet and inexplicable way, and held the small, battered volume against her heart. The reminder of Nicholas's age fairly took her breath away, and she found herself caught up in such a turmoil of conflicting emotions that she could not begin to sort them out.

Being in this meditative state, Olivia did not hear the door of the schoolhouse open, and when the sound of footsteps reached her, she looked up to find Jessie McKeige sweeping along the main aisle, regal as a queen in her elegant morning dress and fashionable hat. She carried a large basket, the handle tucked into the crook of one elbow.

Olivia squared her shoulders and raised her chin, even though—or perhaps because—she felt so small and mouselike. She would have stood, too, except that Jessie motioned for her to remain in her chair.

Managing a smile, Olivia sat stiffly nonetheless, and

Nicholas's primer lay beneath her palm on the desk, like a courthouse Bible. She could feel the echo of her own heartbeat reverberating from its pages.

"I've brought you some refreshment, Miss Drummond, since you clearly do not intend to return to the house for lunch."

Olivia did not know what to say, beyond a murmured thank you. She was not sophisticated, like the woman before her, but for all that, she had no illusions that this visit was about sandwiches and tea.

Jessie set her basket on the desk, looked around for a suitable chair, found one in a corner, and dragged it over. After much pomp and circumstance where dusting off the seat and arranging her skirts were concerned, Miss McKeige sat down. "Now, then," she said briskly.

Olivia's stomach coiled into a knot. Jessie had come to discharge her, here in this place where she so longed to work. No doubt she would be bound for San Francisco, in disgrace, on the very next stagecoach, with no letter of recommendation forthcoming.

Jessie leaned forward slightly and peered at her through narrowed blue eyes. "Dear heaven, you look upset—somewhat green at the gills. What on earth is troubling you, Miss Drummond?"

Olivia swallowed hard, but the blunt truth swelled into her mouth anyway and sprang from the tip of her tongue. "I—I don't want to be sent away."

"Sent away?" Jessie repeated, as though the phrase were foreign and thus unfamiliar to her. "Why would I do that, when you haven't had a proper chance to prove your abilities?" She frowned. "You were completely honest in your letters of application, weren't you? You're not a convict or a married woman?"

Olivia laughed, though nervously. "I was quite honest."

Jessie beamed as revelation struck her, and sat back in her wooden chair. "Ah," she said. "This is about Nicholas, then, and his obvious infatuation with you."

"Yes," Olivia said, somewhat incredulously. No one, to her knowledge, had ever been infatuated with her before; she had always been a wallflower, retiring and tongue-tied, with no names scribbled in her dance book. "It's about Nicholas."

"Foolish boy," Jessie said, but with affection. "I hope you will be patient, Miss Drummond. He's bound to get over it, but there will be no talking sense to him before he does. Nicholas is too much like his father, you see. And, of course, his mother, who is equally bullheaded."

Olivia dared not say that she found Nicholas appealing in wild and primitive ways, that even though he was not yet twenty, he spoke and moved with the innate confidence of a man not only grown but well seasoned by time and experience. His mind was wondrous, a vast network of seemingly endless passageways, with a new and dazzling discovery around every turn. He could make her laugh with a word or a look—reason enough to love him, that, all on its own.

But then there were his physical attractions, which made Olivia's heartbeat erratic and rendered her sleep restless and fitful. Nicholas had made intimate promises, with the look in his eyes and the strength of his hand upon hers, that, God help her, she wanted him to keep.

Olivia cleared her throat softly, uncertain how to respond to Jessie's assurance that Nicholas's fascination would pass. While she did not want to mislead the other woman, neither did she wish to be cast out of Parable for harboring immoral thoughts. She had no place to go, either literally or figuratively, except forward.

"I enjoy Nicholas's company very much," she allowed, conscious that it was surely the greatest understatement of her entire lifetime and willing herself not to blush for making it.

Jessie had opened the basket and smoothed a cloth over one side of the desk and was now setting out small china plates, colorfully painted with images of fruit. "Yes," she said thoughtfully, "I had noticed that."

"And you've come to warn me off," Olivia blurted, in despair.

"No," Jessie said. "Not in the way you think, at least. Olivia—I may call you Olivia?—Nicholas is, I realize, a very charming and attractive young man. Besides his appearance and his sharp mind, there is a certain mysterious and rather wicked element to Nicholas's character—one is never quite sure if one is dealing with an angel or a devil. I suspect he is both." Jessie paused to sigh, then unfastened the lid of a jar and poured steaming fragrant tea into two delicate cups. "Olivia, I know of no other way to say this than with utter directness: Nicholas cannot be trusted—at least in matters of love. He has charmed the garters off more women than I can name—some his own age, some considerably older—and then broken their hearts. I should not like to see that happen to you."

Olivia wanted to bolt and run, but she settled for the closest and most suitable substitute, squirming imperceptibly in her seat and grasping its arms so tightly that her knuckles showed. She knew her color was high, damning her, revealing what she would rather have hidden, but there was nothing for it.

"I shall try to be careful," she promised, with a sort of hopeless bravado. How long could Nicholas have been making these conquests, after all? He was hardly more than a boy.

Whatever his experience, Nicholas's charms were formidable, and Olivia did not know how long she could resist them. Perhaps she didn't truly want to resist, despite the inevitable pain that would result: she had lived nearly thirty years as a virgin and, if she could not have true love and marriage, she wanted a taste of passion, however fleeting—however costly—it might be.

Jessie shook her head. "Trying is not enough," she said, reaching for a sandwich and biting into it with enthusiasm. She chewed interminably, then finally swallowed and went on. "You must be firm with Nicholas. Tell him outright that you do not welcome his flirtations."

Olivia picked up a tidbit from those Jessie had arrayed on a gold-trimmed plate, studied it disconsolately, and set it down again. "But I do, you see."

"My dear," Jessie said, more firmly now, "if you wish to break your contract in favor of marriage, you will certainly not be the first schoolteacher to do so. Gabriel and I will scare up a replacement somehow. But set your sights on another man, someone older and more settled—a nice widower, say." She snapped her fingers, and her classically beautiful face became luminous. "I know just the man, Olivia! His name is Alexander Wellingford, and he has a fine job overseeing Gabriel's mines—he is an engineer, I believe. He adored his wife, but she died of a heart ailment of some sort, five years ago."

Olivia would wonder ever after where she found the boldness to say what she did then. "Perhaps you had better marry Mr. Wellingford yourself, Miss McKeige, since you find him so eminently suitable."

Jessie looked for a moment as though she'd been slapped or doused with cold water. But in the next instant, heaven be thanked, she must have realized that Olivia had not meant the words unkindly but as an observation.

"I couldn't," she said, looking even more luminous than before, as though some flame had been struck within.

Olivia supposed she might be forgiven for a little inward gloating. It was a rarity, she had already discerned, to get the better of a McKeige, and when it happened, one would be wise to relish the moment. "Why ever not?" she asked, genuinely interested. Magically, Olivia's throat had opened, and her stomach was no longer churning. She actually felt hungry and began to nibble at one of the fussy little sandwiches as she awaited a visibly flustered Jessie's reply.

"Well, because I would have to sacrifice my freedom," she finally said, one hand resting, fingers splayed, upon her bosom.

Olivia arched an eyebrow. Whatever happened with Nicholas, she had no intention of giving up her teaching position unless she was forcibly discharged. Which could happen, given the predominating prejudice against married women in the classroom.

Married women? Did she truly expect Nicholas to take her as his wife?

Yes, Olivia concluded, she expected exactly that, though she couldn't have said why.

"Give up your freedom?" she prodded, after a sip

of tea. "What do you do now that you could not do if you were wedded to Mr. Wellingford?"

Jessie was still illuminated, bright as a saint's likeness painted upon a church window, a circumstance that, of course, only made her more beautiful. "Well—suppose I wanted to travel, take the grand tour. Mr. Wellingford is very devoted to his job and would not wish to leave on an extended journey."

"Has he told you so?" Olivia asked between nibbles. She had eaten very little since before her first encounter with Nicholas, at yesterday's tea party, and she was starved.

"Well—well, no, of course not. Mr. Wellingford is my brother's employee. We have never spoken of travel, let alone marriage."

Olivia pursed her lips for a moment, thoughtfully. "Then you believe he is beneath you? Because he works for Mr. McKeige?"

Jessie's eyes flashed with righteous ire. "Of course not," she snapped. "Why, Alexander is a learned man. He went to Harvard, and we have had some fascinating discussions about poetry."

Olivia smiled. "Ah," she said.

Jessie's cheeks flared with tinges of daunting indignation, but the violence in her expression soon subsided to a look of sheepish realization. "You might make a match for Nicholas after all," she said. "You have his talent for turning aside any discussion that is not to your liking."

Olivia looked down at the book, inscribed by the boy Nicholas, and all her inadequacies came flooding back, nearly sweeping her away. "I will keep your advice in mind," she promised, lowering her eyes briefly, while she gathered shreds of courage, here and there, like a tardy gleaner, too late for the harvest. "I will confess that I wish Nicholas were older."

Jessie, seeing that lunch was over, had begun to pick up the debris, setting everything in the basket. "Instead of wishing that you were younger?" she asked, not unkindly.

Olivia sighed. "I feel neither old nor young," she said. "I merely feel like Olivia, and I've never aspired to be different than I am."

Jessie smiled sadly and rose, reaching for the basket's handle. "I have advised you to tread carefully, and I've followed this same counsel myself for many years. Odd, isn't it, that I shouldn't have questioned the wisdom of such circumspection before now?" She reached out and patted Olivia's hand, where it rested upon Nicholas's long-forgotten schoolbook. "What is life, after all, without risk, without passion, without ample measures of pain and pleasure?"

"Nothing," Olivia reflected, surprised by all she had just discovered within herself. Thinking of Nicholas, away for a week on some mysterious errand, and already yearning for his return. "Nothing at all."

Like Gabriel, Annabel awakened before dawn. They were lying inside the silly-looking tent, huddled between two blankets, and for the first few moments Annabel could not rightly tell where she stopped and Gabriel began.

When the enigma was solved, she was startled into full awareness.

"Gabriel McKeige," she protested, but he had taken hold of her hips, and was already moving inside her, slowly, skillfully, deeply.

In the distance the cattle lowed in their mournful voices as cowboys cajoled and whistled, readying the beasts for another long day's travel. The campfire had been built back up to a snapping, cheerful roar, and the aroma of coffee blended with those of crushed grass, fresh air, and rising dust.

Release came quickly for Annabel and, for once, quietly. She lay shuddering beneath Gabriel, and when he reached his own climax, he ground his mouth against hers, and she swallowed his low cries of pleasure.

When it was over, he kissed her again, this time tenderly, then withdrew. While Annabel was still recovering her wits, he pulled on his trousers, shirt, and boots, retrieved his hat and gun belt, and left her behind, plunging headlong into the new day.

Annabel made haste to dress—morning was not her best time, but she would not have the luxury of lolling about in bed today. Not in the middle of the range, with cattle, horses, and cowboys all around. A great tumult of tinkling brass and horses' hooves told her that the cavalry had come to meet them, adding soldiers to the mix.

She squirmed into her clothes, wound her plaited hair into a coronet, and pinned it into place. Then, after drawing a deep breath, she stepped out to face the new day. The instant she'd passed over the canvas threshold, two cowboys began dismantling the tent.

"Mornin', Mrs. McKeige," the cook said, as she neared the main campfire, offering her a mug of coffee and a plate heaped with last night's leftover pork.

Annabel's gorge rose inexplicably, and she shook her head, gripping the rear wheel of the cook wagon for support. "No, thank you," she managed, as politely as she could. "But if there's water . . ."

The grizzled old man took the lid off a barrel affixed to the side of the wagon and ladled out a serving.

Annabel looked at the dipper warily, then accepted it and drank, and the tepid offering soothed her reeling stomach just a little.

"You all right, missus?" the cook inquired, stooping to peer into Annabel's face. His breath smelled of whiskey and bad teeth and nearly sent her stumbling around the side of the wagon to retch. "Shall I fetch the boss?"

"No, please," Annabel protested. "Don't bother. I'll be fine." Sick or well, she was not about to play the prima donna and interfere with Gabriel's work. She had a great deal more pride, and personal strength, than that.

She ran her hands down the thighs of her riding skirt—unlike some women of her acquaintance, who secretly yearned to wear trousers, Annabel preferred ruffles and lace. For all her skill as a horsewoman, for all her temper and her independence and her voracious mind, there was nothing manly about Annabel. She gloried in being female, considering it the best possible fate, for in her estimation, spirit and strength and intelligence were as much womanly traits as much as masculine ones. And the female sex was blessed with other fine and singular qualities as well, qualities that were somewhat rarer in men, such as intuition, empathy, common sense, and compassion.

Annabel quailed with private embarrassment when Captain Sommervale approached, looking resplendent, albeit dusty, in his uniform. His hair and beard were freshly groomed, and he had plainly been to the creek to wash after the ride from Fort Duffield, for his face was still ruddy with the chill. His men mingled with the cowboys, exchanging grunts and grumbles in the first pink-and-gold light.

"Good morning, Mrs. McKeige," he said kindly, taking obvious care not to notice Annabel's rumpled clothing and general air of untidiness. She realized that she was gripping the wagon wheel again, but could not let go.

"Captain Sommervale," she replied, with a nod, cloaking herself in dignity in order to bolster her confidence. She must not impress this man as flighty or weak; he might well hold Nicholas's fate in his hands, and it was up to her to make him see that her son was no cattle rustler.

"I hope you do not find this rough means of travel too rigorous," he said, with sincere concern.

Annabel was self-conscious and not a little queasy. It came to her that the events of the night just past might be common knowledge, but despite her embarrassment, she kept her objective in mind. She smiled warmly and tucked her arm into the captain's. "We must all meet our particular challenges."

"Of course," the captain replied, with a slight and deferential inclination of his head. "But—you'll pardon my presumption, I hope—you seem a bit . . . well, ill."

"I am not ill," Annabel said, with determination. Then, in the very next moment, she pulled free, wheeled about, and barely got around to the other side of the wagon before retching violently into the grass.

When she felt someone beside her, gathering her hair back from her face, offering a ladle of cool and blessed water, this time from the creek, she knew without looking that it was Gabriel.

"I'm sorry!" she wailed, disconsolate.

"Why?" Gabriel asked, sounding honestly puzzled.

But there was something else in his voice, too—a note of speculation, perhaps. Annabel was too weak and distracted to define it exactly.

She rinsed her mouth with water and then drank thirstily, leaning against Gabriel without compunction because her knees were wobbly and she didn't entirely trust her stomach not to raise another rebellion. "You said I didn't belong on the trail. You tried to tell me, but I wouldn't listen—and now I've made an utter fool of myself."

His arms tightened around her, reassuring and strong in that way peculiar to a man's embrace. "Hush," he said, with a chuckle, and grazed her moist temple with a light kiss. "You belong wherever you want to be at the time, Annabel. It's always been that way."

The statement was cryptic, and once again Annabel let it pass undeciphered. "I haven't felt this way since—since—" She stopped in glorious horror and looked up into Gabriel's face. "Since I was carrying Susannah."

Gabriel grinned. Once again he'd been a step ahead of her. "I remember," he said. "Five minutes after we conceived her—Nicholas, too—you started throwing up your shoelaces."

Annabel's eyes stung with tears of jubilation, because she wanted a child so very much, and with tears of sorrow, because this baby, if indeed she was pregnant, would probably grow up in disruption and chaos, just as Nicholas had.

Nicholas, her darling outlaw, the man-child who would not call her Mother.

A sob tore itself from Annabel's throat, and she collapsed against Gabriel's chest, utterly dissolved in a mixture of grief and joy.

Gabriel held her, simply held her, while the cattle drive took shape around them, while cowboys rode past, pretending not to see. The fact that Gabriel did not rush Annabel gave her as much solace as his embrace and the gentle words he whispered to her.

The dogs appeared, worried by Annabel's distraught state, whimpering and prodding her with their long muzzles. Hilditch kept himself to a respectful distance, though he must have been wondering, and even Jeffrey had had the good grace to ride on with the others.

Finally Gabriel cupped Annabel's chin in his gloved hand and kissed her forehead. Then he brushed aside her tears with his thumb and smiled down at her, his golden head rimmed in brand new sunshine.

"We'll work something out, Annabel," he said. "I promise you that."

She believed him, and nodded, sniffling. "You'd better catch up with your men," she told him, with a shaky smile. "I'll be along."

Gabriel kissed her forehead again, then handed her up into the cook wagon—a vehicle she was beginning to wish she had never laid eyes on—mounted his horse, and rode after the drive.

The day was almost unbearably long, and Annabel, sitting stalwartly on the hard seat of that ancient rig, felt every jolt and jostle along the way. Just at twilight, the log walls of Fort Duffield loomed before them.

The soldiers and cowboys drove the bawling cattle into the large, empty corrals awaiting them, while Annabel, Gabriel, and Captain Sommervale rode through the tall, open gates of the fort itself.

Annabel did not know whether to be glad or sorry that there had been no incident along the way. Nicholas was with the wagon loads of ore, traveling in the opposite direction, and he was by no means safe.

There were few women at Fort Duffield, only a handful of officers' wives and daughters, and they were as glad to see Annabel as they had been only a few days before, when she had arrived there in transit, on her way to Parable. If they were shocked by her trousers and shirt, they gave no indication, and while Gabriel conferred with Captain Sommervale and some of the other army authorities, Mrs. Sommervale made Annabel welcome, providing tea, a private room, and a tubful of clean hot water.

Because Annabel had left several of her trunks in Lavinia Sommervale's keeping, she had fresh clothing to put on, and when Gabriel finally appeared, with the captain, he found his wife in improved spirits. She was wearing a dress of soft lavender silk and her hair, still damp from washing, was plaited and loosely coiled at the nape of her neck.

Seated across from Gabriel at the Sommervales' gracious table, Annabel felt restored. She knew her gown, a favorite, was flattering, and so was the dancing candlelight. When Gabriel raised his wine-glass to her in a silent yet eloquent toast, a thrill raced along the traceries of her veins to pulse in her every nerve.

She loved Gabriel, there was no mistaking that, and in a way far beyond anything she had felt for him before. Now that she was older and, at very great cost, wiser as well, she trusted herself, trusted her instincts, enough to open the innermost regions of her being to him. Receiving Gabriel into her body had been easy by comparison. Receiving him into her soul was an intimacy of such magnitude that she had only begun to manage it, and all those years of separation and heartache had gone into the process.

She had lost so much in the making-ready, and so had her husband and son, but there was no point in dwelling on that. Annabel was determined to look to the present, leaving the past behind and the future to its own unfathomable devices.

Later that night, when at last Gabriel joined her in the Sommervales' guest room bed, Annabel had been asleep for a long time. She awakened immediately, however, and even though the lamp had not been lighted, she knew he was troubled.

"What is it?" she asked, touching him tenderly.

Gabriel shook his head, catching moonlight in his hair. "Not tonight," he said.

Annabel was alarmed by his tone; she had never heard such a note of weariness in his voice. What, she wondered, deeply frightened, had been said behind the closed doors of the downstairs study, where Gabriel and Captain Sommervale had passed the evening?

"Nicholas," she whispered. She had not yet spoken to the Captain, for it was vital that she choose the right moment.

"Yes," Gabriel answered, lying down heavily beside her.

She took him into her arms, and they lay curled together, with no further words, until sleep took them.

The night passed all too quickly. They rose early the following morning, dressed, and ate a quiet breakfast with Mrs. Sommervale. The captain, she said, had already gone to his office.

Annabel followed while Gabriel was helping to load

the trunks she had stored at the fort into the back of the cook wagon. A solemn young private admitted her to the army officer's private domain.

Sommervale sighed at the sight of her, but rose from his chair and gestured for her to take a seat near his desk. "I have sons of my own, you know," he said, without preamble, indicating a framed likeness of a young man on a nearby shelf. "That's John, the eldest."

Annabel's heart trembled, but her manner was brave. "Then you've guessed why I'm here."

"Sit down," the captain prompted gently, and only then did Annabel realize that she was still standing.

She sat, silent and sick. It was plain from the expression on the man's face, however kindly, however regretful, that he would not be moved by the testimony of an angel of God in the matter of Nicholas's innocence, let alone the protestations of a frantic mother.

"The proof is quite conclusive, Mrs. McKeige," he said quietly, his hands folded atop of a stack of papers. "I am sorry."

"You are mistaken," Annabel replied, and she meant it, believed it with her whole heart.

"That," the captain answered, with another sigh, "would please me more than anything else could." He met her gaze. "I have no wish to see your son suffer, Mrs. McKeige. But I must do my job."

She merely nodded—there was no more to be said—and numbly took her leave, all her hopes shaken. Here was a situation where persistence would not serve.

At midmorning, with Gabriel riding alongside the chuck wagon, he and Annabel and the cook started back toward Parable, and the ranch. Hilditch had been dismissed earlier, as had the cowboys, and they, able to travel much faster on horseback, were far ahead.

"Tell me what the captain said to you, about Nicholas," Annabel demanded, when they'd stopped for a rest and the cook was out of earshot. She had held the words back as long as she could, waiting to be alone with her husband.

"The army has turned up hard evidence that he was involved in the theft of that first herd, Annabel," Gabriel said. "They mean to prosecute, and he'll be taken into custody as soon as they can find Marshal Swingler and get him to serve the warrant."

Annabel had no right to be surprised, after her own brief interview with the captain, and yet the reality of what was happening was as shattering as a blow. "It's a lie," she murmured, though inside she was screaming. "It's a lie!"

"There are people willing to testify against him," Gabriel replied evenly, his gaze fixed straight ahead. "Good citizens, evidently."

"Who?" Annabel wanted to know. "Who are these 'good citizens'?"

"The captain wasn't about to tell me that," Gabriel answered, "not with Nicholas still on the loose."

Before Annabel could respond, Gabriel touched her arm and, with a nod, indicated a rider in the distance, racing toward them over the rich, rippling sea of grass. It seemed that hours passed before they were finally able to recognize Charlie, spurring his ancient mule to a reckless pace.

"Jesus, Mary, and Joseph," Gabriel muttered. The dogs ran forward, barking.

Annabel's heart had lodged itself in her throat even before the rider reached them, the hooves of his mount sending up great rolling plumes of dust.

Charlie reined in the mule, and for the first time in her memory, Annabel saw desperation in the Indian's usually placid face, and terrible fear.

She wanted to cover her ears, to turn and hurry in the other direction, so she wouldn't have to hear the news he brought. Instead, she stood frozen beside Gabriel, barely breathing, her heartbeat pounding in her ears. Like her, Gabriel was rigid, unspeaking.

Charlie's sorrow was palpable in the heavy summer air. "It's Nicholas," he said at last. "He's been shot."

Fourteen

NICHOLAS WAS ENCOMPASSED, ENCLOSED BY THE FIERY, smothering pain, like a June bug sealed up in a jar, and he could think of little or nothing else. He was, moreover, physically unable to express his suffering with so much as a whimper, and somehow that made it infinitely worse.

Slowly he groped his way toward consciousness, shimmering high above, only to tumble backward, over and over again, into the choking mire. Nothing if not persistent, Nicholas began the climb anew, and finally came within breathing distance of the surface.

He opened his eyes once and saw Marshal Swingler leaning over him. Felt the bed of a wagon beneath him, unyielding, worn smooth by years of hard use.

"You hold on, boy," the lawman commanded. "We got 'em. We got 'em all, you hear me? Don't you let go."

Nicholas could not answer, could not hold his eyes open or shape words with his tongue, which had swollen to fill his mouth, it seemed, and now felt as dry as a mudhole in a summer drought. Like a mind reader, the marshal seemed to know that, and he raised Nicholas's head carefully, to hold a canteen to his mouth.

Nicholas swallowed a capful of water and gagged on the rest, and the resulting spasms in his chest and belly were an exquisite agony. He was glad, that time, to lapse into a confused and merry reverie—whether of dreams or of memories, he could not discern. He was drifting just beneath the deep pulsing layer of pain, aware of the threat but, for the moment, blessedly out of reach.

And then it all came back to him, heartbeat for heartbeat. He was on the road with the wagonloads of silver once again, reliving it all. . . .

The outlaws were on them in an instant. The hair stood up on the back of Nicholas's neck—that was all the warning he had—and the .45 leaped from its holster into his hand, seemingly under its own power, but it was already too late. In the next second the sultry, peaceful afternoon dissolved into chaos. The teams pulling the ore wagons began to shriek and balk in their harnesses while the drivers shouted in angry dismay.

Bullets erupted from the barrels of pistols and rifles and whined in the air. Men bellowed in anguish and in fury, and the dust rose up in a blinding cloud, making it almost impossible to see. Or to breathe.

Riders poured out of the grass on either side of the trail, like snakes suddenly touched by some magician and turned to horse-and-man, pouring out of gullies and dry creek beds and God only knew what other hiding places. Horncastle's gang came from one direction, the marshal and his posse from the other.

Nicholas's instructions were to take shelter under one of the wagons, but it never occurred to him to obey. Just as he wheeled around to take aim at Horncastle's head, the gelding he had raised from a colt keened in agony and folded beneath him, carrying him to the ground as it fell.

Nicholas managed to roll to one side and avoid being crushed, and because the animal was still screaming, hurt, and in terror, Nicholas used the bullet he had intended for Horncastle to put the horse out of its misery. Before the cylinder of the .45 had turned, aligning the next shell in the chamber, Nicholas saw Jack take aim, saw the flare of fire from the other man's pistol.

It happened in a split second, naturally, but still, Nicholas had the strange sensation of standing helpless in the path of that bullet, watching it come at him. The connection was almost graceful, like a dance, sending him spinning away from the dead horse, with his arms flung out from his sides.

The impact had the force of a school yard bat, hard-swung, striking Nicholas beneath his rib cage on the right side, shredding skin and muscle, bone and cartilage, burning deep like a metal spike, fresh-plucked from the forge. . . .

"Nicholas?" The voice might have been his mother's or Jessie's, he didn't know, but it pulled him toward the blessed present. He could not quite rise to meet the sweet sound—nearly unbearable suffering barred the way—but he welcomed the feel of a cool cloth resting on his forehead like the tender sanctification of an angel.

There were more words and phrases, in varied voices, drifting back and forth, and it was as if

Nicholas heard them with his eyes instead of his ears, saw them gliding smoothly back and forth over his head while he looked upward, like a drowning swimmer noting the gleaming, willowy bellies of fish. All emotion had gone, and he was an observer, with no particular opinion on anything.

". . . surgery . . . loss of blood . . ."

". . . whatever is necessary . . . anything . . ."

Nicholas sighed inwardly and let go of all thought.

Annabel sat beside Nicholas's bed, upstairs in Jessie's house, holding one of his hands to her face, wetting his skin with her tears. Gabriel stood behind her, struck dumb by the sorrow and fear they shared. Once before, they had kept a similar vigil beside a child's bed, and they had lost their daughter.

The doctor, a nervous young man reared somewhere back east, had performed what surgery he could, in the circumstances, and now there was nothing to do but wait, hope, and pray. Nicholas had come perilously close to death, and he was still in very great danger, but at least he was not lying in the dirt, where he had fallen.

Others, on both sides of the conflict, had not been so fortunate as he.

Annabel still did not understand exactly what had happened on that far road, and she doubted that Gabriel did, either. A part of her clamored for the truth, even as she kept a desperate watch at her son's side, matching her every breath and even her pulse to his, as if to encourage his lungs and heart by that means and keep them from forgetting.

Softly Annabel began to hum a nursery song she had sung to Nicholas and Susannah long, long ago, before pride and cowardice and despair had taken her so far away. Her tears renewed themselves, drawing on some bottomless well within, as she waited for one sign, one flicker of an eyelash or twitch of a muscle, to indicate that Nicholas was inside that pale, bloodied body, holding on.

Dear God, she prayed silently, if ever he was stubborn, my wayward son, let it be now.

She leaned forward, Gabriel's hand light on her shoulder, and kissed Nicholas's forehead, finding it fevered. Infection was the most deadly peril, now that the crude surgery was over, but Annabel preferred the heat in Nicholas's flesh to the corpselike chill she had felt when she first arrived, breathless, and touched him.

"Annabel." It was Gabriel's voice, and it seemed to come from the back of some distant star, instead of just behind her. "Come away now and rest."

She shook her head and sniffled, unwilling to leave. As long as she was there, she told herself, grasping Nicholas's hand, he couldn't slip away. He would remember to draw breath. Hadn't she left Susannah, just for a few moments, and come back to find her gone?

"I'll tend to Nicholas, Annabel." That was Jessie, standing now on the opposite side of the bed, holding a basin in her arms.

Full of fire and fight, enough to sustain herself and Nicholas, too, Annabel raised her gaze to Jessie. "You have been kind, Jessie," she said evenly, and in a steady tone, "and I owe you a great debt. But I am Nicholas's mother, and I will look after him."

"Annabel—" Gabriel began, reasonably, but she shook his hand from her shoulder.

"No," she said. "I will not leave him."

Jessie glanced at Gabriel, then sighed. "Very well," she capitulated gently. "But at least let me help."

Grudgingly, Annabel nodded her assent.

Jessie set the basin on a nightstand, drew a chair up to Nicholas's bedside, and sat down. "He has a fever," she said, "and he's covered with blood. Let me wash him, Annabel. The water will soothe him, just as it has always soothed you."

Annabel had been about to protest until Jessie mentioned the restorative power of a simple bath. Again, grudgingly, she nodded, and Jessie tore a generous bit of cloth into two pieces.

Together, the women gently wiped away the crimson stains that marred Nicholas's flesh, along with the inevitable residue of trail dirt, missed by the doctor when he made hasty preparations for surgery.

Afterward Nicholas began to sweat profusely, and Annabel hoped that was a good sign. She was near collapse, after the hard ride over the range to Parable—they'd left the chuck wagon behind for the cook to drive, and she'd ridden behind Gabriel, on his gelding—but fright sustained her. It was good for that much, at least, this terror that filled her like a second soul.

Twilight had arrived when Gabriel brought a cot into the room and calmly undressed Annabel to her camisole and drawers. He persuaded her to lie down, like a child told to take a nap, by promising that she needn't sleep.

Still clasping Nicholas's unmoving hand, she dropped helplessly into a shallow and fitful slumber. In her dream she was a young mother again, and Nicholas was small and sick, curled between her and Gabriel in their bed at the ranch house, battling scarlet fever. The disease had carried away many children, not just their own Susannah, but this time Annabel and Gabriel had barred death's way with their own bodies, refusing to let their son go.

"What the hell happened out there?" Gabriel snapped, in Jessie's study, glaring at Jake Swingler over the rim of a brandy glass. Upstairs, Nicholas lay torn apart, maybe dying. Annabel was hardly in better shape; Gabriel knew that if he lost his son, he might well lose his wife as well, from grief. And regret.

The lawman, tall and barrel-shaped, sighed and averted his eyes, gazing with interest at the contents of his own glass. Like Gabriel, he was standing, too agitated to sit, too drained to pace.

"The boy didn't do what I told him to," Swingler replied in a musing tone, as though he were seeing the whole scene unfolding in his brandy.

"Damn it, tell me how my son came to be shot!" Gabriel was ready to throttle an explanation out of Swingler, if that was what he had to do.

"There was a robbery attempt on the ore wagons. Maybe twenty men behind it, some of them hired on by Nicholas himself, as guards or drivers." The marshal's unremarkable face contorted slightly at the memory, but he met Gabriel's gaze straight on. "I was there too, with a posse from over at Sidney, keeping out of sight, of course. When all hell broke loose, Nicholas stood his ground instead of taking cover right away, like we planned. He was caught in the crossfire."

Gabriel closed his eyes for a moment, imagining the incident in all too vivid detail. "Nicholas deliberately hired the thieves?" he asked, because even the pain that thought caused him was a welcome distraction.

"Yes," Swingler admitted, with another sigh. "He had a hand in that, and in the rustling, too. I put him up to it."

"What?" Gabriel rasped the word, and the desire to choke the marshal with his bare hands mounted dangerously.

Swingler had the gall to smile. "That kid's got more guts than a grizzly cub. Came to me about eighteen months ago and said he thought Horncastle and some of his friends were the ones stealing from you, the government, and just about everybody in between. I don't have to tell you how many stage and train robberies there've been in the last year or so, not to mention the cattle you've lost. We didn't have any proof, though. It was Nicholas's say-so against Jack's, and of course Jack had the better reputation of the two. So Nicholas and I cooked up a scheme between us, to catch them good and proper, preferably in the act. Nicholas spent a long time winning a trusted place in that gang."

"Somebody might have mentioned this to me," Gabriel suggested murderously, flailing, inwardly, in a wave of fury, sorrow, and the profoundest relief. "You, for instance. Or that damned fool boy, lying up there with a hole in his belly!"

"That wouldn't have done at all, Gabe, and you know it," Swingler argued fearlessly. "You'd have put a stop to it if I'd spoken up, and there just wasn't anybody else suited to the job. Nicholas was the right age, and he already had a name as a hell-raiser and something of a rebel. Even then, he had to show Horncastle and the others that he had the stomach for holding up trains and stagecoaches."

"Sweet Jesus," Gabriel whispered, as a headache

seized him at the base of his skull and shook him like a rag doll in a dog's teeth. "Trains—stagecoaches? It went that far—Nicholas's part, I mean?"

Swingler nodded with a certain pride. "Always turned his share over to me as soon as he could, of course, and I returned it to the rightful owners."

Gabriel sank into a chair. "By God," he breathed, "if that kid weren't fighting for his life right now, I swear I'd jerk him out of that bed and tan his hide for him."

The marshal's voice was gruff but gentle. "You hold on, you and that lady of yours. Nicholas is tough, and he'll pull through this, if only so he can spit in Jack Horncastle's eye at the trial."

Gabriel looked up, saw Olivia Drummond standing in the open doorway, her eyes big and her skin washed clean of color.

He rose immediately, crossed to her, and took her arm, leading her to a chair.

Oh, yes, Nicholas would fight to live, all right. But not because of his old rivalry with Horncastle, or any hope of glory for all his reckless deeds. No, he'd fight because this young woman was waiting for him—this quiet, unpretentious beauty who had struck the once-impervious Nicholas to the soul with a tea-party smile.

Swingler made his excuses and quietly left, and Gabriel went to the liquor cabinet and poured a dose of sherry for the schoolteacher.

"Drink this," he ordered, holding it out to her.

She accepted the slender glass with trembling hands, sipped, made a face, and sipped again. After a few moments she began to relax a little.

"Will he die?" she whispered, fair choking on the

words, when Gabriel sat down across from her. Her eyes were desolate, pleading. "They say it was a robbery, but that's all I know."

Gently Gabriel explained what had happened, marveling a little himself as he told the tale. At the end, he asked quietly, "Would you like to see Nicholas?"

"His mother—his aunt—" She spread her hands in a small but eloquent gesture.

"They'll make a place for you," Gabriel said. He'd see to it, if that was necessary, though he doubted any problem would arise. Such occasions usually engendered unity among women, not division.

Olivia hesitated only a moment, then bolted from the room. Moments later Gabriel heard her hurrying up the stairs.

His own mood was an almost untenable blend of worry and pride in the brave, if foolish, son he'd raised. He set aside his brandy, rose from his chair, and wandered out onto Jessie's front porch, hoping the evening air would revive him a little.

Instead, leaning against the whitewashed railing, bracing himself with his hands, Gabe found his attention focused on the Samhill Saloon—specifically the third-floor window, the one he knew was Julia's. Already, although it wasn't yet dark, golden light spilled through the glass, warm as a beacon.

Gabe wanted to go to Julia, wanted to tell her about Nicholas, about Annabel and his feelings for her, and, of course, about the child he was certain Annabel carried. He dared not approach his old friend, however, not only because Julia herself had forbidden him to do so but because he knew Annabel would never understand. The peace between his wife and him was a fragile one, and he had no intention of undermining it.

Still, he was lonely in a way unlike anything he'd ever experienced before, not when his mother was captured or when Susannah died or when Annabel left. He felt fractured inside, as though the specter of the bullet that had lodged in Nicholas's body had splintered inside his own.

There was every chance that his only son would not live through the coming night, and no matter if the new baby was a boy, no matter if there were a dozen more to follow, Nicholas could never be replaced.

Gabe wanted to weep, but he would have had to be in better spirits to do that, so he just stood there, counting his breaths, holding himself upright, staring at Julia's window.

"Why don't you go to her?" Annabel's voice startled him to the marrow of his bones; he had not heard her open the door or step out onto the porch. He had, indeed, believed that she was sound asleep.

Gabe stood up straight and turned to meet Annabel's gaze squarely. Her lovely face was ravaged with fear and grieving, her hair slipping from its pins, though she wore a fresh dress. There was no anger in her eyes, no recrimination, only an expression of resignation that broke his heart into brittle pieces.

Gabe ignored the question and drew Annabel into his arms. "How is Nicholas?" he asked, infinitely relieved when she did not pull away but simply allowed him to hold her. Annabel rarely stood still for an embrace unless it was a part of their lovemaking; receiving simple affection was difficult for her.

"I don't know," she said, her voice muffled by his shirtfront. Then she looked up at him, her eyes searching his face. "I was serious before, Gabriel. If you need to see Miss Sermon, then you should go to her."

Gabe shook his head. "It wouldn't be right. You know that as well as I do."

Annabel smiled sadly and pressed her cheek against his chest. He felt her tears through the fabric of his shirt. "Go and sit with Nicholas for a while, then. Olivia is there, poor thing. Jessie and I will be making supper. As Jessie says, the rest of us have to keep body and soul together if we're going to be any good to Nicholas."

Gabe kissed her forehead. "I love you, Annabel," he said.

She touched his hair. "I know you do," she answered. "And since we're making declarations here, let me just say that I love you too, Mr. McKeige."

He embraced her again and went inside, up the stairs, into Nicholas's room.

He had been there for some time, trying to tether Nicholas to earth by sheer force of will, before he realized that Annabel hadn't followed him back into the house.

Annabel entered the Samhill Saloon by the back stairs, paying no heed to the shocked expressions of employees and patrons alike as she walked along the second-floor hallway.

Julia Sermon could have seen Annabel's approach from her window, or perhaps someone had run to her with the news that Gabriel McKeige's wife was on her way. Either way, it didn't matter. Annabel had no energy for wondering; every moment away from Nicholas's bedside was precious to her and dearly bought with the coin of her very soul. Therefore, she was glad when the madam met her halfway.

Annabel had never seen Julia up close, and she

might, under other circumstances, have been taken aback by the woman's dark beauty and innate poise. As it was, she merely said, "Might we speak alone?"

"Of course," Julia replied, and her brown eyes were bright with compassion. She'd heard about the shooting, of course; such news traveled like fire over dry grass in towns as small as Parable. She turned and led the way up another, smaller staircase, and into a well-appointed sitting room.

When Julia indicated that Annabel should take a seat, Annabel shook her head in polite refusal. She couldn't help noticing, even in her distracted state of mind, that the madam, her legendary rival and nemesis, wore a modest, high-collared dress of brown sateen, with her hair in a loose chignon. Nothing like the gaudy silks, laces, and taffetas such women reputedly wore.

Julia smiled gently. "I guess I'm not what you expected."

"No," Annabel answered frankly. She was conscious of Nicholas, pulled toward him by some spiritual umbilical cord, but she was only human and could not help but imagine Gabriel in that feminine, fussy room. All the chairs seemed too small and too flimsy, the tables too timorous, the couch too short.

"I've heard what happened to your Nicholas. I'm sorry," Julia said.

Annabel's throat closed momentarily, and she squeezed her eyes shut to hold back tears. "Thank you," she said. "But I haven't come to talk about my son. It's my husband I want to discuss."

Julia frowned, but her expression was in no way unkind. "Surely this isn't the proper time, Mrs. McKeige—"

"This is the only time, Miss Sermon," Annabel responded. "You are Gabriel's friend, and he is yours, and he needs to confide in you just now."

Julia averted her eyes briefly, and when they returned to Annabel's face, they were full of bewilderment and pride. "I won't pretend that I'm not fond of your husband," she said. "Nor can I say that I understand what you're asking of me. Gabriel and I have never had a—a conjugal relationship."

"If I thought you had," Annabel answered, "I would have brought a shotgun." She approached Julia on an impulse and took both the woman's hands in her own. "Nicholas is Gabriel's only son, and Gabriel loves him more than his own life. He needs to tell someone how he's hurting, and he won't turn to me or to Jessie because he believes he has to be strong for us. Gabriel's told me that you have a gift for listening and that he's found solace in your confidence before. I'm asking you to help him now, for his sake, and for Nicholas's."

Tears glistened along Julia's lower lashes. "If you're certain—"

Annabel interrupted with a nod and urged Julia toward the door with a little tug on her hand.

Julia sniffled, shook her head in wonderment, and followed Annabel's lead.

They walked down the main staircase together, through the smoky saloon, and between the swinging doors that opened onto the street. Annabel felt eyes watching them from every direction, but she paid no heed, for she had just two concerns in all the world just then: Nicholas and Gabriel.

Jessie was standing on her porch when they arrived, one hand to her throat, eyes as big as Charlie's flapjacks. "My Lord," she marveled, but she stepped aside to let Julia pass, followed close behind by Annabel.

Annabel settled Julia in the study and offered her a choice of tea or sherry.

Jittery, Julia chose the sherry, and she was pacing back and forth, sipping from a cordial glass, when Annabel left her to mount the stairs.

Nicholas's condition obviously hadn't changed, but his bandaged chest was still rising and falling rhythmically, and for the moment, that was enough.

Olivia sat beside the bed, her chair drawn up close, one hand resting on Nicholas's forehead and one on his arm. Gabriel was staring down into his son's face as though by doing so he could share his own strength and somehow will him to hold on to life.

Annabel said nothing, but simply watched Gabriel, and presently he felt her gaze and looked up. The bleak suffering she saw in his face all but crushed her.

Olivia did not seem aware of either of them but only of Nicholas, which, Annabel supposed, was just as well. The schoolteacher was probably the only woman in town who didn't know Annabel had just gone into a brothel to fetch her husband's alleged mistress.

"Someone's waiting downstairs to see you," Annabel said.

"They can damn well go away, then," Gabriel answered.

"That would be awkward. You see, it was my idea that she come here, not her own."

Gabriel paled. "Julia?" he asked, incredulous.

Annabel nodded.

Instead of looking pleased or relieved, as Annabel

had expected, Gabriel was clearly angry, not to mention stunned. "Great God," he hissed. "You didn't send for her?"

"I went and got her personally," Annabel replied, undaunted.

Gabriel bent to Nicholas, touched his cheek tenderly with the backs of his fingers, then strode out of the room without a word or glance for Annabel, closing the door rather crisply behind him.

Julia did not, Gabriel noticed, attempt to touch him or even to move toward him. She simply watched him as he entered Jessie's study, where she waited, her dark eyes swimming with sympathy and with sorrows of her own. Sorrows he well knew.

"I am so sorry," she said.

Gabriel kept his distance, closing the study doors but leaning back against them. "Annabel shouldn't have brought you here," he responded, after acknowledging her condolence with a brief nod.

"I know," Julia said, with the specter of a smile. "Mrs. McKeige seemed to believe you would find my presence something of a comfort."

Gabriel sighed. "As little as half an hour ago I thought the same thing," he said. He had always been bluntly honest with Julia, and she with him. The practice had facilitated their unconventional alliance. Both had been crippled by events in their lives, and each had found solace, if not healing, in the understanding of the other.

"And now?"

"And now I'm not looking for comfort. That's my son up there, barely alive, with blood-soaked bandages wrapped around his middle. Why the hell should I feel anything but pain and sadness and anger—and more fear than I ever thought I could sustain without going out of my mind?"

"A good question," Julia said. "You have Annabel now, and that's as it should be. Me, I'm getting tired of this old town, feeling ready to move on. It would seem that we no longer need each other."

Gabriel closed his eyes for a moment. "I'm grateful, Julia," he told her, and he meant it. She had seen him through other, lesser agonies than the one he faced now. But so much sorrow might have been avoided if he hadn't sought his comfort with her twelve years before, instead of going after Annabel and Nicholas, bringing them home. "And I'm sorry."

"Whatever for?" Julia asked, and she looked and sounded sincere. "You were there to look after me when I was little and my pa tried to come sneaking around the ranch. You saw to it that he couldn't hurt me anymore. I was a friend to you, as best I could be, but it's finally over. We both should have moved on a long time ago, Gabe. We were a fine pair of fools, you and I, however honorable our intentions."

"What will you do now?" Gabe asked. She'd often spoken of leaving Parable behind, starting over in some large, bustling city, a place with theaters and symphonies, libraries and emporiums. Someplace where a woman's past didn't matter quite so much, and memories couldn't be reinforced by familiar sights and sounds.

"I'll wait for news of Nicholas," she said. "Then I suppose I'll transfer my money to a bank in San Francisco or Chicago or New Orleans, sell the saloon, and leave. Like I should have done a long time ago."

"Name your price," Gabe said. He meant for the saloon, of course. It was the least he could do, for a friend like Julia.

Julia smiled at the suggestion, then shook her head. "No, Gabriel. I will not sell you the saloon. What chance would you have with Annabel, if you came home one fine day with the keys to a brothel jingling on your belt?"

He returned her smile, though he wanted nothing so much as to turn away, to flee back up the stairs, to kneel beside Nicholas's bed and weep for his son, openly and without shame, the way Jessie and Annabel and Olivia did.

"You're right, as usual," he said, with a break in his voice. "But if you need anything—"

"Just send word over to the saloon when Nicholas gets better. That's all I want or need from you now, darlin'."

"Thank you," Gabe said, with a promissory nod, moving aside and opening the study doors so she could pass.

"For what?" Julia inquired, facing him on the threshold.

"For believing he's going to recover."

Julia reached up and touched Gabe's beard-roughened face. "That's no trick, Gabriel McKeige," she said, with tenderness. "Nicholas is your son, and Annabel's. He's too ornery to give up."

"Let me know if you need anything," Gabe told her again, his voice still somewhat hoarse.

She touched his shoulder. "I need to know you're happy," she replied. "That's all."

With that, Julia left Jessie's house, sparing him not so much as a backward glance, and Gabe blessed her for that, as well as all the times she'd proved herself a fine and trustworthy companion.

"Good-bye," he said under his breath.

Fifteen

NICHOLAS'S FIRST CONSCIOUS THOUGHT WAS THAT HE needed to piss. His second was that he must be alive; in heaven, allegedly, he would have shed his mortal shell and would therefore be untroubled by such mundane matters as passing water. In hell, that simple function might serve to put out too many fires.

He imagined a concerted effort by a singed and repentant population, and a raw chuckle ripped itself from his throat, almost as painful as the wound in his side. It was dark as a pit, and lacking the wit even to catalog his faculties, he wondered if there had been a second bullet. Maybe he'd been struck in the head and gone blind.

"Nicholas?"

His father's voice, the word as broken as the sound Nicholas had made.

"Yeah," Nicholas said, though it cost him. It was just ordinary darkness, he concluded, with relief, when he heard the striking of a match, saw light flare, catch on the wick of the lamp beside the bed, spilling a soft glow into the room.

Gabe produced a cup of water, after some fumbling, and when he held the cup to Nicholas's mouth, using his free hand to raise his son's head from the pillow, Nicholas saw a suspicious glint in his father's eyes.

"It's good to see you, boy," Gabe said.

Nicholas managed a smile; he was too weak to do much else. He took more water, saw his mother appear at Gabe's shoulder, her face weary and rapturous. In that moment many of his most private doubts about her were resolved and put away for the childish things they were.

"Horncastle and the others?" he croaked.

"In jail," Gabe answered. "More than a dozen of them."

Miss Annabel waited until Gabe stepped back, though with visible impatience, and then bent to kiss Nicholas's forehead. The bustle had roused Olivia, who bolted sleepily out of a chair on the opposite side of the bed.

"Is the whole town in here?" Nicholas joked, again at considerable price.

Olivia began to cry softly, smiling at the same time, putting Nicholas in mind of the sun shining through a passing rain shower. She murmured something—a prayer or an imprecation, he couldn't tell which—then left the room.

Nicholas remembered what had awakened him and stated it baldly.

Miss Annabel went out, and Gabe produced the appropriate receptacle. Nicholas hoped the women would give him time to finish before the celebration began.

"You can't be serious," Gabe said, when he saw an old couch of Jessie's being hauled down the main stairway one morning by two hired men, a week after Nicholas's return from the near-dead. He'd been on the range since dawn, with several of his men, branding cattle, and he was too dirty to venture more than a few steps into his sister's spit-polished house.

Annabel, directing the operation from the top of the stairs, with all the concentration of a Roman general, did not spare him a glance. "Of course I'm serious," she replied. "No one buys a house on a whim, Gabriel."

She was actually furnishing the Jennings plase, apparently planning to move in, after all that had happened between them. Did none of it matter—the concessions they'd made, the apologies, the declarations? The promises?

Gabe was stung, and he was furious, but he wouldn't say a damned word, not in front of the men Annabel had hired to wrestle spare furniture down from Jessie's attic.

Annabel looked at him, albeit fleetingly, and he saw that familiar spark of determination in her eyes. He stood aside to allow the couch-bearers to pass onto the porch.

"Damn it, Annabel," he rasped, "what did I do now?"

She sighed. "Good heavens, Gabriel, why do you think everything in the universe is somehow your doing, as though you were some kind of deity? Nicholas is still too ill to travel to the ranch, yet it isn't proper for him to stay here, when everybody in Parable knows he's courting Olivia Drummond."

Outside, the slave-men cursed and muttered as they maneuvered the ugly, cumbersome sofa into the back of a wagon rented from the livery stable. "Wouldn't it be easier to move Miss Drummond?" Gabe asked, in what he hoped was a reasonable and diplomatic manner.

"Where would we put her?" Annabel countered, somewhat impatiently. She had her hands on her hips, and the morning's efforts had raised an appealing moisture around her hairline and neck. Small tendrils of hair clung to her cheeks, her forehead, her throat, and the sight stirred Gabe in a very fundamental way. "No, Gabriel," she went on, "this is the only solution. Please do not make things more difficult by arguing."

Gabe slapped his hat against his thigh, tightened his jaw, and forcibly relaxed it again. "Annabel, you are my wife and—"

She forgot the men jostling the couch into place and looked up. The spark in her eyes would have set wet newspaper ablaze. "Yes, Gabriel, I am your wife. But that never has and never will give you license to order me about, so I hope that isn't what you are about to do."

He closed his eyes, counted mentally. Lost his way among simple numbers. "I apologize," he said in a furious hiss. "I thought we had agreed to reconcile."

"We have agreed not to kill each other," Annabel said in sunny tones.

"But you said—"

"And I meant it," Annabel broke in. "I love you. Perhaps the best way to continue our present truce is to maintain separate residences. For the time being, at least."

Gabe's mouth dropped open, and before he could assemble a sensible response, Annabel rushed on into new and different atrocities.

"Did I tell you I bought the saloon?" she asked, as lightly as if she were confiding the purchase of a particularly expensive hat.

Gabe could barely force his answer past his teeth. "You did what?"

Annabel smiled, pleased, as always, that she'd shocked him. "I think you heard me quite clearly, Gabriel," she said, with eminent reason. "You needn't worry that I plan to operate the place, of course. I intend to close it down."

"Close it down?" Dazed, Gabe imagined a townfull of cowboys, just back from a long cattle drive, with nowhere to vent a head of steam. No saloon? Hell, a town without a church or a general store had a better chance of surviving.

Annabel stepped out onto the porch. "Mind you don't scrape the woodwork, carrying that in," she called to her beleaguered drudges. "I want it in front of the bay window, facing the fireplace."

"Yes, missus," one of the men called back, ducking his head and tugging at his hat. His partner was busy tying down the load of miscellaneous loot, generously donated by Jessie. Or had she just seen a chance to get shut of it?

"Annabel," Gabe warned.

She smiled up at him in that deliberately beatific way calculated to stick under his hide like a burr. "Yes?"

He spat a swearword. "You can't just shut down the

saloon. There won't be anywhere for men to go of a night."

"They can stay at home," Annabel suggested, as though the idea were a concept freshly born. "Talk with their wives. Go over school lessons with their children. Read good books. That sort of thing."

"You don't understand," Gabe insisted. He was doing pretty well at holding his temper, he thought, considering that he'd have chucked just about anybody else over the porch rail into the flowerbed by that point.

"I do," Annabel countered sweetly. "This is the beginning of a new age in Parable. Why, without a saloon, the place will be a regular Eden." She was baiting him, he knew it, and yet he could not resist taking the hook.

"Without a saloon," Gabe argued hotly, and in all sincerity, "there will be chaos!"

She was undaunted, as usual. When Annabel got into one of these moods, there was no reasoning with her. On some level, of course, this temperance campaign had its beginning in the ways of her ne'er-do-well father and how he'd dragged her from pillar to post, but she would never admit that, damn cuss-headed woman.

"We'll see, won't we?" she said.

"No," Gabriel responded, "we won't see, because if you close that place, I'll just put up another one, bigger and better. I'll build ten of them. Damn it, Annabel, I'm not Ellery Latham, and you don't have to fight me as if I were!"

Annabel put her hands on her hips and narrowed her eyes, but he knew he'd pierced her supercilious attitude, however small the puncture. "You would, wouldn't you, just to spite me!"

He bent until his nose was a fraction of an inch from hers. "I would indeed, Mrs. McKeige. And you'd be wise not to make a challenge out of it," he advised. Even though Gabe was angry, he was exhilarated, too, like a man who had just set a flag on a high peak.

Annabel rose on tiptoe, arms still akimbo. "And you would be wise not to interpret it as one," she shot back. "I am merely trying to make a contribution to this community. Do you want your child to grow up in a pit of sin?"

Gabe found himself grinning, somewhat after the fact. It wasn't all amusement, though; some of it was surprise. He supposed that was one of the things he found most endearing—not to mention exasperating—about Annabel. A man had a better chance of predicting spring weather or a turn of the cards than guessing what she would do or say next.

"Annabel," he said patiently, "the world is a pit of sin."

"Well, I plan to sweep one corner of it clean," Annabel answered, flushed with righteous resolution. "If you won't help, kindly don't hinder."

Gabe laughed, hooked his arm around Annabel's waist, hauled her close, and kissed her smartly. Then he turned, whistling, went back to his horse, which was tethered at the gate, mounted, and rode away. He couldn't rightly remember why he'd made the trip in the first place, but he supposed it would come back to him in time.

The conversation on his aunt Jessie's front porch rose softly to Nicholas on the summer air, like faint music riding on curls of smoke, and made him smile. He was sitting up, at long last, propped against the headboard with what seemed like every pillow in the house fluffed up behind him.

He'd thought a lot about his parents in recent days, perhaps because of his enforced idleness—that made a man consider many things he might otherwise have kept at bay. It had come to him that the exchange between his pa and Miss Annabel was some kind of game, not a frivolous one, either, but an exercise of the intellect and the spirit, and probably unconscious on both their parts.

Miss Annabel's original flight, he'd decided, had been a move, like the challenging advance of a pawn on a chessboard, and a daring one. One that, for some reason, his father had chosen not to counter.

Or maybe, by not responding, Gabriel McKeige *had* countered. They were a mystery, those two, and even though they had established a truce of sorts, it was plain that the game was far from ended. They had simply learned to play it with more skill and patience.

Nicholas sighed and turned his head to look at the woman he had met only a few days before. Olivia was dozing in the chair beside his bed, snoring prettily, a copy of *Gulliver's Travels*—his perennial favorite—open in her lap.

He wondered how it would be, a union between the two of them. There'd be no lack of passion, that was for certain. Nicholas felt that profoundly, and he knew by the few kisses they'd contrived to steal that Olivia, though innocent, wanted his lovemaking, would give herself up to it with abandon, allowing him to teach her and, by her very lack of experience, teaching him.

Beneath the thin sheets of his sickbed, Nicholas felt himself stir and then harden. He tilted his head back and closed his eyes, willing the damn thing to go limp again, since there would be no relief in the foreseeable future, but his efforts met with resounding failure.

It looked, he mused, upon opening his eyes again, like somebody had set up a tent between his legs.

Olivia, he discovered in a sidelong glance, was awake and looking too. Her color was high, and she swallowed, but she didn't shift her gaze. Not, that is, until she realized that Nicholas was watching her.

She dropped her head.

"It will never do, your being so shy," Nicholas said quietly. Gently. In the three or four years since he'd lain with his first woman, an eager employee of Miss Julia Sermon's, he'd never bedded a virgin. While he ached to make Olivia his own—the proof couldn't be denied—he was nervous about it, too, and glad there was plenty of time. "When we're married, you'll see a hell of a lot more than a rise in the bedclothes."

Olivia was smiling, though tentatively, when she made herself meet his eyes. An instant later her expression was agitated again. "I never heard of anybody falling in love the way we did," she fretted. "I keep thinking it must be a mistake, that it's impossible. And yet . . ."

Nicholas reached out, at some cost, and clasped her hand. "And yet?" he prompted, because her sentence had fallen away, like a pebble into a deep ravine.

"It's like something out of the love stories I've been reading ever since I was a girl. I looked at you and . . . well, it wasn't as if we'd never met but rather as if we'd been parted a long time ago and just found each other again."

"Come here," Nicholas said, "and kiss me."

She glanced with alarm and no little interest at the monument to his desire, but then she came to sit beside him on the mattress, blushing and a little stiff.

He laid a hand on the back of her neck and pulled her down, so that her mouth met his, but before he could soothe her fears and get down to the serious business of kissing her as he'd intended, the door sprang open.

"I knew I was right," Miss Annabel announced, without recrimination, causing Nicholas to wilt instantaneously. "Nicholas McKeige, you have no name as a gentleman, being a scoundrel of wide renown, and your reputation can only be enhanced by such an episode. Olivia, on the other hand, has a great deal to lose. Get off that bed immediately, Miss Drummond."

Olivia scooted back onto the chair, mortified, but Nicholas regarded his mother with a level and unrepentant stare. He knew Olivia would have bolted from the room if it hadn't been for his firm grip on her hand.

"You will please excuse us for a few minutes, Miss Drummond?" Miss Annabel inquired, in that same sweet, chimelike voice—a trill nobody but Nicholas or his father, and maybe Jessie, would have had the temerity to ignore. "I'm sure you'd like a nice cup of tea and a few minutes to recover your dignity."

Olivia flung an imploring glance at Nicholas and tugged, and he released her hand, so that she could make her escape. Which, of course, she immediately did.

Miss Annabel closed the door behind her and came to stand looking down at Nicholas. Her expression would have made it clear enough that she was about to give him what-for, even if her elbows hadn't jutted out, pointed, from her sides, like the wings of a ruffled hen.

"I think she may be too timid for you," Miss Annabel said.

Nicholas chuckled, partly because his mother had surprised him again and partly because he was relieved. "Seems to me, this family could use someone with a little less temperament," he observed.

Miss Annabel sat down in the chair Olivia had occupied. *Gulliver's Travels* lay on the bedside table now, and she lifted it, perused its worn pages, and then set it aside again. "That's one of the things I never suspected about you, Nicholas," she said, in a tone of sad thoughtfulness. "That you read as voraciously as your father, I mean."

"There wasn't much else to do," he answered carefully, "once the chores were done and supper was over." Things were better between him and Miss Annabel—since his shooting he could not doubt that she bore him a mother's pure and devoted love—but that didn't mean he wasn't furious with her. He was.

She touched his hair. "So many prayers, never heard. So many stories, never read. Oh, Nicholas, I'm sorry—sorry for my own sake as well as yours."

He looked away. "I'm not that little kid anymore, Miss Annabel. You don't need to apologize."

She laid a hand on his cheek and turned his face toward her, though gently. "Oh, but you are that very same boy, Nicholas. Somewhere, deep inside, he's there, outraged because I didn't come when he called out at night after a bad dream or too many green apples." She sighed. "I was wrong to let you go. I've admitted that on several occasions. But if you're not willing to come part of the way to meet me, I don't know what else I can do."

Nicholas didn't recognize the sound of his own

voice, "Is that why you came in here? To talk about the past?"

Miss Annabel's hand fell away, to lie in her lap with its counterpart. "I came to tell you that you and I are moving to my house down the street," she said. "And it's obvious from the tomfoolery going on when I walked into this room that I've made the decision none too soon."

Nicholas rolled his eyes and would not permit the smile tempting his mouth to settle there. "The irony of that statement, Miss Annabel, is almost too much for me to resist. Because I am more of a gentleman than you will allow, I'll let it pass. Once."

Her flawless skin glowed with indignation and the undeniable fact that he was right. "Your father should have paddled you far more often," she blustered.

Nicholas laughed. "He might have, except he was never able to catch me. And when Pa's temper got the better part of his patience, Charlie always stepped in."

"Speaking of Charlie," Miss Annabel said, frowning, "I don't believe I've seen him since the day you were shot. Where do you suppose he's gotten off to?"

The question had never troubled Nicholas—until now. Charlie was first and always an Indian, and even though he'd been around as long as Nicholas could remember, he did what he pleased, when it pleased him. Still, Miss Annabel was right—it was odd, his not being there.

Nicholas felt the hairs rise on the nape of his neck, but for his mother's sake he made light of the matter. "I suppose he's up in the hills someplace, taking a little rest from his cooking duties or parlaying with his patron saint—it's a bobcat, I think."

Miss Annabel pretended to swat him. "You are irreverent, and I don't like it."

Nicholas made a face. "I don't care," he said. "Would you send Olivia back in here?" He indicated the book on the night table with a toss of his head. "She was right at the part where Gulliver meets the Yahoos."

"I'll give you Yahoos," Miss Annabel said with mock sternness. It clearly pleased her to mother him, however belatedly, and because it sometimes pleased him to be mothered, he tolerated it. "And don't look for Olivia to return anytime soon. I mean to keep her busy helping me establish my household."

"I have the same thought in mind," Nicholas answered, "with a few variations, of course." All he had to do was survive—not such a simple trick, even now. He felt as if he'd been taken apart at the hinges and scattered six ways from Sunday.

"Get out of that bed, you malingerer," Miss Annabel teased, albeit with a straight face. "You are obviously well enough to resume your normal schedule."

Nicholas winked at her, reached for his book, and, frowning with concentration, tried to lose himself in the familiar exploits of Gulliver in the land of Yahoos. In reality, he was thinking about Charlie's disappearance, Jack Horncastle's gang, down the street in that inadequate jailhouse, and the fact that his draw, thanks to injury and inactivity, would be about as formidable as a preacher's handshake.

In Annabel's opinion, Miss Julia Sermon's departure from Parable was a modest affair when compared with her own stirring arrival. The former madam, dressed as circumspectly as a pastor's wife and carrying only a small valise, boarded the stagecoach tha passed through on Tuesday morning. Her other be longings had either been consigned to the freigh company for shipping or parceled out among her girls who wailed sonorously on the wooden sidewalks an waved their tattered silk handkerchiefs in farewell a the stage pulled out.

Watching the phenomenon through the bank's fron windows, Annabel examined her conscience, where the purchase of the Samhill Saloon was concerned and could not acquit herself of selfish motives. Al though her plan to rid the town of free-flowing whiskey, card playing, and prostitution was a worthy one—if somewhat grandiose, even for her—Annabe could not deny, in the privacy of her own mind, a least, that she'd wanted Miss Sermon gone. Forever.

She bit her lower lip, chastened by these reflections. Miss Sermon was merely a woman, not a monster—a mere mortal with sorrows aplenty of her own. Gabriel was a man grown, with a good mind and a conscience; he would always do what he thought was right, which meant she could safely trust in him. And she suspected he'd been correct, that recent morning on Jessie's front porch, when he'd told her, in so many words, that shutting down the saloon would cause more problems than it would solve.

The bank manager, Oldmixen, came to stand beside Annabel, smiling and rocking back on his heels. He had a habit of sucking on his teeth that made her queasy.

"I don't suppose word has gotten out yet that you plan to turn the saloon into a hotel," he said. They had just finished signing the contracts for the purchase of the saloon, though Miss Sermon had not come in person to see to her part.

Annabel didn't meet his eyes. It was bad enough to listen to the man, without looking at him, too. "I'll make the announcement on Sunday morning, after church," she replied, perhaps a bit defensively. She was not feeling well, and Nicholas, ensconced against his will in the house she had bought and furnished with a jumble of Jessie's castoffs, was proving to be a recalcitrant patient. Worst of all, she had not seen Gabriel since she'd first told him she intended to purchase the saloon and close its doors, and she found that she missed his company most sorely.

Annabel's pride wouldn't allow her to search Gabriel out, and yet the temptation grew stronger with every passing day. It wasn't so much that she wanted his lovemaking, though of course she did. More than Gabriel's tenderness, more than his passion, however, Annabel missed their verbal sparring matches. She missed seeing him put on his spectacles and read.

Still, it was a heady thing to win a point against Gabriel McKeige—difficult to do and therefore rightfully relished.

". . . we'll all rest easier, once Captain Sommervale sends an armed guard to fetch Jack Horncastle and his men to Fort Duffield for trial."

Annabel's attention returned to Mr. Oldmixen. She had not thought much about the outlaws—there were a dozen or so of them, everyone knew, locked up in Parable's one-cell jailhouse. Hadn't thought of them, except for an occasional, wholly unchristian wish to avenge her son's shooting against their leader, that is.

"Nicholas will be called to testify at the trial," she said, realizing the import and the peril of her words only as she spoke them.

"Oh, yes," Oldmixen agreed. "It was a shock to this

town to learn that one of their favorite sons was nothing better than a common thief."

"Jack Horncastle is considerably more than that," Annabel said, recalling, with fresh anguish, the way Nicholas had looked the day of the shooting, broken and bleeding. So near death that, at times, he'd seemed almost transparent, and Annabel had thought once or twice, in her distress, that she might be able to put her hand right through him, like a mirage. Now, recalling it, she felt a chill settle deep into her spirit. "He would have killed my son, but for the grace of God."

The banker gazed uneasily toward the jailhouse; there was nothing much to see on the street, now that the stage was gone and Miss Sermon's girls, with no inkling that they were about to be dismissed, had straggled back into the shadowy confines of the saloon.

"I hope Captain Sommervale's detachment gets here soon," Oldmixen mused. "Holding a dozen men in that cell is like trying to force as many rattlers into a tobacco can. The walls are bound to give way to the pressure."

The pit of Annabel's stomach quivered, and her breakfast roiled dangerously close to the back of her throat. Since the day she realized Nicholas would recover, she had been rejoicing, but now she knew for certain what she had not allowed herself to suspect before—that he was not out of danger. He was up and about, his side thickly bandaged, but he tired easily, and when he wasn't sleeping or charming Miss Olivia Drummond in the parlor, he was fiddling with that .45 of his. Drawing it repeatedly, awkwardly, from its holster, drawing again, over and over, until he was white with fatigue and fresh pain.

Of course, Annabel thought, with growing horror. Nicholas wanted to regain his lost deftness for a specific reason, not just on general principle. How could she have thought he was merely passing the time? He expected to face Horncastle again, and not in the safety of an army courtroom.

Annabel's heart fluttered into her throat, like a small bird scared up from the brush, and she was so agitated that she made several grabs at the doorknob before she managed to catch hold of it.

"Mrs. McKeige," the bank manager cried, hurrying after her. "You've forgotten your deed."

Annabel paid him no mind, but instead dashed into the street. She nearly collided with Jeffrey Braithewait on the dim hay-and-manure-scented threshold of the livery stable, and for once she was glad to encounter him.

The rugged life seemed to agree with Jeffrey; he'd passed through the greenhorn stage with admirable quickness. Now he was almost appealing, and his manner was no longer abrasive.

"Annabel," he said, laughing, as he gripped her shoulders to steady her. "Where are you off to in such a hurry?"

She dragged in several deep breaths and released them slowly, but the technique failed to calm her as it usually did. "Jeffrey, tell me where to find Gabriel—take me to him."

Jeffrey's expression became somber, not out of jealousy, she was relieved to see, but with concern. "He's at one of the mines. The Silver Shadow, I think. Come along, and we'll hire a buggy to take us there."

Annabel's surrey was at the ranch, supposedly undergoing some kind of repair. "Thank you," she said, regaining her composure by slow degrees.

"What is the matter?" Jeffrey pressed, while one of the hands at the livery stable prepared the rig. "You look dreadful—not your usual blooming self at all, I'm afraid."

Annabel put a hand to her forehead, tried to smile, and couldn't. She wasn't given to panic, as a general rule, but the sudden awareness of this new and ominous threat had utterly unnerved her. "It's just that—well, I'm sure I'll sound like a hysterical mother, but . . . I'm afraid, Jeffrey."

The buggy was driven out into the sunlight, and Jeffrey helped her into the passenger seat before climbing in to take the reins. "Surely Nicholas is mending in a satisfactory fashion . . . ?"

How could she have been so blind? How could Gabriel?

"Annabel?" Jeffrey persisted, starting the horse and buggy toward the ranch with a smart slap of the reins.

"Damn it, Jeffrey," Annabel cried, "just drive!"

The trip to the Silver Shadow was made in difficult silence; Annabel could not bring herself to apologize, though she knew she must, and Jeffrey was understandably reluctant to pursue any sort of conversation. When they arrived, after almost an hour of hard driving, and Gabriel was summoned from the depths of the mine, black with dirt from head to foot when he came out of the ground, she felt a little foolish.

A fact that did not diminish her sense of purpose in the least.

"I must speak to you in private," she informed Gabriel, scrambling down from the buggy seat before either he or Jeffrey could help her, and nearly getting both feet tangled in her hem in the process.

"Nicholas . . . ?"

Annabel took Gabriel's arm and half pulled, half

dragged him away, paying no further heed to the state of his clothes and person. "Nicholas is fine," she hastened to assure her husband. "For the moment, at least."

Gabriel balked, glaring down at Annabel. "Damn it all to hell, Annabel, you nearly gave me a heart attack," he hissed, making precious little effort to keep his voice down. "What the devil is this about?"

Annabel ran her tongue over her lips. "It's—it's the way Nicholas keeps practicing—"

"'Practicing'?" The word seethed out of Gabriel, like froth from a boiling pot.

"With his forty-five," Annabel hastened to explain. "I don't know why we didn't see it, didn't realize—Gabriel, Nicholas fully expects to face Jack Horncastle and maybe others besides, in a gunfight."

At first, Gabriel looked baffled, but then Annabel could have sworn she saw him go pale beneath all that dirt. "Horncastle's in jail—you know that. So is the rest of his gang."

For the second time that day, a shiver traced its way down Annabel's spine. "No," she said. "There's someone else, don't you see? Someone who might be able to help the others break out."

Gabriel looked grim, and his grasp on Annabel's arm tightened. "Maybe that's where Charlie's been all this time," he speculated. "Hunting the man or men who slipped out of the trap."

Annabel nodded, and it wasn't until Gabriel wiped her cheek with a grubby thumb that she realized she'd been weeping.

Sixteen

GABRIEL'S JAWLINE WAS HARD, UNDER THE SOIL OF THE mine. Behind him, grim-looking mechanisms clattered and creaked, and men moved in their midst, garnering treasure from the earth. "I'm taking Nicholas home to the ranch, Annabel," he said, "and before you trouble yourself to protest, let me just say that I don't give a damn whether you approve or not."

Annabel was relieved, though in almost any other instance Gabriel's imperious and arbitrary attitude would have galled her.

"Go back to town and get his gear together," he went on, gesturing to one of the men to bring his horse. "I'll be there as soon as I've taken care of a few things here."

Annabel didn't raise the possibility that Nicholas would balk at leaving town—and specifically Olivia Drummond—because she knew that wouldn't matter to Gabriel any more than it did to her. He and Nicholas would just have to thrash that out between them.

Anyway, it was inevitable: Nicholas was going home, and, because she wasn't about to be parted from her son at this juncture, so was she.

Jeffrey dutifully drove Annabel to her house in Parable, where she thanked him hastily at the front gate. On that leg of the journey, they had talked, at least, though about relatively inconsequential things.

Nicholas, as Annabel had suspected, was not happy about the prospect of returning to the ranch, where he would be separated from Olivia, but he wasn't strong enough to fight back, and when Gabriel came for him, he had to content himself with arguing a futile case.

For the first time since her return, Annabel saw herself in her son, instead of just Gabriel, and she was mildly amused. She hadn't done Nicholas any favors by passing on to him her contrary nature, her obdurate independence, but at least she could be assured that he wouldn't stand by idle while life flowed past him like a river.

Olivia, grown less timorous in recent days, through almost constant exposure to one McKeige or another, was firm with Nicholas, ignoring his grumbling, helping Annabel to gather the few of his belongings she'd brought to her house—a shaving brush and razor, a comb, his favorite books, and two changes of clothes.

Gabriel, still clad in his mining clothes, escorted his son to the buckboard waiting in the street, helped him up into the box, and then returned to the gate to confer with Annabel. Olivia remained on the porch, at a diplomatic distance.

"You'll be coming to the ranch?" Gabe asked Annabel.

She nodded. "In a little while," she answered. "I have more to pack than Nicholas."

For a beat, Gabriel just looked at her, absorbing

what she'd said. "I'll send some men back with the buckboard in a few hours."

"I'll be ready a lot sooner than that, Gabriel McKeige," Annabel answered, with a lift of her chin, "and I don't need an escort."

Gabriel glanced at Nicholas, looking battered and a little disconsolate on the high seat of the wagon, and then turned back to Annabel. "This house is yours; you're free to give the orders here. On the ranch, I run things. You'll have men to accompany you, and that's the end of it."

Annabel sighed. "Very well," she said, but behind the concession was a small, hot pleasure that she would never, ever admit to feeling. "I'll see you at home, then."

With that, she waved at a scowling Nicholas, then turned and went back up the walk. Olivia, she noticed, was wearing a slight smile.

Two hours later, with a buckboard full of trunks and boxes behind her, Annabel set out for the ranch, with Hilditch for a driver and two armed cowboys for guards.

It was a surrender of sorts, her going back with most of her belongings, but she didn't care. She told herself that Nicholas was more important than her pride and her seemingly relentless need to prove to Gabriel that she could survive on her own.

And she had done just that. Gabriel had always been generous with her financially, but she could have paid her husband back every cent he'd ever given her, with interest—she kept a running tally in her head and knew exactly how much that was—and still lived on quite a grand scale. She wasn't about to do so, of course, being above all a prudent woman.

Upon reaching the ranch house, Annabel discovered straightaway that Nicholas had been deposited in his room. He was sound asleep, exhausted, looking guileless and very young.

Annabel crept out into the corridor and closed the door softly.

Gabriel was somewhere about; she didn't know precisely where, and it didn't matter. For a time—and Annabel was certain it would not be long, whether or not fortune favored the McKeiges—they were all three under one roof. She wanted to savor that, hold it as a talisman against the forces that might destroy them, or at least drive them apart.

Downstairs, in the kitchen, a lonely, too-tidy place without Charlie, Annabel built up the fire in the cookstove and began pumping water into kettles and pots. The room was steaming when, after forty-five minutes or so, Gabriel came in and collided with the bathtub in the fog.

"Surely you're not taking a bath in the middle of the day," he said. Through the mist, Annabel could see that he was still wearing the same clothes he'd had on when she'd summoned him from the bowels of the silver mine.

"No," Annabel said briskly, pouring the first kettleful into the tub. "You are. You look as though you've been digging for coal rather than silver, and furthermore, you're all done in and could use a bit of coddling. Take off your clothes."

Gabriel was taken aback by this command; he was used to giving orders, not taking them. "I have work to do," he said, but not very forcefully.

"Nonsense," Annabel replied, upending another kettle into the tub and raising a fresh geyser of steam. "The ranch can spare you for one afternoon, and it's not as if you have to scrabble for a living. Now stop fussing and get undressed before this water turns cold."

He sat down heavily on the bench next to the table, kicking off his boots as he unfastened his blackened shirt. He still looked very somber, as though he suspected an ambush of some sort.

After an anxious glance toward the doors and the window above the sink, Gabriel shed the last of his clothes and stuck one foot into the tub.

He gave an immediate howl and drew back, dirt-streaked and magnificent in his nakedness. Annabel decided to seduce him, even as he glowered at her.

"Damn it, woman, are you trying to scald the hide off me?"

She laughed and shook her head. "No, Gabriel," she answered. "I simply wish to make you fit for a lady's bed."

He flushed at that, under the layers of grime, and waited while Annabel pumped a bucketful of cold water and poured it into the tub.

"We can't make love in the middle of the day," he said, with a distinct lack of conviction, testing the bath again and finding it to his liking this time.

"This from a man who took me against a wall only last week?" Annabel teased, and had the pleasure of watching his manhood, impressive even at rest, take on exalted proportions. "Sit down, Gabriel—I'd need a ladder to wash you, standing up like that."

Gabriel lowered himself into the water and, on contact, gave a lusty sigh. "What's this about, Annabel?" he asked a moment later, clearly having retained his suspicions.

Annabel knelt beside the tub, the well-splashed floor wetting her skirts through at the knees, and took up a washcloth and a cake of soap. "Must everything be about something?" she countered. "I'm in a wifely mood—it must be the pregnancy."

"In that case," Gabriel said, with another sigh, closing his eyes in shameless bliss as Annabel began to lather and scrub his chest, "remind me to keep you pregnant from now on."

She laughed softly and continued her gentle but nonetheless brazen ministrations, rinsing the soapsuds from his midsection, then lashing each of his flat brown nipples once with the tip of her tongue.

Gabriel groaned. The tub was too small for his long legs, and his knees protruded from the water, along with something else—something Annabel took particular care in bathing.

Just when he seemed ready to take her on the kitchen floor amid pools of spilled water, Annabel withdrew to fetch a kettle she'd set aside for washing his hair.

"You are a demon," he said. His eyes held a hot, unholy glow as he watched her, and when she'd soaped and rinsed his hair, turning it golden again, he caught her around the waist, as she knelt there beside his tub, and opened the bodice of her dress, freeing her breasts from the flimsy camisole that had restrained them.

He took hungry suckle at her nipples, one and then the other, and she stroked his hair while he partook of her, her head flung back in capitulation and in conquest. It was at that point that Annabel's eager body betrayed her, and all power shifted to Gabriel.

He kissed her, consuming her, and would not allow her to close her dress.

Her every nerve seemed to pulse; her every inhibition had vanished with the rising steam.

"Go to our bedroom, Annabel," Gabriel said,

against her mouth, against her seeking, hungry mouth. "But do not take your clothes off. I want to do that."

She got, somehow, from her knees to her feet, every limb trembling. Perhaps Gabriel helped; she did not know. "Gabriel—" she pleaded.

"Go," he said again. Gruffly.

Annabel half fled, half stumbled up the rear stairway, and she was standing in front of her harp, so long silent and out of tune, when, mercifully, Gabriel entered the room, wearing only a towel around his middle. His flesh, newly scrubbed, sparkled with droplets of water, and his hair was thrust back from his face and still bore the ridges left by his fingers.

He closed the door, latched it behind him. His eyes burned as he regarded Annabel.

"Your shoes," he said, coming no nearer. "Take them off."

Annabel bent, her bodice and camisole still open, and unbuttoned her boots with hasty, awkward motions.

"The stockings."

Trembling, Annabel put one foot up onto a chair seat, raised her skirts, unhooked her garters, and rolled down her stocking, and all the while her gaze was locked with Gabriel's.

One by one, she shed her garments, at his command and at the pace he set, and by the time she was naked, her body glowed with a moisture that had nothing to do with spilled bathwater.

"Play," he said, nodding toward the harp.

In a daze of anticipation and sweet agony, Annabel sat down at the instrument and struggled to render some simple tune from the long-neglected strings, and the sound, though discordant, found some answering note within her and resonated there.

Gabriel crossed the room—until then he had not moved—plunged his fingers into Annabel's hair and drew her head back, painlessly, for a lethal, soul-splintering kiss. She was Eve, before the Fall and before the fig leaf, and while he devoured her mouth, Gabriel slid his free hand down her belly with excruciating slowness, found the thicket of damp curls, parted them.

Annabel's cry echoed inside his mouth.

Gabriel's attentions were at once a benefaction and a discipline; he caused Annabel to surge and rock against him, played her with exquisite skill, as she had once played the harp that was whispering now in a breeze from the window. Again and again he brought her to the brink of glory, but he would not allow her to pass over, and at last she was unable to stand.

He carried her to the bed, laid her down, and stretched out beside her.

"I'm going to make you want to howl like a she-wolf," he promised, tasting her mouth. Then, raising his head to smile into her eyes, he added, "But you'll have to be quiet, won't you? Like a lady?"

Annabel whimpered. Nicholas's room was at the other end of a long hall, and the walls, formed of heavy logs, were thick. Still, she felt like screaming in demand even now, when the ritual had barely begun. What sounds would she make at the critical moment, when those demands were fully, thoroughly met, as she knew they would be?

Gabriel found a nipple and nibbled there, then indulged himself in a long pull of his mouth that left Annabel fitful and feverish. She was perspiring from her toes to her scalp; her hair clung to her neck and cheeks and forehead and spilled wildly over the pillows.

"Is it the lady," he mused, and went to the other nipple, to perform the same devil's trick, "or the she-wolf?"

"Damn you," Annabel gasped, and somewhere in that wondrous desperation he'd spawned in her, she found strength, and slipped out of his embrace to move downward, over his hard belly and his thighs. "Damn you," she said again, and took him, and reveled in the fierce upward thrust of his hips as he surrendered to her, the low, raw exclamation as she conquered.

Their lovemaking became a tender battle after that, a test to see who could drive the other one mad first. The final conflict was elemental, a storm confined to that room, bright with lightning, loud with thunder, and the victory was blinding, a cataclysm of fire. In such a union Zeus or Apollo must have found conception—or Nicholas McKeige.

When Annabel drifted back into her exhausted and still shuddering body, she was surprised and perhaps a little embarrassed to find herself upright, pressed against the bedroom wall, with Gabriel at her back, her arms widespread and clutching, feet hooked round the backs of Gabriel's thighs. He cupped her breasts in his hands and made a slow, shivery trail down her spine with his lips. He was still deep inside her and only beginning to turn supple, which meant he might well recover and have her again before she caught her breath.

"How did this happen?" Annabel asked, with a little whimper.

Gabriel traced the jutting lines of one shoulder blade with the tip of his tongue. "Oh, in the usual fashion, I think," he answered, at his leisure. Sure enough, he was hardening again, and it was a minor humiliation that this was virtually all he had to do to arouse her.

"Bloody hell," Annabel sputtered, as her fingers curved against the rough wood of the log wall, "I didn't mean that."

He pushed aside her hair, nuzzled her neck, tasted it. A violent shudder of sheer, primitive accommodation went through her. "What," he asked, "did you mean, then?"

She moaned as Gabriel caressed her sensitive nipples and, at the same time, began to move inside her, with slow, rhythmic command. "Oh, God—"

"Surely this is no time for a theological discussion," Gabriel admonished.

Annabel gave a strangled cry of frustration and of rising passion. "Aren't we—aren't we supposed to make love on the bed—and rest once in a while?"

Gabriel laughed, massaging her breasts fully now, and her belly, and moving faster and then faster still. "I don't know," he ground out. "I've never done this with anybody but you—sweet God, Annabel, when you move like that—"

But Annabel could not answer him, for the second release came quickly and with power, and she was a mindless and nameless being, utterly lost, knowing no language but that of surrender, a soul set free and flailing among folds of light.

Annabel was deeply asleep when Gabe roused himself from their bed, groped for fresh clothes, and struggled into them. He had no idea what time it was; the house was quiet and dark, the stars out in profusion, but he supposed it couldn't be too late. After all, the sun had been up when Annabel lured him into that bathtub, like the siren she was.

He grinned at the memory, picked up his boots in one hand. Annabel's harp stood in a pool of starlight, draped with a single fluttering stocking. Her dress and frilly underthings were scattered on the floor around it.

Gabe went out, closed the door softly behind him. Annabel needed her rest.

The stairs creaked as he descended by the back way; he sat down two steps from the bottom to pull his boots on. That done, he lit a lamp and surveyed the kitchen. It resembled the aftermath of a shipwreck.

Taking care to be quiet, Gabe put the kettles away, carried the tub out into the backyard, and emptied it there. Then he went back inside to mop the floor and build up the fire.

He was hungry, and it was likely to be a long night, followed by an even longer day.

Within a few minutes Gabe had brewed coffee and scared up a can of beans from the back of a pantry shelf. With Charlie gone, the pickings were slim.

When he was finished eating, Gabe strapped on his gun belt and set out for the study to fetch his favorite rifle and scabbard. He'd planned to write a hasty note of explanation to Annabel, but that thought was forgotten when he stepped over the threshold and found a lamp burning and Nicholas sitting behind the desk, fully clothed.

The .45 lay before him, gleaming with gun oil from a recent and thorough cleaning.

"Kind of late to be going out," Nicholas remarked, wiping his fingers on the same cloth he'd used to polish the Colt. He'd had the pistol since his fifteenth birthday, the boy had, knew it better than his name, could take it apart and put it back together in the dark. Gabe had seen to all that, personally.

"Is it?" Gabe asked, taking the rifle from its cabinet, the scabbard from the drawer beneath, along with an ample supply of shells.

"You're going looking for Charlie," Nicholas said. He spoke in a quiet voice, calculated, Gabe knew, to make him listen.

"You'd rather I didn't?" Gabe asked, loading the rifle.

"No, sir," Nicholas clarified. "He's been gone too long, and something's wrong. I just want to go with you." He could be patient, as well as soft-spoken, when it served him.

"That's a pity," Gabe answered. "You'd fall out of the saddle, if you even managed to mount up in the first place, and your mother would peel off my hide for letting you try it."

"You don't know where to look. I do. I've been up in those hills with Charlie a thousand times."

"So have I. I don't suppose you plan to tell me where to find him?"

Nicholas grinned. "No," he said. "Furthermore, if you leave without me, I'll set out on my own. There'll be nobody to stop me."

"I think you're underestimating your mother."

"Maybe. I looked in on her before I came downstairs, though—while you were sprucing up the kitchen. My guess is, Miss Annabel is going to sleep until sometime tomorrow afternoon."

Gabe felt heat climb his neck, waited a moment before he spoke. "You're no match for me, boy—not on a good day, let alone with your belly trussed up in bandages like that. I guess if I wanted to make you stay put, I could find some way to do it."

"You're welcome to try, Pa." Nicholas's tone was cordial and easy. "Like as not, you'd win, all right. But it sounds like a hell of a lot of trouble to go to, when you must know I'm going to saddle up and ride out anyway. Wouldn't you rather be around to keep an eye on me?"

Gabe laughed hoarsely. "Hell. Trying to reason with you is like trying to reason with Annabel."

Nicholas touched the tips of his fingers together in a steeple, elbows on the desktop, thumbs under his chin, and regarded Gabe with a gleam of humor and pure cussedness in his eyes. "I am like Miss Annabel," he conceded generously. "On those rare occasions when I don't take after you, that is."

Gabe watched as his son stood, slipped the freshly cleaned .45 into his holster, and rounded the desk. "Who's going to look after her, with both of us gone?"

The ploy failed; Nicholas merely arched an eyebrow and shook his head, as if to say it was a pitiful attempt. They both knew Annabel could have held Troy against the Greeks, practically single-handed, but neither would risk testing the theory. In the end, the foreman and several of Gabe's most trusted men were assigned to stand guard, watching the house from all sides.

For one of the few times in his life, Gabe gave in to pressure, though not graciously. "Well, damn it, then," he growled, sliding the rifle into its scabbard and striding toward the door, "try to keep up. I'm not about to double back every five minutes, looking for you."

Nicholas answered with a nod, and he made a creditable job of matching his father's pace, though when they got to the barn, Gabe softened a little and saddled a spirited sorrel he'd planned to give him later, as a gift. He'd lost a few horses himself, in his time, and he knew the sorrow of it.

Stubborn as the proverbial ox, the boy reached up, grasped the saddle horn, and dragged himself onto the sorrel's back. He was white with pain and soaked in sweat from that effort alone, and Gabe wouldn't pretend he hadn't noticed.

"You might have been better off with other parents," he said. "Folks with a little more 'give' in them."

Nicholas laughed. "And you might have been better off with another son," he retorted. "One with any 'give' at all."

Gabe watched his son in silence for a moment, and in respect. Then he shook his head. "No," he said. "You'll do just fine." Having heard them getting the horses ready, the foreman appeared, and Gabe gave the order to see that Annabel was kept safe at all costs. When he and Nicholas were alone again, he swung up into the saddle. "Now tell me where to look for that knothead Indian."

Nicholas tilted his head toward the east, where the mountains rose against the night sky, and they set out toward the foothills, moving at a slow but steady pace. "Charlie will have left some kind of a trail for us," he said, with quiet certainty. "Assuming he wants to be found, of course."

When Annabel awakened, the sun was high and hot, and Gabriel's side of the bed was empty. He would have been up and about his business long ago, but she was content to take her time.

She lay still until the inevitable spate of nausea passed—she had never been surer of anything than she was of this new pregnancy—and when it had gone, she rose, poured water into the washbasin, and performed what ablutions she could.

She put on a lightweight dress with only one petticoat, out of deference to the heat, and blushed a little as she gathered up the garments she'd left spilling around the base of the harp. She ran her fingers across the strings of the splendid instrument, and smiled.

Once, she'd been quite a good harpist; she had taught herself, by trial and error. Perhaps later in the day, when she'd seen to Nicholas, fed the chickens, and made an inventory of the pantry, she would take the time to tune the instrument, then try to recall some of the music she'd made with such ease in times past.

Reaching the door of Nicholas's room, she rapped smartly.

No answer.

Annabel knocked again, frowned at the silence, and opened the door.

Nicholas was gone, his bed unmade. The room was unbearably stuffy, so Annabel opened all the windows and stripped the linens from the mattress. He'd probably gotten hungry, she concluded, waiting for her to get up and fix his breakfast. That was it. She would find him in the kitchen.

She gasped. Dear Lord, the kitchen! Anyone seeing the tub, the spilled water, the scattered kettles, couldn't help but conclude . . .

But that room was empty, too, and all traces of Gabriel's bath were gone.

"Nicholas?" Annabel called, after depositing the bed linens on the back porch, by the wash table.

There was no sign of him, or of Gabriel, anywhere.

She was about to inquire at the barn when Jeffrey appeared, with her hounds frolicking at his heels.

Evidently the old enmity between man and beasts had been resolved, probably by means of bribery.

"You look a bit better this morning," Jeffrey said, "though I daresay you're still leaning towards the peaky side."

Annabel smiled. "I must apologize to you, Jeffrey," she said. "I was very sharp yesterday."

Jeffrey touched the brim of his hat and drawled, Gabriel-like, "Don't you give it another thought, ma'am."

Annabel laughed, and the dogs, pleased, came to snuffle at her palms. She patted them both and ruffled their great floppy ears.

"Have you seen Nicholas this morning?" she asked, inviting Jeffrey inside with a nod of her head.

"Isn't he here?" Jeffrey asked. He followed her into the house, and so did the dogs, who were promptly shooed back to the porch. Through the open door, Annabel saw them choose sunny places to lie, tongues lolling, gleaming sides heaving as they breathed.

"No." Annabel washed her hands at the sink, then put a fresh pot of coffee on to brew. She was getting rather good at small domestic tasks, having made a home for herself and Nicholas in town, however briefly, and she had ambitious plans to tackle the laundry.

Jeffrey accepted a cup of coffee, and Annabel sat down across from him with a cup of her own.

He smiled. "Pardon me, madam," he teased, "but can you tell me how I came to be in the Wild, Wild West? Last thing I knew, I was in London, reading a newspaper and sipping brandy in my gentlemen's club."

"You've always been adventurous," Annabel allowed. She thought Jeffrey had been in Australia for the past year. "What will you do now? You must be getting bored with riding the range—after all, you've been at it at least a week."

Jeffrey pulled a face. "I'm afraid this life is a bit too picturesque for me. I'll be moving on to San Francisco one day soon."

"And from there?"

"Who knows? Perhaps Hong Kong, perhaps some country yet unnamed."

Annabel sighed. For all that she was happy in America, for all its perils, with Gabriel and Nicholas and the new baby to look forward to, she had cherished the dream of reclaiming Evanwood, her family home, too long to let it go easily. "Not back to England?"

Jeffrey wore, for a moment, an expression of sadness, but it was quickly masked. "Not for a while," he said. "I had planned to live there with you. Can't quite face going back yet—too many broken hopes to stumble over."

"I'm sorry," Annabel said sincerely. "But you must admit that I never encouraged you to think—"

"Oh, I know," Jeffrey admitted charitably. "I've always been optimistic, though. Nothing for it. It's just my way." He paused for a breath, though barely. "What about you, lovely Annabel? Will you sell your English house and all your pretty belongings?"

"I don't know," she answered, musing. She couldn't imagine her paintings and ornaments, trinkets and pillows, on display here in this rustic frontier place, however sturdy and spacious it was. "Things I thought of as treasures are beginning to seem more like clutter. It's people that matter, Jeffrey, not bits of porcelain and glass. Why did it take me so long to learn that?"

Jeffrey reached across the table and patted her hand. "You know it now—probably knew it all along." He began to chatter merrily then, in that fashion so typical of him, about his plans for the journey to San Francisco and points beyond.

Annabel tried to be attentive, but her mind wandered. The room, full of light, slipped into shadow for just a second or two as the sun went behind a cloud, and though it was very warm, she shivered.

Where was Nicholas?

Seventeen

GABE FELT EVERY JAR AND JOLT, EVERY STUMBLE OF HIS son's horse, in his own flesh and bones as Nicholas rode grim-faced and uncomplaining beside him.

The country around them grew more thickly wooded, rocky, and rugged, as they climbed. The night air was as cold as October would be in the lowlands, though it was still mid-July, and the calls of small animals and the whisper of the wind harmonized to make their particular music, never striking the same note twice.

Gabe supposed they were headed toward a specific campsite, or the first of a series of them, and from there it was an easy conclusion that Charlie had taken Nicholas to those places over the years. Probably often.

The insight was a small but keenly felt revelation to Gabe; Charlie had, in many ways, been more of a father to his son than he had. Oh, he himself had taught the boy to ride and shoot, among other things, and he didn't suppose Nicholas had ever questioned his devotion quite the way he had Annabel's, but the plain truth was, Gabe knew, that he had spent too much of his time trying to outrun his own pain. He'd left the gentle side of Nicholas's upbringing to Jessie and, in less obvious, day-to-day ways, to Charlie.

"You as worried about him as I am?" Gabe asked, more to start a conversation than anything else. Neither he nor Nicholas had said more than a few necessary words since they'd ridden out a couple of hours before.

"Oh, yeah," Nicholas answered, but he seemed sure of the trail. More than once he'd spotted some mark Charlie had left—a pile of stones, a slash cut into the bark of a tree.

Gabe sighed. "I didn't think much of his being gone until your mother came to me and said you'd been practicing your draw. She'd worked out that you were expecting trouble, and that put Charlie's sudden yen to wander in a new light." He paused, went on. "How many more men are there?" he asked. "In Horncastle's gang, I mean."

"Horncastle isn't the ringleader," Nicholas said, somewhat reluctantly and after a long time spent considering matters. "He's the fool."

"You still haven't answered my question."

"Not many. Two or three, I guess."

"I don't suppose you plan to tell me who runs the outfit?"

Nicholas straightened his hat, a habit that manifested itself, in Gabe's experience, when he wanted to change the subject or just delay things a bit. "I would," he finally answered, with a long sigh, "if I knew."

"Marshal Swingler seems to think he's got the whole bunch of them."

"He's wrong," Nicholas said flatly, his face in shadow. "He'll get around to facing it, though, once he's got that cell full of snakes off his hands."

"What makes you—and Charlie—so sure there are others?"

"Horncastle. I've known him for most of my life, and he hasn't got the guts or the skill to steal a pie from an old lady's windowsill. Neither do any of the men who rode with him—just a bunch of misfits and stragglers."

"Seems to me they were damn hard to catch, all the same."

Nicholas turned his head, grinned. "They had me to advise them," he said. "I'm a born outlaw, Pa; I won't lie to you—I enjoyed the planning and even the robberies themselves. It was like a game. Only problem is, I've got a conscience, and I didn't like scaring people. That pretty much took the fun out of it."

Gabe shifted in the saddle, wishing the sun would rise. Wishing they'd find Charlie safe and sound. "You must have some idea who's behind that gang," he persisted.

"Some folks think it's you," Nicholas said.

Gabe was stunned, though he supposed, in the next instant, that he shouldn't have been. "What motive would I have? I could throw away money with both hands from now till my dying day and still go to the grave a rich man."

Nicholas grinned, his strong teeth flashing in the relative darkness. He didn't often get the best of Gabe, and it was obvious that he was enjoying the moment. "Maybe you're more like me than you want to let on, Pa. Maybe it wasn't the figures in that master ledger of yours that drove you to work like you have, to build one of the biggest and best ranching and mining operations in the state. Could have been the simple challenge, a way of sharpening your wits." He shrugged, and Gabe saw that the motion was painful, that Nicholas was holding himself in the saddle by the power of his will alone. "Other men have stepped outside the law for lesser reasons."

"You don't actually think—"

Nicholas laughed; the sound was raw. "No. Your conscience would get in the way, just like mine did. I was just making a case for the hell of it."

Gabe muttered a curse.

"Too bad Miss Annabel didn't come back sooner," Nicholas went on, bent, evidently, on pushing his luck. On the other hand, in his condition, he knew he had nothing to fear. "She seems to keep you from getting bored."

"You'd best have meant that in a respectful way," Gabe said.

"Oh, I did," Nicholas assured his father. "I surely did. Miss Annabel's like a puzzle to you, I think, and you're the same to her. Keeps your mind busy, trying to work out what she's up to and find a way to trip her up."

Gabe chuckled. "I suppose that's right," he admitted. Right then he missed Annabel with the whole of his being, for all her sharp tongue, reckless ideas, and harridan's ways. The eastern sky was beginning to glow with the first promise of light, though it would still be several hours before the sun rose, and he wished he was back home with her, lying warm in their bed.

"It's different with Olivia and me," Nicholas said. For him, that was an unprecedented confidence; Gabe had never heard so much as a woman's name from his son, let alone a reference to his feelings for one. "When I'm around her, it's like standing close to a fire on a cold night, or taking shelter from a rainstorm." He stopped for a few moments and then, with some difficulty, went on. "The passion's there too. Sometimes I think I'm going to go crazy if I can't bed that woman soon, but the waiting has a sweetness all its own."

Gabe merely listened, a trick he had made too little use of in the past. He didn't like the way Nicholas looked, but at the same time he knew he couldn't have stopped him from coming along.

"I can't ask Olivia to marry me until this other business is over and done with," Nicholas said, reasoning as much with himself, Gabe suspected, as with him. He looked down at the bandages, bulky beneath his shirt. "Until I can be a fit husband." He turned his gaze toward Gabe, serious and a man, in every sense of the word. "I'll be putting up a house on the ranch, soon as I can figure out where it ought to be."

Gabe was quiet, partly rejoicing because his son was grown up, partly mourning the spirited, mischievous boy he'd been. He wouldn't speak until Nicholas presented him with a direct question; a wise course, since Gabe wasn't at all sure he could trust his voice.

"It bothers Olivia that she's older than I am."

No question, no answer. Gabe held his tongue. Unlike Annabel and Jessie, he didn't see the schoolteacher's age as a problem. It appeared that his theory was right: Miss Olivia Drummond had a settling influence on Nicholas, and that was a good thing from any perspective.

"For my part, I don't believe age has a damn thing to do with anything," Nicholas went on, gaining steam, like a lawyer making a case in front of a stone-faced jury. "Even if it made a difference in her looks, which it doesn't, I wouldn't care. It's the way Olivia makes me feel that matters. The way she makes me want to be somebody better than I am."

Gabe smiled and waited.

"You like her, don't you, Pa?"

"Yes," Gabe said. "And so does your mother. She might be a bit reluctant to lose you, though."

Nicholas's jawline hardened, relaxed again. He kept his gaze ahead, on the moon-washed trail. "It's a little late for her to start worrying about that, it seems to me."

Gabe broke his own rule and offered advice. "Make your peace with Miss Annabel," he said quietly. "The effort it takes to hate her would be better spent making the rest of your life work."

Even in the darkness, Gabe saw a brief wash of color in Nicholas's face, but the boy wouldn't look around. "I don't hate Moth—Miss Annabel," he said grudgingly. "It's a lot more complicated than that."

"The hell it is," Gabe answered readily, and calmly. "She wasn't here when you needed her, and that makes you mad as a scalded rooster. You'd be better off admitting it, to yourself and to her."

"If I start in telling Miss Annabel what I think, I don't know how I'll stop. And she'll be destroyed."

Gabe made a wry sound, akin to a chuckle. "You're not giving Annabel due credit if you think mere words could ever be the end of her." He fell silent, watching Nicholas's obstinate profile for a time before going on. "It's true that your mother may shed a few tears, and she'll feel pain, hearing what you have to say. But she's strong enough to take that and a lot more, Nicholas, and if it will break down the barriers between you, she'll welcome whatever she has to suffer."

Nicholas turned his head, regarded his father from beneath the brim of his hat. "Did you make that speech for my benefit, Pa," he asked, "or were you talking to yourself?"

Gabe heaved a sigh. He and Annabel had reconciled, at least physically, and probably conceived a child in the process. But there were still things that needed settling, agreements that had to be reached.

"You have a streak of good sense in you, Nicholas," he said, at length, "and I don't always find it easy to deal with."

Nicholas reached over, patted his father's shoulder in a comradely way. "Me, either," he admitted.

After that, they rode on in silence, each one leaving the other to his own thoughts, though their separate wills were attuned to one purpose: finding Charlie.

Annabel wondered if it was a sign of favorable change in her nature that she didn't immediately go out searching for Nicholas, or if it was, instead, a manifestation of some new cowardice, born of sensual satisfaction and pregnancy.

After Jeffrey had finished his coffee and gone, she hung her son's blankets on the clothesline to air, took stock of the pantry's contents, and set two of the cowboys hanging around outside the house to building a fire in the yard and pumping water for the washtubs. She found soap flakes and bluing and gathered dirty clothes from the master bedroom and from the floor of Nicholas's armoire. A few had been kicked under his bed.

She supposed this frenzy of domesticity would pass soon, given the fact that keeping a house without servants was backbreaking work, but Annabel was determined to enjoy the penchant while it lasted. These normal household tasks, however homely, made her feel wholly genuine, in a way that other more elegant pursuits never had.

By noon the clotheslines fluttered with clean shirts and trousers, sheets and pillowcases, and several of her own skirts and shirtwaists. Her undergarments—camisoles and drawers and petticoats made of the finest silks and linens—being no concern of the cowboys who came and went all day, hung on folding wooden racks in the master bedroom.

When she was through with the wash, Annabel made a careful list of necessary supplies and asked Mr. Hilditch to hitch up the surrey and bring it around. She had expected her energy to wane after a morning of joyous drudgery, but it only seemed to multiply.

Humming, Annabel donned a fresh gown, put up her hair, and went to town, shopping list in hand. Gabriel's foremen and two other men insisted on accompanying her, but they kept a respectful distance.

Passing the Samhill Saloon, a dispirited-looking place now that Miss Sermon was gone, Annabel felt her mood dampen, though only temporarily. The following Sunday after church, as planned, she would announce that the establishment was being closed, but that would not be the end of the matter, she knew.

For one thing, the dancing girls could not simply be turned out in the street, though she reckoned there was little chance of redeeming most of them. Each one would need money for stagecoach and train tickets, not to mention a new start in some hopefully distant place. The copious supplies of whiskey would have to be disposed of, the gambling tables turned to better uses, the sawdust floor swept clean and replaced with good, serviceable wood.

Considering the enormity of her plan to turn the place into a reputable hotel, an amenity the growing town sorely needed, Annabel felt the first twinge of fatigue. Who would run the establishment, once the restorations had been completed? It was all well and good to say she could do it herself, but she was carrying a child—a child who would, she vowed, have all the love and attention Nicholas had missed. And there was Gabriel, food of her mind and spirit, joy of her body. She could not, would not, deprive herself of him.

She sighed, jerked from her reverie, when Mr. Hilditch brought the surrey to a snappy halt in front of the general store. Unlike Jeffrey, Hilditch did not enjoy his cowboy duties, and driving for Annabel was a welcome respite.

"Here we are, Mrs. McKeige," he said, jumping down to offer her a hand.

Annabel put all thoughts of enterprise aside and swept into the store, where she was met with a mingling of smells—leather and onions, dust and rosewater, paper and pepper. She expected to be greeted with more curiosity than cordiality, and she was neither disappointed nor disturbed; one could never entirely outdistance one's past, and she would always be the woman who had once run away, leaving a good man behind and taking his son.

With the quick efficiency that was as much a part of

her nature as her temper and her determination, Annabel selected the items she needed to make the ranch house comfortable: flour and other staples, spices and yeast, canned foods and soap, a cookbook.

She ordered a porcelain bathtub with brass spigots from the catalog, along with a sink, a flush toilet, and all the required pipes and valves—the first such purchase in Parable's admittedly brief history, she gathered from the excitement generated among the other shoppers—and she enjoyed the small flurry of notoriety. Assembling the collection and getting it into working order, of course, would be Gabriel's problem.

A second mail-order purchase caused almost as much of a stir: Annabel bought a washing machine, with an agitator operated by a pedal, and a wringer that could be turned by hand.

Olivia was standing on the sidewalk, quietly waiting, when Annabel finished her spree and went out to supervise while Mr. Hilditch loaded boxes and crates behind and beneath the seats of the surrey.

"Mrs. McKeige?" Olivia ventured. She was not shy, exactly, Annabel had concluded during the recent ordeal, nor was she passive, which would have been a disastrous attribute in any woman who hoped to make a life with Nicholas. No, she decided, Olivia was the type to bank her fires and then blaze like the heart of hell when the situation called for it.

Annabel smiled. "Hello, Olivia."

"I've been wondering about Nicholas . . ."

"So have I," Annabel said. "He's vanished."

Olivia's dark eyes widened. She might have been close to thirty, but in that moment she looked no older than sixteen, and hardly more sophisticated. "Vanished?"

Annabel sighed. "Actually, I was hoping you'd seen him—that he'd come to call on you at Jessie's."

Olivia shook her head. She was wearing a bonnet and a simple calico dress; after all, she had been engaged to teach school, and the term was scheduled to begin, according to Jessie, in just a few weeks. "No," she said worriedly, casting a troubled glance toward the marshal's office, with its bulging jail. "I'm worried, Mrs. McKeige. The army men still haven't come for the prisoners, and, well, there's a sort of tension in the air."

"I feel it," Annabel confessed ruefully, pulling Olivia a little aside, out of the stream of traffic. "Maybe I'll send a wire to Captain Sommervale and inquire about the delay." The act would come under the heading of meddling, a habit Annabel had resolved to curtail, but it was plain that someone had to do something.

"Would you?" Olivia asked. "It would be such a relief, having those dreadful men in proper custody."

Annabel quite agreed, though she sensed that circumstances were already in motion, like some vast machine, foreordained and therefore unstoppable. "Why don't you come back to the ranch with me, and we'll have a visit? Maybe Nicholas will be there, and you can see for yourself that he's getting better."

Olivia blushed prettily. She had thick lashes, in double rows, and perfect skin. Annabel wondered why she had ever thought the other woman was plain.

"I would like that," Olivia said. "I just have to buy six eggs for Miss McKeige, as I promised, and let her know where I'm going. Is there time for that?"

Annabel nodded. "I'll send the wire, and we'll pick you up at Jessie's house on our way out of town."

Olivia nodded in eager agreement and hurried into

the general store, where she would no doubt be regaled with the tale of Mrs. Gabriel McKeige's flush toilet and pipe-fed bathtub. Annabel, meanwhile, made her way to the impossibly skinny building squeezed in between the bank and the jailhouse, which served as the telegraph office.

The message to Captain Sommervale was a succinct one: "Captain. Regards to yourself and Mrs. Sommervale. We await removal of prisoners with impatience. Expediency appreciated. Annabel Latham McKeige."

Annabel wrote it out carefully on a yellow pad, paid the operator, and waited while the code was transmitted over the wires stretching between Parable and Fort Duffield. The town, she knew, aspired to a railroad, now that the telegraph had linked it to the rest of the world; Parable was a place with plans for the future.

It needed a hotel.

Annabel smiled as she stood patiently waiting for her wire to go through, because she liked being right.

Barely fifteen minutes had passed when a response came: "Mrs. McKeige. Volunteers dispatched in good time. Please advise immediately if they have not arrived before day's end. Cordial regards, etc., etc., J. D. Sommervale."

Frowning, Annabel read the wire through twice. Fort Duffield was less than a day's ride away for young, fit men on horseback such as Captain Sommervale's soldiers. For her, "immediately" was not soon enough; she wondered what was keeping them and considered communicating her concerns in a second telegram.

In the end, she decided that making a pest of herself, at this juncture anyway, would not serve her purposes. Annabel folded the captain's reply, tucked it into her handbag, and took her leave of the telegraph office.

When she and Mr. Hilditch reached Jessie's house in the surrey, Jessie was waiting on the porch. She insisted that they both come in for lunch, and Annabel, ravenously hungry and knowing a losing argument when confronted with one, agreed.

Mr. Hilditch ate in the kitchen while Jessie, Annabel, and Olivia took their meal at the dining room table, chatting pleasantly as they nibbled at dainty sandwiches, tea cakes, and Jessie's wonderful cinnamon pear preserves.

If Annabel's stamina had been flagging a little, the food revived her, and she was in a cheerful mood when she and Olivia set out for the ranch at last, with Mr. Hilditch humming at the reins and the watchmen tagging dutifully along behind. Surely Nicholas would be home again by the time they returned, back from whatever mysterious errand had taken him away. After all, he simply wasn't strong enough, or well enough, to go far.

An hour past dawn, they reached the first camp.

It was clear that neither Charlie nor anyone else had been there in the recent past; the charred stones that had enclosed the last fire were scattered through the grass, and the embers were cold.

Nicholas looked bad, as if he might roll back his eyes and fall right out of the saddle at any moment. Hell and damnation, he shouldn't have let the boy leave the house; Annabel would have known better. And she'd raise the devil's dead uncle when she found out.

Gabe thrust a flask into his son's hand. "Take as much as you can swallow," he commanded.

Nicholas opened the flask, raised it to his lips, and tilted his head back. He swallowed several times and then gave a low, lusty yowl of appreciation as he screwed the lid in place and handed the small bottle back to his father. His eyes were mischievous, if sunken and far too bright, when he spoke. "That was almost worth getting shot for," he said.

"How far is the second camp?" Gabe demanded, tucking the flask into the inside pocket of his coat.

"Five miles or so," Nicholas answered, after dragging his hand across his mouth. He nodded to indicate the place where Gabe had stored the whiskey. "Was that breakfast?"

"If you can hold it down, it wasn't," Gabe replied. "If you can't, there isn't much use in feeding you anything else, is there?"

Nicholas laughed, but the sound was too sharp, too shrill, and painful to hear. "Miss Annabel is going to have you skinned and pickled for this," he said, evidently relishing the idea. "First you drag her baby boy out into the wilderness, looking for an Indian who probably doesn't want to be found, and then you give him rotgut booze for breakfast."

Gabe wasn't amused, partly because Nicholas was right—Annabel *would* do him bodily harm for this one—and partly because the boy looked like a parody of death.

"I wouldn't blame her if she shot me," Gabe said glumly. "I'd do the same, in her place." He reached out and snatched the reins from Nicholas's hands. "We're going back, right now."

Nicholas swore, but when he tried to grab the reins back, he swayed, and Gabe barely caught him in time to prevent a headlong pitch onto the ground.

"I think I could stand a little more of that whiskey,"

Nicholas mumbled, thick-tongued. Then he turned his head and vomited into the grass.

After that, Nicholas shook so badly that Gabe had to tie his hands to the saddle horn, just to keep him mounted. They rode back to the first camp at an agonizingly slow pace, with Nicholas drifting in and out of consciousness, and Gabe silently cussing himself for letting him come along. If the boy lived through this, Gabe thought, it wouldn't be because his father hadn't done his level best to kill him.

The front of Nicholas's shirt was soaked in blood and sweat by the time Gabe got him off the horse and laid him out in the shimmering shade of a cottonwood tree.

Nicholas arched his back and laughed like a maniac, and then, in the next minute, he sobbed fit to break a hangman's heart. There were tears on Gabe's own face as he spread a bedroll on the ground for his son and built a fire in the hope of keeping him warm. And, please God, of attracting Charlie.

Charlie, with his calm spirit and knowledge of the ancient ways, would be able to help Nicholas.

Gabe found a spring and refilled his canteen, then used the water and a worn bandanna to soothe the boy's fever. The bleeding had stopped, at least, but when he pulled back the bandages and examined the wound, he was alarmed by what he found—swelling and a putrid seepage. He was no doctor, but he knew that infection had set in and that it was often fatal.

He used every dry twig and stick of wood he could find to build up the fire, and prayed under his breath while he waited. The image of a gravestone carved with Nicholas's name and set next to Susannah's kept coming into his mind, but he fought it off every time.

It was midafternoon when Charlie finally showed up, wandering into camp with a skinned rabbit in one hand. For once in his life, the Indian was rattled.

"Nicholas," he gasped, at the sight of the boy lying there out of his head, and threw the rabbit down in the dirt to kneel at his side. After examining the nasty mess under Nicholas's shirt, he turned furious eyes on Gabe. "What were you thinking, bringing him out here like this?"

Gabe was too weary to explain. "Never mind that now, damn it. I've burned up half the timber on the mountain trying to get your attention, so do something!"

Charlie appeared overwhelmed for a moment, but then his serenity returned. "You got any whiskey?" he asked.

Gabe produced the flask. It was about half full, thanks to Nicholas's thirst earlier in the day.

Muttering to himself, Charlie removed the lid, tossed it aside, into the brush, and upended the bottle over Nicholas's naked wound. Nicholas made a primitive, terrible sound as the liquor made contact with his flesh—it must have felt like being branded, even in his semiconscious state—and writhed to evade the searing pain.

"Jesus," Gabe breathed, and dragged the back of one hand across his face.

"While you're praying," Charlie snapped, raising Nicholas's lids with his thumbs and peering into his eyes, "ask your Great Spirit to keep those outlaws I've been trailing away from here. If I saw your fire, they probably did, too. There are six of them, and they're armed and wearing cavalry uniforms."

"What?"

Charlie was concentrating on Nicholas. "Clean up that rabbit and put it on a spit over the fire. I'll get some blankets and medicine."

"From where?" Gabe demanded, furious and scared that his only son would die after all. If Nicholas didn't survive, the blame was his, Gabe's, alone.

"Never mind where," Charlie retorted. "I don't have time to answer your stupid questions." He got Nicholas behind the arms and dragged him closer to the fire. "The whiskey might do some good, but it won't be enough on its own. I should have known better than to leave him to that white doctor."

Charlie checked the spit, where the rabbit was beginning to roast, to make sure Gabe had followed his instructions, then cast another glance at Nicholas and disappeared into the trees. He left the camp the same way he'd come in—on foot.

The Indian had been gone maybe half an hour when Nicholas opened his eyes, looked at Gabe without recognition, and then passed out again.

Gabe pressed his ear to the boy's chest. Nicholas was breathing, and his heart was beating. For the moment, it was enough.

He sat next to Nicholas, his back braced against the trunk of a tree, his rifle lying across his lap. Only then did he take the time to really think about what Charlie had said: there were half a dozen outlaws somewhere in those foothills, and they were dressed as cavalrymen.

"Son of a bitch," Gabe groaned, as he finally realized what was about to happen. He was pretty sure that he and Nicholas were in no immediate danger, but that was precious little consolation, considering the wider picture.

Marshal Swingler was expecting army men to relieve him of the prisoners crowding his jail, and when six men in government blue appeared in Parable, smartly mounted and probably carrying official papers in the bargain, he would hand Horncastle and the others over to them without hesitation.

Thereby setting them free.

Eighteen

Marshal Swingler was in a foul temper that hot July afternoon when the army finally appeared at his jail to collect Jack Horncastle and the others. As if the outlaws weren't enough trouble, jammed into that one cell, always fighting among themselves, filling chamber pots, and wanting tobacco, his rheumatism had been acting up, making him feel old. On top of it all, his daughter, Callie, was in an everlasting snit because Nicholas McKeige had taken up with the new schoolmarm.

The marshal privately thought it a blessing that McKeige had lost interest in Callie. He was clever, that kid, with the courage of an Apache warrior and a brain full of wheels and gears that never stopped turning, and without him, bringing in Horncastle's gang would have been nigh unto impossible. Still, Nicholas was and always would be untamed—too much for Callie, being a simpler soul, to handle.

She was by no means innocent, his Callie—she'd run a little wild since her mother died, two years back—but she was gullible and wanted some firm guidance. The marshal had a young farmer in mind for her, and when things settled down, he'd get her to invite the lad to supper.

It was a sweet mercy Callie and Nicholas hadn't started a little McKeige before Miss Olivia Drummond came along. That would have complicated matters.

He sighed to himself as he signed the papers presented to him by a young lieutenant; the lad looked familiar, and he decided they must have crossed paths around Independence Day, when Sommervale had brought what seemed like a full legion to Parable. Surely the soldier had been in town on leave often enough, too. A man couldn't be expected to know them all by name, coming and going the way they did.

The lieutenant saluted when Swingler handed over the papers, there in the office, with the prisoners crowded up to the bars, looking on, quiet for the first time since they'd been brought in. It troubled him, some quality of that silence. Made him twitchy.

"Thanks, Marshal," the boy soldier said.

Swingler frowned. It was the first time he'd noticed that none of the soldiers carried handcuffs or shackles. He hoped they didn't expect him to supply the necessary gear for transporting prisoners; there was no place in the town budget for conveniences the army should pay for themselves.

"You sure you can handle these rascals?" he asked. He was getting a headache and wanted nothing so much as to sit back in his chair for an hour, with his feet on the desk and his hat shading his eyes.

The lieutenant looked like he wanted to smile, though he didn't indulge the whim. "We can handle them, all right," he said, and nodded toward the cell. "If you don't mind, Marshal, we're in something of a hurry."

Swingler grunted assent and, taking his keys from his belt, turned his back on the young officer. In the few instants of consciousness that followed, it seemed as if the roof fell in, a beam striking him hard across the back of the head. He felt an explosion of gut-wrenching pain, and then darkness billowed up around him like smoke, bringing with it merciful oblivion.

His awakening was rude; someone flung a dipperful of cold water into his face, and Swingler roused, sick with the ache in his head and the knowledge that he'd made a bad mistake.

At first he thought the first visitors were back, for the man standing over him, holding the dipper in one hand, wore cavalry blue, with plenty of brass. He was a lieutenant, too, but that, unfortunately, was where the similarity ended. This man was short and slight, with a blond beard and mustache, neatly trimmed, and his eyes were fairly popping with fury.

"Where are the prisoners?" he demanded, through his teeth.

Swingler got to his feet without help, hoping the ensuing conversation would be short, so he wouldn't have to endure the added humiliation of losing his lunch on the lieutenant's boots. "There were some men here"—he glanced at the clock on the wall—"about an hour ago. They were wearing calvary uniforms and carrying papers."

The soldier flushed furiously, and the men who had crowded in behind him looked at one another out of the corners of their eyes.

"That seems to be a favorite trick with these

particular individuals," the lieutenant snapped. "It seems to me, Marshal Swingler, that you might have been a little suspicious, given the fact that two hundred cattle were stolen by virtually the same means, less than two weeks ago."

Swingler's yearning for retirement, always with him, was keener than ever. He'd get Callie married, he decided, then court the widow he'd been seeing for the past year, right and proper. She had good land going to waste, and he'd saved a considerable sum over the years; he'd make a rancher of himself and live a peaceful life. Let someone else have this miserable job, where you were damned if you did and damned if you didn't.

"I guess our time would be better spent catching up with those polecats," Swingler said, resigned, "instead of standing here yammering."

The army man couldn't very well deny that, but before he turned to set his men on the trail of Horncastle and his band of outlaws, he made a quiet, scathing declaration. "I'll have your job for this, Marshal."

"It's yours," Swingler replied.

"Where do we start looking, if you please?"

Swingler thought, and even that was painful. "Christ," he breathed, "they'll go after Nicholas McKeige. Last I heard, Gabe and Miss Annabel had taken him out to the ranch."

"Lead the way," the lieutenant said, with a gesture.

Charlie didn't come back until long after the rabbit was cooked through, which was well past noon. Gabe had forced himself to eat, and spent the rest of the time either fussing over Nicholas or pacing back and forth, muttering to himself.

The Indian brought a pouch full of dried herbs, which he mixed with water from Gabe's canteen, making a poultice, and chanted over Nicholas like a sideshow medicine man.

Gabe was something less than impressed. "Hell," he said, "I'm going to town for the doctor."

Charlie paid him no mind, but simply opened Nicholas's shirt, cleaned the wound with water and a rough cloth, and then applied the mixture. It stank so bad it made Gabe's eyes water.

He took to pacing again. He'd get halfway to his horse, then stop, torn. There were a lot of dangerous variables in between.

Finally, his work finished, Charlie went to the spring and squatted to wash his hands. Gabe loomed over the Indian, not sure whether to throttle the man or name his next child after him.

"Damn it all to hell," Gabe sputtered, when Charlie failed to initiate a conversation, "that had better not have been some ancient mixture of pine needles, bird shit, and dirt!" He gestured wildly toward Nicholas, referring, of course, to the poultice.

Charlie rose slowly, giving his friend and employer a look that would have melted roofing tar. "It's the same medicine I used on you five years back when you cut your hand on that barbwire and didn't take the time to attend to it. If I remember right, your fancy Boston doctor had given you up for dead."

Gabe thrust his hand through his hair; he had long since thrown his hat aside. "Is he going to die?"

Charlie regarded Nicholas for a long moment. "No, probably not. The poultice will draw out the poison, and then the real recovery will begin."

Because he believed Charlie, and because he was weak with relief, Gabe sagged against a nearby tree, one arm curved high on the trunk, to cushion his face. Charlie slapped him once on the back and then left him alone until he'd recovered his composure.

When he returned to the campfire, Nicholas, though still not awake, was already looking better. There was a promise of color in his face, and the rhythm of his breathing indicated that he was no longer unconscious, but merely sleeping.

"It's a natural process," Charlie said, with a shrug, when Gabe thanked him. "Infection is the body's way of flushing poisons from the blood and tissue and sloughing them off." He was crouched near Nicholas as he spoke, devouring a crisply roasted flank of the rabbit. "We've got other problems, boss."

Gabe nodded. "The outlaws," he agreed. It was rare for him to feel as dazed as he did then; usually he knew exactly what he wanted to do about everything, when he wanted to do it, and how to proceed. A dozen bloodthirsty thieves were about to be turned loose on Parable and the surrounding countryside, if they hadn't been already, by six more of their ilk. It was his duty to aid in their capture, and yet he couldn't leave Nicholas unguarded and ill. He hadn't given the outlaws proper thought from the beginning, in fact, because he'd been so worried about his son, and about Charlie.

Even if they'd been at the ranch, with Nicholas tucked up in his bed and his mother to look after him, Gabe wouldn't have gone anyplace.

Charlie must have been reading his thoughts. "If Nicholas is the target," he said, rising, wiping rabbit grease on his buckskins as he did so, "he is also the bait."

"They want him, all right," Gabe agreed. That fact was hardly a comfort; he'd have been happier if the gang had simply ridden to Mexico, to live out their lives drinking and chasing senoritas, but he knew they wouldn't. Not until they'd killed Nicholas, avenged his betrayal of them.

"He knows their names," Charlie said, with a solemn nod. He looked at Nicholas for a few moments, then turned his dark gaze to Gabe. "When you've got a man's name, you have power over him." He paused. "We don't have time to get back to the ranch. And if Horncastle and the others catch us here in the open, we won't have a chance."

"You know these foothills better than I do," Gabe replied. Unlike Nicholas and Charlie, he'd spent most of his time in the low country, running cattle, digging up silver. Doing his damnedest to forget Annabel. "What do you suggest?"

Charlie looked away and then, with visible effort, made himself meet Gabe's eyes again. "If we hurry, we can get to your mother's place."

After delivering what amounted to a cudgel blow, the Indian kicked dirt over the fire and dropped to one knee at Nicholas's side. With minimal effort, he raised the boy up in his arms. Nicholas roused briefly, then passed out.

"He'll ride with you," Charlie said, speaking boldly into Gabe's stricken and thunderous silence. "It isn't far. I'll lead the way on Nicholas's horse."

Gabe swung into the saddle and bent to receive his son as Charlie handed him up. He felt numb, and the world around him seemed to throb in time with his own heartbeat.

"I'm sorry," Charlie said, mounting the bay. "I wouldn't have told you that way if I'd had a choice in the matter."

"You wouldn't have told me at all," Gabe answered

furiously, securing Nicholas with one arm and grasping the reins in the other hand. *All this while, she'd been somewhere nearby—the mother he had mourned for most of his life.*

Charlie made no answer; there wasn't time. He spurred the gelding into the timber, and Gabe didn't hesitate to follow.

They rode for most of an hour and once or twice had to stop while Charlie doubled back to make sure they weren't being followed. Finally, however, the thick birches and cottonwoods, pines and furs, gave way to a grassy clearing, with a creek and a small cabin at its center.

A woman wearing a worn buckskin dress awaited them in the doorway, her golden hair trailing down her back and stranded through with silver that caught the light, her chin high. She would be an outcast among her own people, and yet she seemed as proud and regal as a queen, standing there, watching their approach.

He had believed her dead, or far away. Instead, he realized now, carrying his broken son in his arms, she had been within a day's ride. But she'd chosen—*chosen*—to let him and Jessie wonder and grieve. Had she known, he asked himself, the horrible fate he had imagined her enduring? The stories he had heard as a boy on the school ground? Jesus, sometimes he still had nightmares about what her captors might have done to her.

He hated her for the deception, for the pain, and the expression in her blue eyes told him she knew it.

"Gabriel," she said, approaching, and laid her hand on his lower leg. Her gaze was fixed on Nicholas. "What's happened?"

Gabe looked down at the boy, still delirious. "He

knew you were here, didn't he?" he countered. "Didn't he?"

"There will be time for that later," Charlie said, dismounting, striding over, reaching up to claim Nicholas.

"Yes," Louisa said, hurrying into the cabin, with Charlie right behind her.

Gabe tied the horses up out back and unsaddled them. He heard nothing, and he saw nothing, and yet the odd prickling sensation at the nape of his neck told him they weren't alone, the four of them, in that hidden, idyllic place. At any other time he would have investigated; as it was, he could hardly stay in his skin, he was so agitated.

"Why?" he demanded of Louisa, inside the tidy, sparsely furnished cabin, where Nicholas was lying on a narrow bed, stripped of his clothes. Gabe's mother was re-bandaging his son's wound, and Charlie went outside, pistol in hand, ostensibly to gather wood for the coming night.

She looked at him with eyes full of sorrow. "Because I knew you would never understand why I had to leave. And I was right. You don't."

"You're damn right I don't!" Gabe rasped. "Do you know what it was like, wondering—"

"Keep your voice down," his mother said calmly. "Nicholas needs to keep his mind on his mending, and shouting will disturb and distract him."

"You weren't captured," Gabe accused, albeit in a quiet, if no less furious, tone of voice. "You *wanted* to go."

"Yes," she admitted, with a forlorn sigh. "Oh, yes."

"Why?"

"Because I had fallen in love, Gabriel. Deeply. helplessly in love."

"You were married."

"Your father was twenty years older than I was, and not the kindest of men. Not to me, at least. I never loved him, and he never loved me."

"What about Jessie and me?" Gabe demanded, suddenly five years old again and left behind in the care of an uninterested father. "Did you give a damn about either of us?"

"I couldn't raise you among the Indians, Gabriel. You wouldn't have belonged."

"Does she know? Jessie, I mean?"

Louisa sighed again, brushing a tender hand over Nicholas's hair. "Perhaps, if she's read my journals. It's all there—how I met Gray Cloud by accident one day when I was picking berries for a pie." She paused, smiled sadly at the memory. "He was a shaman, a medicine man, not a warrior, and he was gathering herbs. We seemed to encounter each other again and again after that first time, though I can't pretend it was accidental.

"Eventually we became lovers. He got me with child, Gabriel—and make no mistake, I was willing—but once that happened, I knew I could no longer live in two worlds. If I'd presented your father with an Indian baby, he would have killed both of us and been given a medal for it. So Gray Cloud arranged for us to run away together, and made it look as if I'd been taken captive."

Gabe grasped the back of a chair, for support. "You had a child?"

She nodded and indulged in a small smile very reminiscent of Nicholas's frequent wicked grins. "I called him Charles, for my father, and he grew up to be a fine man. A shaman, among other things."

"Charles?" Gabe swung the chair around and sank

onto it, sitting astraddle. All the starch had gone out of him. "Charlie?"

She laughed quietly, her eyes shining. "You never suspected?"

He searched his innermost self and found that he *had* known, somehow. Charlie had always been more brother than friend, and he had been family to Nicholas as well. And to Annabel. "Did Nicholas know?"

She sighed. "He probably guessed. Charlie's brought him here many times, but we never actually told him the whole story. It was enough of a strain on a little boy's loyalty, keeping a secret from his father. Nicholas idolizes you, Gabriel. I hope you know that."

Gabe swallowed a lump the size of an apple. "Your . . . husband, what happened to him?"

"Gray Cloud died ten years ago, and after that there was no longer a place for me in the tribe. The white world wouldn't have accepted me either, naturally, so Charlie helped me build this cabin, and I've been here ever since."

Nicholas's eyes fluttered open; he looked at his grandmother, then at Gabe. Then he blinked and went through the whole process all over again.

"Oh, shit," he said, when he'd assured himself that he wasn't seeing things.

"You're in it, boy," Gabe assured him. "Right up to your backside."

Louisa straightened her grandson's covers and stood up. "It isn't fair to blame Nicholas," she told Gabe, as indulgent as any grandmother anywhere. "I made him promise never to tell you or Jessie that I was here."

Nicholas grinned in the old devil's way, and the